SWEET TALK

SUSAN MALLERY

WHEELER
CHIVERS

LIBRARY OF CONGRESS CATALOGING-IN-PUBLICATION DATA

Mallery, Susan.
   Sweet talk / by Susan Mallery.
     p. cm.
   ISBN-13: 978-1-59722-830-5 (alk. paper)
   ISBN-10: 1-59722-830-3 (alk. paper)
   1. Pianists—Fiction. 2. Large type books. I. Title.
PS3613.A453S94 2008
813'.6—dc22   2008027430

BRITISH LIBRARY CATALOGUING-IN-PUBLICATION DATA AVAILABLE

Published in 2008 in the U.S. by arrangement with Harlequin Books S.A.
Published in 2009 in the U.K. by arrangement with Harlequin Enterprises II B.V.

U.K. Hardcover: 978 1 408 42109 3 (Chivers Large Print)
U.K. Softcover: 978 1 408 42110 9 (Camden Large Print)

Printed and bound in Great Britain by
CPI Antony Rowe, Chippenham and Eastbourne

To my agent, Annelise Robey. With
heartfelt thanks for all the
support and hard work. You're amazing
and I adore working with
you. Here's to all the success in the
world . . . for both of us.

CHAPTER ONE

Claire Keyes jumped to answer the phone when it rang, deciding an angry call from her manager was more appealing than sorting the pile of dirty clothes in the middle of her living room.

"Hello?"

"Hi. Um, Claire? It's Jesse."

Not her manager, Claire thought, relieved. "Jesse who?"

"Your sister."

Claire kicked aside a blouse and sank onto the sofa. "Jesse?" she breathed. "It's really you?"

"Uh-huh. Surprise."

Surprise didn't begin to describe it. Claire hadn't seen her baby sister in years. Not since their father's funeral when she'd tried to connect with all the family she had left only to be told that she wasn't welcome, would never be welcome and that if she was hit by a bus, neither Jesse nor Nicole,

Claire's fraternal twin, would bother to call for help.

Claire still remembered being so stunned by the verbal attack that she'd actually stopped breathing. She'd felt as if she'd been beaten up and left on the side of the road. Jesse and Nicole were her *family.* How could they reject her like that?

Not knowing what else to do, she'd left town and never returned. That had been seven years ago.

"So," Jesse said with a cheer that seemed forced. "How are you?"

Claire shook her head, trying to clear it, then glanced at the messy apartment. There were dirty clothes piled thigh-high in her living room, open suitcases by the piano, a stack of mail she couldn't seem to face and a manager ready to skin her alive if that would get her to do what she wanted.

"I'm great," she lied. "And you?"

"Too fabulous for words. But here's the thing. Nicole isn't."

Claire tightened her grip on the phone. "What's wrong with her?"

"Nothing . . . yet. She's going to have surgery. Her gallbladder. There's something weird about the placement or whatever. I can't remember. Anyway, she can't have that easy surgery with the tiny incisions. The

8

lapi-something."

"Laparoscopic," Claire murmured absently, eyeing the clock. She was due at her lesson in thirty minutes.

"That one. Instead, they're going to be slicing her open like a watermelon, which means a longer recovery time. With the bakery and all, that's a problem. Normally I'd step in to help, but I can't right now. Things are . . . complicated. So we were talking and Nicole wondered if you would like to come back home and take care of things. She would really appreciate it."

Home, Claire thought longingly. She could go home. Back to the house she barely remembered but that had always placed so large in her dreams.

"I thought you and Nicole hated me," she whispered, wanting to hope but almost afraid to.

"We were upset before. It was an emotional time. Seriously, we've been talking about getting in touch with you for a while now. Nicole would have, um, called herself, but she's not feeling well and she was afraid you'd say no. She's not in a place to handle that right now."

Claire stood. "I would never say no. Of course I'll come home. I really want to. You're my family. Both of you."

9

"Great. When can you get here?"

Claire looked around at the disaster that was her life and thought about the angry calls from Lisa, her manager. There was also the master class she was supposed to attend and the few she had to teach at the end of the week.

"Tomorrow," she said firmly. "I can be there tomorrow."

"Just shoot me now," Nicole Keyes said as she wiped down the kitchen counters. "I mean it, Wyatt. You must have a gun. Do it. I'll write a note saying it's not your fault."

"Sorry. No guns at my house."

None in hers, either, she thought glumly, then tossed the dishcloth back into the sink.

"The timing couldn't be worse for my stupid surgery," she muttered. "They're telling me I can't go back to work for six weeks. *Six*. The bakery isn't going to run itself. And don't you dare say anything about me asking Jesse. I mean it, Wyatt."

Her soon-to-be-ex-brother-in-law held up both hands. "Not a word from me. I swear."

She believed him. Not because she thought she frightened him but because she knew he understood that while some of the pain in her gut came from an inflamed gallbladder, most of it was about her sister

10

Jesse's betrayal.

"I hate this. I hate my body turning on me this way. What have I ever done to it?"

Wyatt pushed out a chair at the table. "Sit. Getting upset isn't going to help."

"You don't actually know that."

"I can guess."

She plopped into the chair because it was easier than fighting. Sometimes, like now, she wondered if she had any fight left in her.

"What am I forgetting?" she asked. "I think I've gotten everything done. You remembered that I can't take care of Amy for a while, right?"

Amy was his eight-year-old daughter. Nicole looked after her a few afternoons a week.

Wyatt leaned forward and put his hand on her forearm. "Relax," he told her. "You didn't forget anything. I'll look in on the bakery every couple of days. You've got good people working for you. They love you and are loyal. Everything will be fine. You'll be home in a few days and you can start healing."

She knew he meant from more than just the surgery. There was also the issue of her soon-to-be-ex-husband.

Instead of thinking about that bastard

Drew, she stared at Wyatt's hand on her arm. He had big hands — scarred and callused. He was a man who knew how to work for a living. Honest, good-looking, funny.

She raised her gaze to his dark eyes. "Why couldn't I have fallen in love with you?" she asked.

He smiled. "Back at you, kid."

They would have been so perfect together . . . if only there had been a hint of chemistry.

"We should have tried harder," she muttered. "We should have slept together."

"Just think about it for a minute," he told her. "Tell me if it turns you on."

"I can't." Honestly, thinking about having sex with Wyatt kind of set her teeth on edge, and not in a good way. He was too much like a brother. If only his stepbrother, Drew, had caused the same reaction. Unfortunately with him, there had been fireworks. The kind that burned.

She pulled back and studied Wyatt. "Enough about me. You should get married again."

He reached for his mug of coffee. "No, thanks."

"Amy needs a mother."

"Not that badly."

"There are great women out there."

"Name one that isn't you."

Nicole thought for a minute, then sighed. "Can I get back to you on that?"

Claire arrived at the SeaTac Airport early in the afternoon, feeling very smug about making her own travel arrangements. She'd even booked a car for herself. Normally she would have used a car service, but she would have to drive back and forth to the hospital, then to the bakery. Nicole might need her to run errands. Wheels of her own made sense.

After wrestling her two very large suitcases off the baggage claim belt, she grabbed one in each hand and dragged them toward the escalator. The catwalk to the parking garage was long and the bags heavy. She was breathing hard by the time she reached a bank of elevators she had to take down to the rental car place. By the time she got to the Hertz office, she was regretting the long wool coat she'd shrugged on. Sweat trickled down her back, making her cashmere sweater stick to her.

She waited in line, excited about being here, nervous and filled with resolve to do whatever it took to reconnect with her sisters. They were being given a second chance. *She* wasn't going to blow it.

The woman at the counter waved her forward. Claire dragged the two suitcases along as she approached.

"Hi. I have a reservation."

"Name?"

"Claire Keyes." Claire handed over her driver's license and her platinum credit card.

The woman studied the driver's license. "Do you have insurance or do you want coverage on the car?"

"I'll take your coverage." It was easier than explaining that she didn't own a car and had, in fact, never owned a car. The only reason she had a driver's license at all was because she'd insisted on lessons when she'd turned eighteen and had studied and practiced until she'd passed the test.

"Any tickets or accidents?" the woman asked.

Claire smiled. "Not one." Getting a ticket or an accident would require actual driving. Something Claire hadn't done more than once or twice in the past ten years.

There were a couple of forms to sign, then the woman handed back the license and credit card.

"Number sixty-eight. It's a Malibu. You said midsize. I can get you something bigger, if you want."

14

Claire blinked at her. "Number sixty-eight what?"

"Your car. It's in slot sixty-eight. The keys are inside."

"Oh, great. I'll pass on something bigger."

"Okay. You need a map?"

"Yes, please."

Claire tucked the map into her purse, then dragged her suitcases out of the glass structure. She saw rows of cars and numbers at the end of each parking space. Counting as she went, she found number sixty-eight and stared at the silver Malibu.

It had four doors and looked huge. She swallowed. Was she really going to drive? A question for later, she told herself. First she had to get out of the parking lot.

Challenge number one turned out to be getting her luggage into the trunk. There didn't seem to be any way to open it. No buttons, no knobs. She pushed and pulled, but it wouldn't budge. Finally she gave up and maneuvered her two big bags into the backseat. Then she slid behind the wheel.

It took her a couple of minutes to get the seat moved up so she could actually reach the pedals. She managed to get the key in the ignition and turned it. The engine caught immediately. Claire carefully adjusted her mirrors, then drew in a breath.

She was practically on her way.

Next she turned to the GPS system. It greeted her in French.

Claire stared at it. What on earth?

She pushed a few buttons. Yup, it was speaking French. Okay, sure, she also spoke the language, but not well enough to deal with it while driving. The potential to freak while on the road seemed big enough without adding a foreign language to the mix.

She punched buttons until she'd scrolled through Dutch and Japanese. Finally she heard the pleasant female voice in English.

The need to run screaming into the night faded slightly.

She continued reading the instruction card, then carefully punched in the address of the bakery. She'd forgotten to ask Jesse for the name of the hospital where Nicole would have her surgery, so the bakery seemed like the best place to start. Finally, she braced herself to drive out of the space.

Her chest was tight. She ignored that, along with the prickling that started on her back and moved over her whole body.

Not now, she thought frantically. Not now. She could panic later, when she wasn't about to drive.

She closed her eyes and breathed, pictured

her sister lying in a hospital bed, in desperate need of help. That's where she needed to be, she reminded herself. With Nicole.

The sense of panic faded a little. She opened her eyes and began her journey.

The parking structure seemed dark and closed. Fortunately there weren't any cars in the row in front of her, so she would have extra room to turn as she drove out.

Slowly, carefully, she put the car in Drive. It started to move right away. She jammed her foot on the brake. The whole car jerked. She eased up on the brake and it moved again. Moving six or eight inches at a time, she managed to make it out of her space. Fifteen minutes later she'd made her way out of the parking structure and onto the road that led out of the airport.

"In five hundred feet, stay to the right. I-5 is on the right."

The voice from the GPS system was very commanding, as if it knew Claire was totally clueless about driving in general and where she was going in particular.

"I-5 what?" Claire asked before she saw a sign for the I-5 freeway. She shrieked. "I can't go on the freeway," she told the GPS. "We need to go on regular streets."

There was a ding. "Stay to the right."

"But I don't want to."

She looked around frantically, but there didn't seem to be any other way to go. The road she was on just sort of eased into the freeway. She couldn't move to her left — there were too many cars in her way. Cars that suddenly started going really, really fast.

Claire clutched the steering wheel with both hands, her body stiff, her mind filled with images of fiery crashes.

"I can do this," she whispered to herself. "I can do this."

She pressed a little harder on the accelerator, until she was going nearly forty-five. That had to be fast enough, didn't it? Who needed to go faster than that?

A big truck came up behind her and honked its horn. She jumped. More cars came up behind her, some getting really, really close. She was so busy trying not to be scared by the cars zipping around her that she forgot about merging until the GPS system reminded her, "I-5 north is to the right."

"What? What right? Do I want to go north?"

And then the road was turning and she was turning with it. She desperately wanted to close her eyes, but knew that would be bad. Fear made her sweat. She really wanted to rip off her coat, but couldn't. Not and keep from crashing. She was clutching the steering wheel so hard, her fingers ached.

She was doing this for Nicole, she reminded herself. For her sister. For family.

Her lane merged onto I-5. Still going forty-five, Claire eased into the right lane and vowed to stay there until it was time to exit.

By the time she got off, just north of the University district, she was shaking all over. She hated driving. Hated it. Cars were awful and drivers were rude, mean people who screamed at her. But she'd made it and that was what mattered.

She followed the directions from the GPS and managed to make her way into the parking lot next to the bakery. She turned off the car, leaned her forehead against the steering wheel and did her best to breathe.

When her heartbeat had slowed from hummingbird rate to that for a medium-size mammal, she straightened, then stared at the building in front of her.

The Keyes bakery had been in the same location for all of its eighty years of operation. Originally, her great-grandparents had rented only half the storefront. Over time, the business had grown. They'd bought out their neighbor's lease, then had bought the whole place about sixty years ago.

Pastries, cakes and breads filled the lower half of the two display windows. Delicate lettering listing other options covered the top half. A big sign above the door proclaimed Keyes Bakery — Home of the World's Best Chocolate Cake.

The multilayer chocolate confection had been praised by royalty and presidents, served by brides and written into several celebrity contracts as a "must have" on location shoots or backstage at concerts. It was about a billion calories of flour, sugar, butter, chocolate and a secret ingredient passed on through the family. Not that Claire knew what it was. But she would. She was confident Nicole would want to tell her immediately.

She got out of the car and smoothed the front of her sweater. It was cool enough that she kept on her coat, hoping it wasn't too wrinkled from the drive. After collecting her purse, she carefully locked the driver's door. Taking a deep breath, she walked into the bakery.

It was midafternoon and relatively quiet. There were two young moms sitting at a corner table with pastries and coffee. Two strollers with babies were between their chairs. Claire offered a smile as she made her way to the long counter. The teenage girl there looked at her.

"Can I help you?"

"Yes. I hope so. I'm Claire. Claire Keyes."

The teenager, a plump brunette with big, brown eyes sighed. "Okay. What can I get you? The rosemary garlic bread is hot out of the oven."

Claire smiled hopefully. "I'm Claire Keyes," she repeated.

"Heard that the first time."

Claire pointed to the sign on the wall. "Keyes, as in Nicole's sister."

The teenager's eyes got even bigger. "Oh, my God. No way. Are you really? The piano player?"

Claire winced. "Technically I'm a concert pianist." A soloist, but why quibble? "I'm here because of Nicole's surgery. Jesse called and asked me to —"

"Jesse?" The girl's voice came out as a shriek. "She didn't. Are you kidding? Oh, my God! I can't believe it." The teenager backed up as she spoke. "Nicole is so going to kill her. If she hasn't already. I just . . ." She held up her hand. "Wait here, okay? I'll be right back."

Before Claire could say anything, the girl took off toward the back.

Claire adjusted her bag on her shoulder and looked at the inventory in the glass

21

case. There were several pies, a couple of cakes, along with loaves of bread. Her stomach growled, reminding her she hadn't eaten all day. She'd been too nervous to have anything on the plane.

Maybe she could get some of that rosemary garlic bread and then stop at a deli for —

"What the hell are you doing here?"

Claire looked at the man walking toward her. He was big and rough looking, with tanned skin and the kind of body that said he either did physical work for a living or spent too much time at a gym. She did her best not to wrinkle her nose at the sight of his plaid shirt and worn jeans.

"I'm Claire Keyes," she began.

"I know who you are. I asked why you were here."

"Actually you asked me why the 'hell' I was here. There's a difference."

He narrowed his gaze. "Which is?"

"One question implies a genuine interest in the answer, the other lets me know that somehow I've annoyed you. You don't really care why I'm here, you just want me to know I'm not welcome. Which is strange, considering you and I have never met."

"I'm friends with Nicole. I don't have to

have met you to know all I need to about you."

Ouch. Claire didn't understand. If Nicole was still mad at her, why had Jesse called and implied otherwise? "Who *are* you?"

"Wyatt Knight. Nicole is married to my stepbrother."

Nicole got married? When? To whom?

A deep, deep sadness followed the questions. Her own sister hadn't bothered to tell her or invite her to the wedding. How pathetic was that?

Emotions chased across Claire Keyes's face. Wyatt didn't bother to try to read them. Women and what they felt were a mystery best left unsolved by mortal man. Trying to make sense of the female mind would drive a man to drink, then kill him.

Instead he studied the tall, slender blonde in front of him, looking for similarities to Nicole and Jesse.

Their eyes, he thought, taking in the big, blue irises. Maybe the shape of the mouth. The hair color . . . sort of. Nicole's was just blond. Claire's was a dozen different shades and shiny.

But nothing else was the same. Nicole was his friend, someone he'd known for years. A pretty enough woman, but regular looking. Claire dressed in off-white — from her too-long coat to the sweater and slacks she wore underneath. Her purse was beige, as were her boots. She looked like an ice princess . . . an evil one.

"I'd like to see my sister," Claire said firmly. "I know she's in the hospital. But I'm not sure which one."

"No way I'm going to tell you. I don't know why you're here, lady, but I can tell you Nicole doesn't want to see you."

"That's not what I heard."

"From who?"

"Jesse. She said Nicole was going to need help after her surgery. She called me yesterday and I flew in this morning." She raised her chin slightly. "I'm not going away, Mr. Knight, and you can't make me. I *will* see my sister. If you choose not to give me the information, I'll simply call every hospital in Seattle until I find her. Nicole is my family."

"Since when?" he muttered, recognizing the stubborn angle of her chin and the determination in her voice. The twins had that much in common.

Why had Jesse done this? To make more trouble? Or had she been trying to fix a desperate situation? The truth was Nicole *would* need help and she was just difficult enough not to ask. He would do what he

24

could, but he had a business to run and Amy to look after. Nicole wouldn't want Drew around, assuming his good-for-nothing brother hadn't run off somewhere to hide. Jesse was a worse choice. Which left exactly no one else.

Why did he have to be making this decision? He swore under his breath. "Where are you staying?"

"At the house. Where else?"

"Fine. Stay there. Nicole will be home in a couple of days. You can take this up with her then."

"I'm not waiting two more days to see her."

Selfish, spoiled, egotistic, narcissistic. Wyatt remembered Nicole's familiar list of complaints about her sister. Right now, every one of them made sense to him.

"Listen," he said. "You can wait at the house or fly back to Paris or wherever it is you live."

"New York," she said quietly. "I live in New York."

"Whatever. My point is you're not going to see Nicole until she's had a couple of days to recover, even if that means I have to stand guard on her hospital room myself. You got that? She's in enough hurt right

25

now from the surgery without having to deal with a pain in the ass like you."

CHAPTER TWO

Claire deflated like a punctured balloon, leaving Wyatt feeling like the biggest asshole this side of the Rockies. He told himself it was just an act, that she was born to play people and had only gotten better at it as she'd gotten older. For someone who claimed to care so much for her sister, she'd never once shown up here in all the years he'd known Nicole. Not for birthdays or even her sister's damn wedding. She'd missed Jesse's high school graduation. She was good at playing the victim, that was all, and he wasn't going to get sucked in to her game.

Just when he thought she was going to turn around and go away, she straightened. Her shoulders went back, her chin came up and she looked him square in the eye. "My sister called me."

"So you said."

"You don't believe me."

"I don't care enough to think about it one way or the other."

She tilted her head so that her long, shimmering blond hair fell over one shoulder. "Nicole has a good friend in you. I hope she appreciates that."

So she'd moved on to sucking up. Probably an effective plan on anyone who wasn't clued in to her style.

"Jesse called me," she continued. "She told me about the surgery. You have to know that much is true, otherwise how would I know? Jesse also told me that Nicole wants me to help out afterward and is happy I'm here. Under the circumstances, I'm more inclined to believe her than you."

"I can tell you that as of twenty minutes before the surgery, Nicole had no idea you were going to show up. Trust me. She would have mentioned it."

Claire frowned slightly. "Nothing about this makes sense. Why would Jesse lie? Why would you?"

"I wouldn't."

She looked genuinely confused and Wyatt almost believed her. This messed-up situation had Jesse written all over it. The question was, why had the kid done it? To make a bad situation worse or did she really want to help Nicole? With Jesse it wasn't easy to tell.

"I'm staying," Claire told him. "Just so you're clear. I'm staying. I'm going to the hospital and —"

"No."

"But I —"

"No."

She looked at him. "You're very determined."

"I protect what's mine."

Something flickered in her eyes. Something sad and small that he didn't want to identify.

"Fine. I'll wait at the house until Nicole is ready to come home," Claire said at last. "Then she and I can figure out what's going on."

"It would be easier if you just went back to New York."

"I don't do easy. Never have. Career hazard, I suppose."

He had no idea what she was talking about. Did she think anyone believed that playing the piano for a bunch of rich people in fancy European cities was hard?

He shrugged. He couldn't force Nicole's sister to disappear. As long as she didn't try to bug Nicole in the hospital, he would stay out of it.

"So Nicole will come home in a couple of days?" Claire asked.

"Something like that."

She smiled at him. "You're very determined not to give up any information, Mr. Knight, but as I'm going to be living in the same house it will be difficult to conceal Nicole's arrival from me."

"Wyatt. I'm not your boss and you're not my banker."

"Your employees call you by your last name?"

"No. I was making a point."

"My banker calls me Claire."

"My banker doesn't."

Her smile faded. "You don't like me very much."

He didn't bother to answer that.

"You don't even know me," she continued. "That hardly seems fair."

"I know enough."

She stiffened, as if he'd hit her. Egotistical and sensitive, he thought grimly. Hell of a combination.

Claire turned and walked out of the bakery. Wyatt followed to make sure she really did get into her car and drive away.

He glanced around the parking lot, half expecting to see a stretch limo or a Mercedes. But Claire's rental was a midsize four-

30

door with luggage piled in the backseat.

"How much crap did you bring?" he asked before he could stop himself. "It wouldn't even fit in the trunk?"

She came to a stop and looked at him. "No. That's all I brought."

"What have you got against the trunk? Afraid you'll break a nail?"

"I, as you put it so elegantly, play piano. I don't have long nails." She straightened again and seemed to brace herself. "As I said before, I live in New York, where I don't keep a car. I don't drive much anywhere. I couldn't figure out how to open the trunk."

Now he knew why she'd braced herself. She was waiting for him to rip her a new one. It was a pretty sweet setup and he could think of a hundred cheap shots. Who didn't know how to open the trunk? His eight-year-old could do it.

What stopped him from saying that and more was the fact that she was expecting to be trashed and that, even knowing he didn't like her, she'd still exposed a vulnerable spot. Wyatt didn't mind being a mean bastard, but he wouldn't be a bully.

He moved next to her, took the keys from her hand and pointed to the attached fob. "Ever see one of these before? The little pictures tell you what the buttons do." He pushed the one that opened the trunk. It popped open.

Claire grinned at him. "Seriously? That's it?" She walked over and stared down into the space. "It's huge. I could have brought more luggage. Are there more buttons?"

She was thrilled on a level the key fob didn't deserve. "You don't get out much, do you?"

The smile widened. "Even less than you think."

"Door lock, door unlock, panic button."

"That is so cool."

She was like a kid with a new toy. She had to be jerking him around.

"Thank you," she told him. "Seriously, I felt like such an idiot at the car rental place, standing there not knowing what to do." She wrinkled her nose. "If only driving were this easy. Do people have to go so fast on the freeway?"

He had no idea what to think of her. Based on Nicole's infrequent comments about her sister, he knew not to trust her. But while she was as useless as Nicole had claimed, she wasn't nearly as cold and distant.

Not his problem, he reminded himself.

He handed the keys back to Claire. She reached out and took them. For a second, maybe two, they touched. His fingers on her palm, a brush of skin. Inconsequential. Except for the sudden burst of fire.

Goddamn sonofabitch, he thought grimly, jerking back his hand and stuffing it in his jacket pocket. No way. Not her. Dear God, anyone but her.

Claire was babbling on, probably thanking him. He wasn't listening. Instead he was wondering why, of all the women in all the world, he'd had to feel that hot, bright, sexual heat with her.

The calm-voiced woman in the GPS system led Claire to the house where she'd spent the first six years of her life. She found a parking space on the narrow street in front. It was by a driveway, so all she had to do was pull forward to claim it. There was no way she would ever be able to parallel park.

She turned off the engine, got out of the car and locked it, using the fob. Feeling foolishly proud of herself, she walked around to the back of the house and found the spare key where Jesse had said it would be. She unlocked the rear door and stepped into the house.

She hadn't been inside it for years. Nearly twelve, she thought, remembering the single night spent under this roof after her mother had died. One night with Jesse staring at her as though she was a stranger and Nicole glaring with obvious loathing. Not that Nicole had settled on communicating silently. At sixteen she'd been very comfortable speaking her mind.

"You killed her," she screamed. "You took her away and then you killed her. I'll never forgive you. I hate you. I hate you."

Lisa, Claire's manager, had taken her away then. They'd checked into a suite at the Four Seasons where they'd stayed until after the funeral. From there they'd gone to Paris. Springtime in Paris, Lisa had said. The beauty of the city would heal her.

It hadn't. Only time had closed the wounds, but the scars were still there. Springtime in Paris. The words always made her think of the song and whenever she heard the song, she thought about her mother's death and Nicole screaming that she hated her.

Claire shook off the memories and moved into the kitchen. It looked different, more modern and bigger somehow. Apparently Nicole had renovated the place, or at least parts of it. She continued through the downstairs and found several small rooms had been opened up into a larger space. There was a big living room with comfort-

34

able furniture, warm colors and a cabinet against one wall that concealed a flat-screen TV and other electronics. The dining room looked the same. The small bedroom on this floor had been converted into a study or den.

The place was dark and cool. She found the thermostat and turned up the heat. A few lamps helped add light, but didn't make the house any more welcoming. Maybe because the problem wasn't the house. It was her and the memories that wouldn't go away.

The last time she'd come to Seattle had been for their father's funeral. She'd received a terse phone call from a man, probably Wyatt, Claire thought as she sat on the edge of the sofa, saying her father had died. He'd given the date, time and place of the funeral, then had hung up.

Claire had been in shock. She hadn't even known he was sick. No one had told her.

She knew what they thought — that she couldn't be bothered with her own family. That she didn't care. What she'd tried to explain so many times was that she was the one who had been sent away. They'd been allowed to stay here, where it was safe, where they were loved. But Nicole had never seen it that way. She'd always been so angry.

Claire rubbed her hands against the soft fabric on the couch. None of this was familiar. Wyatt had been right — she didn't belong here. Not that she was leaving. Nicole and Jesse were the only family she had left. They might have ignored her phone calls and letters over the years, but she was here now and she wasn't leaving until she somehow got through to them. Until they made peace.

Claire stood and went up the stairs. There were three bedrooms on the top floor. She paused by the master suite. Based on the color scheme and items scattered across the dresser, she would guess that Nicole slept there now. At the other end of the hall were the two remaining bedrooms and the bathroom they shared.

One looked like a typical guest room with a too-tidy bed and neutral colors, while the last was done in purple, with posters on the walls and a computer on a desk filling one corner.

Claire walked into that room and looked around. The space smelled of vanilla.

"What have you done?" she asked aloud. "Jesse, did you set me up? Is Nicole really ready to forgive me?"

She desperately wanted to believe her sister, but found herself doubting. Wyatt had been very convincing in his dislike of her.

The unfairness of it, a stranger judging her, made her chest hurt, but she ignored the sensation. Somehow she would get this all fixed.

She returned downstairs and walked toward the front door. On the way, she saw a narrow staircase leading to the basement. She knew what was down there.

Every cell in her body screamed at her not to do it — not to go look — yet she found herself walking toward the opening, then slowly, so slowly, moving down.

The stairs opened into a basement. But what should have been an open space was closed off with a wall and a single door. Nicole hadn't destroyed it, Claire thought, not sure what to make of that. Did it mean there was hope, or had the project simply been too much trouble?

Claire hesitated, her hand on the doorknob. Did she really want to go in?

When she and Nicole had been three, their parents had taken them to a friend's house. It was a place neither girl had been before. At first the visit had been unremarkable. A rainy Seattle day with two toddlers trapped inside a house full of adults.

One of the guests had tried to entertain the girls by playing the piano. Nicole had grown bored and wandered away, but Claire had sat on the hard bench, entranced by the keys and the sound they made. After lunch, she'd gone back on her own. She'd been too short to see the white and black keys, but she'd known they were there and she'd carefully reached above her head and started to play one of the songs.

Despite how young she'd been, Claire remembered everything about that afternoon. How her mother had come looking for her and stared at her for the longest time. How she'd been put on her mother's lap in front of the piano, where she could make the pretty music more easily.

She had never been able to explain how she knew which key produced which sound, how the music had seemed to begin inside of her, bubbling up until it spilled out. It was just one of those things, a quirk of an, until then, unremarkable gene pool.

Nicole had also sat on her mother's lap, but she'd shown no interest in the piano and when she put her tiny hands down, there was only noise.

That moment had changed everything. Within two days, Claire started lessons. Then the work on the basement began and

38

a soundproof studio was built. For the first time in their lives, the twins weren't doing exactly the same thing at exactly the same time. Music, and Claire's gift, had come between them.

She pushed the door open. She could see the piano that had seemed so beautiful and perfect when she'd been a child. She would guess the cost of it had decimated her parents' savings account and then some. Claire had played on many of the most famous pianos in the world, but this was the one she remembered most.

She stared at it now, at the dust on the cover. It probably hadn't been touched in years. It would need tuning.

She had no desire to play. Just the thought of sitting down on the bench made her chest tighten. She forced herself to keep breathing. She didn't have to play if she didn't want to. Everything was fine. She didn't even have to make up excuses to avoid her masters classes. She was a whole continent away from that world.

Panic haunted the edges of her conscious mind. She pushed it away. When it stayed stubbornly in place, she retreated upstairs, to safer ground. Once on the main floor, she could breathe more easily.

She would ignore the piano, she told

herself. Pretend it wasn't here at all. Except for getting it tuned. A lifetime of training wouldn't allow her to let it sit untended.

With the monster in the basement, if not vanquished at least momentarily glared at, she went out to the car and wrestled in her two suitcases. After dragging them up the stairs and putting them in the guest room, she returned to the kitchen to make herself something to eat.

There wasn't a lot of food in the house. She found a can of soup and started heating it on the stove. In the meantime, she located a phone book and started calling hospitals until she found one that said her sister had been admitted and offered to connect her to the nurses' station. Claire declined and hung up.

The good news was the surgery had gone well, since Nicole's room had been on a regular floor, not in ICU. The bad news was that according to Wyatt, Nicole knew nothing about Claire's visit and had no interest in seeing her. Had she come all this way for nothing?

She checked her cell phone out of habit and saw she had two messages from Lisa. As her manager couldn't possibly say anything she wanted to hear, Claire deleted them without bothering to listen.

Standing at the sink, she ate soup out of the pot and stared into the small, fenced backyard.

She knew when things had gone wrong with Nicole. She knew what the problem was. So why couldn't she fix it?

Did it matter? She was here now. Here and determined to make Nicole and Jesse a part of her life. No matter what they said or did, they weren't getting rid of her. She was going to make them love her and she was going to love them back. They were her family and that mattered more than anything.

Nicole did her best not to move. She hurt. The pain was dulled by the miracles of modern drug therapy, but it was still there, lurking, threatening. She ignored the heat of it and blessed whoever had invented beds that raised and lowered with the push of a button. She would just lie here for the next six or eight years and eventually she would be fine.

Someone walked into her room. She heard the footsteps and braced herself for the inevitable poking and prodding that followed. Instead, there was only silence. She opened her eyes and saw Wyatt standing next to the bed.

She felt like crap and figured she didn't

look a whole lot better. At times like this she was grateful they had only ever been friends.

"It's going to be a hell of a scar," he told her.

"Guys are into scars," she whispered, her mouth dry. "I'll have to beat them off with a stick. Not that I can ever imagine having the strength to lift a stick. Can I beat them off with a straw? I could handle a straw."

"I'll be there to help."

"Lucky me."

He touched her cheek, then pulled up a chair and sat down. "How are you feeling?"

She managed a smile. "That falls under the category of really stupid questions. Did you get the whole concept of surgery? I've been sliced and diced and I'm thinking of getting hooked on painkillers."

"You won't like rehab. You're too cynical."

"And crabby. Don't forget crabby." She pointed to the plastic cup on the tray beside her bed. "Could you hand me that?"

Wyatt picked it up and passed it to her. She took it and risked a sip. The last one had nearly made her throw up but a very mean-looking nurse had informed her she had to start drinking and peeing. Nicole didn't see the point, but the nurse had been insistent.

She took a tiny sip and winced as a wave of nausea washed through her. At least it was less intense than the previous one. She sipped again and didn't feel much of anything. Progress.

She handed him the water and drew in a breath. "You talk. I'll listen. But please, don't be funny. I don't want to laugh. It will hurt too much."

Wyatt leaned forward and took her fingers in his. "I went by the bakery. Everything is fine."

"Good. They'll be okay without me. They know how to handle the business. I don't have to worry about anything."

She would worry because it was her nature, but it was nice to know it wasn't required.

"So, um, I met someone there."

Despite the pain and the drugs, Nicole opened her eyes. There was something about the way Wyatt wouldn't look at her. Something almost . . . guilty.

"A woman?"

He nodded.

She didn't understand. What was the big deal? He'd met someone. That was a good thing. "So ask her out."

"What?" He straightened and stared at her. "You're not —" He leaned toward her again. "I didn't mean I'd met someone I liked. I met someone I didn't expect to be there."

"Maybe it's the surgery and everything, but you're not making sense."

"I met Claire."

Claire who? But even as the question formed, she already had the answer. Claire, her sister. Claire, the perfect one, the princess. The concert pianist and soloist. World traveler. Rich bitch. Her selfish, narcissistic, shallow, cruel, awful sister.

"Not possible," she murmured as her eyes closed. Sleep would be good, she told herself. She would sleep now and this would all go away.

"Apparently Jesse called and told her about your surgery and she flew in."

Nicole's eyes opened. "What?"

"She's here to help during your recovery."

If Nicole hadn't been so uncomfortable and drugged, she would have laughed. "Help? She wants to help? Where the hell has she been for the past twenty-two years? Where was she while I was stuck here, raising Jesse and working in the bakery? Where was she when our mother went off to be with her and then died? Where was she when Dad died? Does she bother to show up even once? I can't believe it. She needs to leave right now. She needs to get her designer-wearing ass out of my city and back to her cocktail party circuit or wherever it is she spent her —"

Nicole made the mistake of trying to sit up on her own. Pain ripped through her, stealing her breath and making her moan. She sank back into the bed and closed her eyes. Claire here? Because Nicole's life wasn't sucky enough already?

"I hate her."

"I know." Wyatt squeezed her fingers. "She thinks she's helping."

It was too much, Nicole thought. "I can't deal with her right now. Just keep her away from me. I mean it, Wyatt. Don't let her come to the hospital."

"I won't," he promised, then kissed her forehead.

He was a good guy, she thought as sleep beckoned. One of the best. Why hadn't she been smart enough to fall in love with him? Instead she'd fallen for Drew. Talk about a disaster. All of it. And now Claire? What was next? Locusts?

Claire arrived at the hospital in plenty of time to take Nicole home. The previous day she'd made the drive twice so she was familiar with the route. Driving was a little less scary, as well. As long as she stayed off the freeway, she felt almost competent. She'd also talked to Nicole's nurse, explaining that they were family and that she, Claire, wanted to pick her up. They had given her the approximate time of release. Now Claire was here and ready to help.

She tried not to think too much about Wyatt's claim that Nicole knew nothing about her visit and wasn't going to be happy to see her. Despite repeated calls to Jesse's cell phone, she'd been unable to catch her, nor had Jesse answered any of her messages. Obviously something was going on, but Claire was confident it was little more than a misunderstanding that could be easily cleared up. At least that's what she told herself every time her stomach flipped over or her chest started to constrict.

She tightened her grip on her handbag as she exited the elevator and started down the long hallway. The signs pointed to the nurses' station, but before she got there, she saw Nicole in a wheelchair being pushed by a nurse, with Wyatt bringing up the rear.

Emotions flooded Claire, bringing her to a stop as she just stared at the sister she hadn't seen in years. Nicole looked good, pale, but that made sense. The woman had just had surgery. She wore a zip-up hoodie over a T-shirt, with her hair pulled back in ponytail. Claire instantly felt overdressed.

"Nicole," she whispered, fierce joy filling her. They were together again. Finally.

"Oh, crap," Nicole muttered. "Can I get more drugs?"

"Your sister?" the nurse asked. "You look alike. Almost like twins."

"Fraternal and don't make a bad situation worse by talking about it," Nicole said.

Wyatt put his hand on her shoulder. "I'll take care of this." He walked to Claire. "What are you doing here? I told you not to come."

She ignored him and Nicole's snarky comments, instead rushing forward, then crouching in front of her sister. She wanted to hug her, but was afraid of hurting her. She settled on touching her arm and smiling into her eyes.

"You look great. How do you feel?"

Nicole stared at her. "Like I had an organ ripped out. What are you doing here?"

"I'm taking you home."

"No, you're not," Wyatt said. "That's why I'm here."

"What are you doing in Seattle?" Nicole asked. "Please tell me it's a short visit that ends in an hour."

"I heard about your surgery, so I flew here

to take care of you."

"That's so sweet," the nurse said.

"I don't need your help," Nicole said. "Go away."

Claire was doing her best not to react to all the hostility. She told herself that her sister was in pain, that Wyatt didn't know her and that a lot of time and bad feelings had come between the Keyes sisters. It was going to take more than a day to heal old wounds.

What she wanted to do was stand up, stomp her foot and point out that she was the wronged party here. That Nicole had turned her back on Claire years ago and refused to reconsider her position. That she'd been blamed for things that had hurt her just as much as them. But there was no point in starting there. She was here for a purpose.

She stood. "I'm not going anywhere. You need me."

Nicole groaned. "I need a lot of things, but you're not one of them. Wyatt, did I tell you to shoot me before? Did you listen?"

Wyatt put his hand on her shoulder. "I told you I couldn't do that."

"All men are useless," Nicole muttered, then looked back at Claire. "You want to get up so I can get out of here? I hurt, I'm tired and I just want to go home."

"My car is right out front," Claire told her. "I know the way. I practiced the drive."

"We're all so proud."

The nurse gave Claire a sympathetic smile, then pushed her patient toward the elevators. Claire trailed after them, not sure what to say or do. She couldn't force Nicole into her car. Maybe it would be better to let Wyatt deal with getting Nicole to the house and Claire could take over from there.

Still, it hurt to be rejected and ignored. She'd hoped things would be different.

"I'll change them," she told herself as they walked out into the cool, spring morning.

There was a large truck parked in front of the entrance. Wyatt opened the passenger door, then lifted Nicole inside and put her on the seat.

Claire watched, aching at the sight of the tenderness and care Wyatt displayed. She wanted a little of that for herself. Not from Wyatt, but from someone. She wanted a man to care about her, worry about her. She wanted friends and family. She wanted a life.

Which was mostly what she'd come home to find.

CHAPTER THREE

"I thought you were lying," Nicole said as they pulled out of the hospital parking lot. "I thought I was having drug-induced hallucinations. I can't believe she's here. She's possibly the most useless human being on the planet. Why me? Why now?"

Wyatt didn't have any answers, so he kept quiet. He'd heard enough about Claire over the years to form an unflattering opinion of her. But today, at the hospital, she'd looked so hopeful and wounded at the same time. He'd almost felt bad for her.

Which only proved what a fool he was when it came to women. He always picked wrong. He had the divorce to prove it. Nicole knew her sister a whole lot better than he did, and he trusted Nicole. What she said went.

"What are you going to do about her?" he asked.

"I supposed asking you to shoot her would

be a waste of time." She sighed. "I don't know. Ignore her and hope she goes away."

"You're going to need some help, at least for a couple of days. You won't be able to take care of yourself."

He kept his eyes on the road, but felt Nicole's angry stare. "You have got to be kidding me. You're not suggesting I let her stay and attempt to take care of me. Do you know how incredibly useless she is? She's not a person, Wyatt. She's a trained monkey. I'm amazed she can even drive a car. Oh, wait. I haven't seen the car. I'll bet you money it's a limo, with a driver. Claire wouldn't want to risk her delicate and valuable hands by actually doing work. Holding the steering wheel might impact her performance and we wouldn't want that."

He'd known the sisters didn't get along and the bare bones of the estrangement, but he'd never understood the depth of Nicole's anger and bitterness before.

Nicole had been hurt when Claire had gone away, but until now, he'd never known the wounds went so deep. Sarcasm and black humor concealed a lot of pain. It was just like her to play the bitter bitch to protect herself.

"I can come over in the evenings," he said. "After work."

She slumped down in the seat, then pressed her arm into her midsection and groaned. "I don't want that. You have to take care of Amy. I'll be fine."

"No, you won't."

"I don't want to think about it. Not right now."

None of this was supposed to be a problem, he reminded himself. When the surgery had been scheduled, Drew, Nicole's husband, had still been in the picture.

Wyatt thought of his stepbrother and instantly wanted to pound him into the ground. What a total idiot. Talk about screwing up big-time. Drew had crossed the line and Nicole was never going to forgive him. Wyatt wasn't sure he would be able to forgive his brother either.

He glanced in his rearview mirror and saw Claire in the car behind them. Even from a couple of car lengths away, he could see her death grip on the steering wheel and the determination in her face.

"You should move in with me and Amy," he said. "That's the easiest solution."

"No."

"You're being stubborn."

"It's part of my charm."

Under normal circumstances, Jesse could have pitched in, but that wasn't going to happen anytime soon.

"If you don't want me, you'll have to have someone," he said. "At least for the first couple of days. Claire can keep food in the house, bring it to you."

"Ha. You think the piano princess can cook?"

"She can order takeout."

"I can do that."

"And check on you."

"Did I mention a trained monkey? It would be a lot more helpful. Or one of those service dogs."

"She's your sister."

Nicole glared at him again. "She was the start of my bad luck streak."

"You're overreacting. Use her. There should be some pleasure in that."

"Less than you would think."

They arrived at the house. After parking, Wyatt came around to the passenger side and opened the door.

Nicole looked at him. "Don't even think about carrying me. I can walk."

"When was the last time you let a man sweep you off your feet?"

"I would never do that."

"You need to work on your trust issues."

With that, he gathered her in his arms. Claire had already opened the back door.

She followed them inside.

He went up the stairs and into Nicole's bedroom. Someone, probably Claire, had pulled back the covers. When he set Nicole in the bed, she sucked in a breath, then forced a smile.

"Thank you."

She'd gone pale. He knew she had to be hurting. "When can you take something for the pain?"

"Not for a while. I got a shot in the hospital. I'll be fine."

She didn't look fine.

He pulled off her athletic shoes, then unzipped her sweatshirt. She eased out of it and he tossed it on a chair.

She wasn't wearing a bra. He could see her breasts moving under her thin T-shirt and wished the curves tempted him. Falling for Nicole would solve a lot of problems. Unfortunately, he felt nothing.

He pulled the covers over her, then sat on the edge of the bed.

"It's just for a few days," he told her. "I'm happy to hang out here in the evenings and you know Amy loves you but you'll need help during the day."

She closed her eyes.

"It won't be so bad," he said.

"I hate you."

"Is that a yes?"

She sighed. "Yes."

He stood. Claire hovered in the doorway. He went past her then waited until she'd trailed after him into the hallway and downstairs. Once they were in the kitchen, he faced her.

"You said you came here to look after your sister," he said.

"Yes. Obviously. Why else?"

"Fine. Then that's what you're going to do. Help. This isn't about you. Nicole is in a lot of pain. She's going to be healing and your only job is to make her life easier. You don't get to run off to visit clubs or hang out with your friends. You're to be here and be responsible. This is a serious commitment. I'll be checking in every night and I promise you, if you screw this up, you'll be sorry."

Claire looked at him as if he were an alien life form. "I have no idea what you're talking about."

"What was unclear?"

"Is that really what you think of me?" She shook her head. "Never mind." She crossed to the counter and leaned against it. "Part of me wants to ask what she's told you, but I don't really want to know. I mean, why would I set myself up that way? I'm bad and she's good and that's how it's always been."

She paused and swallowed. Wyatt had the sudden sense that she was fighting tears. While he was a typical guy and would do almost anything to make a woman stop crying, he told himself that this was nothing more than an expert performance. He refused to be engaged by the play.

But Claire didn't cry. She took a couple of breaths, then faced him.

"You don't know me. Regardless of what Nicole has told you, you know nothing about me. I could say the same about her, which is sad. We're twins. Fraternal, but still. I hate how much we've messed over each other's lives. I hate how things are now. I don't . . ." She stopped and pressed her lips together. "Sorry. You don't actually care about any of this, do you."

He watched her without saying anything.

She squared her shoulders and raised her chin. "I'm here to help. I have no interest in nightclubs, I never have. I don't have any friends here in Seattle, so you don't have to worry about distractions. I want to take care of Nicole and reconnect with her. Nothing more. Those are the only words I have. You'll either believe them or you won't. The bottom line is, I'm not going anywhere. Not until Nicole is better."

She spoke with a quiet dignity that appealed to him. His instinct was to believe her, but Nicole had always talked about how Claire played people with the same easy skill that she played the piano.

Still, he didn't have a choice. He couldn't take off from work and he had a daughter to deal with.

"I'll be around," he told her. "Watching."

"Judging. There's a difference."

He shrugged, not caring if he offended her.

He pulled a business card out of his shirt pocket. "My cell is on this. You can always reach me on it. If there's a problem, call."

"There won't be."

He handed her the card, instead of just putting it on the counter, then realized his mistake the second their fingers touched.

The heat was so bright and raw, he expected the kitchen to explode. He swore under his breath as he glared at Claire, blaming her for the unwelcome chemistry flaring between them. She stared at the card, then looked at him.

"That was weird," she said.

There was genuine confusion in her voice and questions in her eyes, as if she'd felt it, too, but didn't know what it meant.

Yeah, right, he thought to himself. She *was* playing him.

Play away. He didn't care. It didn't matter how he reacted when he touched her — he would never act on those feelings. He wasn't controlled by his hormones. He was a rational man who thought with his head, not his dick.

Still, when she smiled at him and said, "Thank you for taking care of her," putting her hand on his arm, he wanted to pull her hard against him and kiss her until she begged for mercy. The image was so powerful, his mouth went dry and he got hard in a heartbeat. Talk about humiliating.

He stalked out of the kitchen without saying goodbye and vowed he would keep his distance from Claire. The last thing he needed in his life was another useless woman making him crazy and ruining everything she touched.

Claire stared at the clothes she'd laid across the bed and sighed. Apparently packing was not an intuitive skill. She'd been so careful with everything. Yet here were all her clothes, horribly wrinkled.

Normally Lisa's assistant du jour would whisk the clothes away and bring them back perfectly pressed. If she wasn't around,

Claire could call the valet service at the hotel herself. But this wasn't a hotel.

She studied a silk blouse and wondered if it was safe to iron. With another sigh, she reminded herself she didn't know how to use an iron and if she wanted to practice, perhaps a designer silk blouse was not the place to start.

"Am I really totally useless, or is this an isolated incident?" she asked herself, speaking the words softly aloud. Better to know the truth than pretend. Her goal was to change — to fit into the real world. She needed to know where she was to find out how much work was required to get where she needed to go.

A sound from down the hall caught her attention. Still holding the blouse, she hurried toward Nicole's room and found her sister coming out of the bathroom. She was bent over at the waist, one arm pressed across her midsection. Her face was drawn, her mouth pulled in pain.

"You should have yelled for me," Claire said as she hurried to her side. "I'm here to help."

"If you figure out a way to pee for me, I m all ears. Otherwise, stay out of my way."

Claire ignored the snarky comment and rushed to the bed where she quickly smoothed the sheets and pulled back the covers. Nicole ignored her and what she'd done as she slowly, carefully, crawled back in bed. Claire reached for the covers.

"If you tuck me in, I swear I'll kill you. Not today, but soon and when you least expect it."

Claire stepped away from the bed.

When Nicole was settled she closed her eyes. After a second, she opened them again. "Are you just going to stand there?"

"Do you need anything? More water? Ice chips? They'll help you stay hydrated without making you nauseous."

"How do you know that?"

"I was reading some articles on the Internet."

"Aren't you mama's little helper?"

Claire clutched her blouse in one hand. "They didn't say anything about surgery making one ill-tempered, so I guess the sarcasm is all you."

"I wear it proudly, like a badge of honor." Nicole shifted and winced. "What are you doing here, Claire?"

"Jesse called me a few days ago and told me about the surgery. She said you were going to need my help." Claire didn't want to say the rest when it was obviously untrue, but she couldn't think of a way to avoid it.

She'd already told Wyatt and she suspected he had passed it on to Nicole. "She said you were sorry we were still estranged and that you wanted us to be a family."

She spoke without shaking, without her voice giving away her potential hurt. But it was still there, hidden. Because connecting was the one thing she wanted.

"You believed her?" Nicole shook her head. "Seriously? After all this time, you think I'm suddenly going to change my opinion of you?"

"Your opinion of who and what you *think* I am," Claire told her. "You don't actually know me."

"One of the few blessings in my life."

Claire ignored that. "I'm here now and you obviously need help. I don't see anyone else lining up for the job. Looks like you're stuck."

Nicole's expression tightened. "I have friends I could call."

"But you won't. You hate owing anyone anything."

"Like you said, you don't actually know me."

"I can guess." Claire hated being obligated, too.

"Don't pretend we have anything in common," Nicole snapped. "You're no one to me. Fine, if you think you can help, help. I don't care. The good news is I don't think you're capable of anything beyond being served, so my expectations are fairly low."

This was so not what she'd imagined, Claire thought sadly. She'd hoped they would be able to find their way back to each other. She and Nicole were twins . . . fraternal, but connected from conception. Had all the time apart, the anger and misunderstandings really broken that bond?

She was here to find out.

"You probably want to rest," Claire said. "I'll get out of your way."

"If only."

She ignored that and started to leave, then paused. "Do you have a cleaning service you use?"

"For the house? No. I managed to scrub it all by myself."

"Oh. Okay. I didn't mean . . . Never mind."

Nicole stared at her. "What didn't you mean?" Her gaze dropped to the blouse in Claire's hand. "You mean a service to clean my clothes?"

Claire took a step back. "It's not important."

"Yeah, right. Let me guess. A piano princess like you couldn't possibly be expected to take care of your own clothes. I'd tell you how to use the washer, but that's probably not going to help, is it? Too much silk and cashmere, I'll bet. Poor, poor Claire. Never owned a pair of jeans. You must cry yourself to sleep every night."

Claire did her best to deflect the hurtful darts that jabbed at her. "I won't apologize for my life. It's different from yours, but that doesn't make it any less valuable. You've changed, Nicole. I've always remembered you being angry before, but I don't remember you being mean. When did that happen?"

"Get the hell out of here."

Claire nodded. "I'll be down the hall if you need me."

"That is not going to happen. I'd rather starve than deal with you."

"No, you wouldn't."

Ignoring the burning in her eyes and sense of loss weighing her down, Claire returned to her room, determined to fix whatever had gone wrong.

The alarm went off at three-forty-five in the morning. Claire turned it off and then stared at the unblinking red light. What had she been thinking? Who got up this early?

People who worked in a bakery, she reminded herself. She was one of the Keyes sisters. She had an obligation to the family business. As Nicole was in no position to check on things and Jesse had disappeared for reasons still not clear, it was left to Claire.

She got up and pulled on clothes. Wrinkled clothes made only marginally better by their time in a steamy bathroom. She washed her face, applied some light makeup, pulled her long hair back in a ponytail and quietly crept downstairs. Less than fifteen minutes later, she had arrived at the bakery and parked in the back by the other employee cars.

There were lights on in the building. Claire hurried to the rear door and walked inside.

The space was warm and bright, smelling of sugar and cinnamon. Equipment filled counters and lined walls. Huge ovens radiated an impressive amount of heat. There were deep fryers and massive mixers, stacks of flour and sugar and what smelled like the richest chocolate in the world.

Claire paused and breathed in the delicious scents. She'd only been able to fix soup again the previous night, not that Nicole had been all that interested in eating. But three days of a nearly liquid diet had left Claire starving.

A middle-aged man dressed entirely in white saw her and frowned. "Hey, you. Get out of here. The bakery opens at six."

She gave him her best smile. "Hi. I'm Claire Keyes. Nicole's sister. I flew in because of her surgery. I'm helping out."

"Sister? She doesn't —" The man was small — a couple of inches shorter than her, but built like a bull. He drew his bushy eyebrows together. "You're the one who plays the piano? The snooty one?"

"I do play the piano," Claire said, wondering what Nicole had been telling people about her. "I'm not really snooty. Nicole, um, asked me to come by to help, what with her being laid up and all."

The man frowned. "I don't think so. She doesn't like you."

Something she'd apparently shared with the entire world. Claire had felt guilty about lying, but she didn't anymore. She was going to find a way to fit in and the bakery was the obvious place to start.

"We've come to an understanding," she said, still forcing a smile. "There must be something I can do to help. I'm her sister. Baking is in my blood."

Or it should be. Claire had never tested the theory by actually baking anything.

"Look, I don't know what's going on, but I don't like it. You need to leave."

The man walked away. She trailed after him. "I can help. I'm a hard worker and I'm really good with my hands. There has to be something. I'm not asking to work on the famous Keyes chocolate cake or anything."

The man spun back to face her. "You stay away from the chocolate cake, you hear me? Only Nicole and I do that. I've been here fifteen years and I know what I'm doing. Now get out of here."

"Hey, Sid? Come here for a sec."

The voice calling came from behind a wall of ovens. Sid gave her a scowl, then hurried off in the direction of the voice. Claire used the alone time to explore the inner workings of a real bakery a little more. She smiled at a woman injecting yummy-looking filling into pastry shells. The woman ignored her. Claire kept moving.

She found another woman working a machine that applied frosting to doughnuts. The smell was heavenly and Claire's stomach began to grumble in anticipation. She took a step toward the machine and bumped into a man carrying something.

As they struggled to get their balance, the bag he'd been carrying flew up in the air. Claire instinctively reached for it. But

66

instead of catching it, she only bumped the side, sending it tumbling, sprinkling its contents on them, the floor and onto the already frosted doughnuts moving on the narrow conveyor belt. It spun and spun before landing, open end up, in a massive vat of dough.

"What the hell did you do?" the man demanded, as he began to swear in a language she didn't recognize.

Sid came running. "You! You're still here?"

The woman managing the doughnuts flipped off the belt and hurried over to inspect them. "Salt," she muttered. "It's everywhere. They're ruined."

Claire wished she could slink away. "I'm sorry," she began. "We ran into each other and —"

"You're not supposed to be here," Sid yelled. "Did I tell you to leave? Did you listen? Jesus, no wonder Nicole talks about you the way she does." He leaned over the vat of dough and swore. "Salt," he yelled. "There's a five-pound bag of salt in the French bread dough. You think anyone's going to want that? It's our batch for the day. The *day*."

Oh, no. "Can't you make some more?" she asked in a tiny voice, feeling so awful.

"Do you understand anything about making bread from scratch? What am I asking? Of course you don't. Get out. Just get out. We can't afford any more disasters this morning."

Claire wanted to say something to make it better, but what was the point? All four of them stared at her as if she was the lowest form of life they'd ever seen. They wouldn't care that she'd only been trying to help. That she hadn't meant to run into the other guy. That it had only been an accident.

Not knowing what else to do, she turned and left.

It was after five when she arrived back at the house. Claire checked on Nicole, who was still sleeping, then went down to the kitchen and made coffee. The first pot smelled funny and tasted worse. She threw it out and started over.

The second batch was drinkable. She poured herself a cup and sank into a chair at the table.

How could her day have started so horribly? How could she have messed up so badly without even trying? It wasn't fair. She wasn't a bad person. Okay, yes, she lived a strange, twisted life that most people couldn't relate to, but that didn't change who she was on the inside.

But it seemed existing outside of her

gilded cage was going to be harder than she'd first realized.

"I'm not giving up," she said aloud. "I'm going to figure this out."

She didn't have much choice. If she couldn't play the piano anymore, she was going to need to have a life without music.

No music. The thought of it made her sad. Music was everything to her. It was her reason for breathing.

"I'll find another reason," she told herself. "I have unexplored depths." At least she hoped she did.

A little after six, she went looking for the toaster. There was plenty of bread in the freezer. She managed to burn the first three slices she put in before getting the adjustment right. She was digging around for a tray when the back door opened.

She straightened and saw Wyatt walking into the kitchen. Wyatt, who hated her nearly as much as Nicole. Wyatt, who'd made her hand tingle so strangely the previous day.

But before she could wonder what that all meant, she saw the pretty little girl who trailed behind him.

Wyatt set several grocery bags on the counter. "Something smells bad."

"I burned some toast." Claire couldn't

look away from the girl. "Your daughter?" she asked. Wyatt had a daughter? Which meant he had a wife.

The realization caused her to take a step back, although she couldn't say why. Still, she wanted to meet the girl. Claire had always liked children and dreamed of a family of her own.

"This is Amy," he said, moving his hands as he spoke. "Amy, this is Claire." He used his fingers in an odd way. "Amy's deaf."

"Oh." She looked at the child and noticed hearing aids in both ears.

She'd never known a deaf person before. No sound. What would that be like? Never to hear a Mozart concerto or a symphony? No melody or rhythm. Her whole body clenched at the thought.

"How horrible."

Wyatt glared at her. "We don't think so, but thanks for sharing your enlightened and sensitive opinion. When you see a one-legged guy walking down the street, do you kick it out from under him?"

She blushed and glanced at his daughter. "No. I'm sorry. I didn't mean it that way. I was thinking about music and how . . ." There was no recovery from this, she thought as guilt swamped her. "I didn't mean anything bad."

70

"People like you never do."

He wouldn't understand, mostly because he didn't want to. He assumed the worst about her and she seemed to do nothing but prove his point.

He began taking groceries out of the bags. She thought about offering to help, but knew he would refuse. Instead, she retreated to the living room and wondered if she should simply hire a nurse for Nicole and escape back to New York. At least there she fit in.

She sank onto one of the sofas and did her best not to cry. Why was everything going so wrong? How could she make things better? Because as easy as escaping would be, she didn't want to be a quitter. She'd never quit. Not once — no matter how hard things got.

But this situation was impossible.

Amy walked into the room. Claire started to apologize for what she'd said, only to realize the child probably hadn't heard her. Which meant she would have to explain why she was apologizing, assuming she could even get her point across. She sat there, feeling both stupid and awkward, not sure which was worse.

Amy didn't seem to pick up on any of that. Instead she walked over to a bookshelf

71

in the corner and picked up a large picture book. She carried it back to the sofa and handed it to Claire.

"You want me to read to you?" Claire asked, looking at the book. "Aren't you too old for this book?"

Amy waved her hands to get Claire's attention, then touched her chin. She motioned to her lips, then her eyes.

"See you speak."

The words were spoken slowly, with exaggerated pronunciation.

Claire's eyes widened. "You can talk?"

Amy raised her right hand and waggled it sideways, then held her thumb and index finger an inch or so apart.

"A little," Claire said, feeling triumphant. "You can speak a little."

Amy nodded. "My school teaches me."

"Your school is teaching you to talk?"

Amy nodded. She pointed to her mouth again. "Lips."

"And read lips?"

More nodding. The girl smiled. She pointed at the book. Claire opened it. There was a girl holding a book. Amy pointed at the girl, then made a fist and rubbed her thumb across her cheek.

"Girl." Amy repeated the motion. "Girl."

Understanding dawned. "I get it," Claire

told her. "This is the sign for girl?"

Amy grinned and pointed to the book. She held both her hands together, as if she was praying, then opened them.

Claire repeated the gesture. "The sign for book?"

Amy nodded.

Claire flipped the page. "This is so cool. What else can you teach me?"

Wyatt walked into Nicole's room with coffee and the bagels he'd brought.

"Hey, sleepy."

She opened her eyes and groaned. "Hey, yourself."

"How do you feel?"

"How do I look?"

"Beautiful."

She winced as she pushed into a sitting position, then leaned back against the pillows. "You are such a liar, but thank you for that. I feel awful. I have to tell you, the drugs in the hospital are much better than the stuff you get at the pharmacy. Is that coffee?"

"Yes, but I wasn't sure if you were allowed any."

"So you brought it to taunt me?" She reached for the mug. "I'm supposed to take it easy and eat what sounds good. Coffee sounds like a miracle, right now."

He set the tray on the nightstand, then pulled up a chair. After she'd taken her first sip and sighed with pleasure, he asked, "You doing okay with Claire?"

Nicole rolled her eyes. "Do I have a choice? She's staying away, which is my preference. Sid called my cell about a half hour ago." She motioned to the small phone by the tray. "She went to the bakery this morning, apparently to help. He sent her away. Instead she managed to run into Phil and dump a five-pound bag of salt into a batch of bread dough. It's totally ruined."

"How did that happen?"

"I have no idea."

"She didn't do it on purpose, did she?"

Nicole glared at him. "Probably not, but don't you dare take her side."

"Not my plan."

"Good, because I'm not sure I could handle that. She's even more useless than I'd first thought. She actually asked me about a cleaning service for her clothes. Apparently a few things are wrinkled and she doesn't know how to deal with that. We should all have such problems. I hate her."

"You don't hate her."

"I know, but I wish she'd go away."

So did Wyatt. As it was, he was keeping his distance. The last thing he needed was another raging fire keeping him up at night . . . in both senses of the word.

Why her? Why couldn't he have chemistry with someone else? Someone normal? Someone like Nicole? His body sure had a sense of humor.

Nicole glanced at the clock. "Where's Amy?"

"Downstairs with your sister."

"Check her before you leave. Who knows what Claire might do to her."

"I'll make sure she's in one piece." He stood and crossed to the bed, then kissed Nicole on the top of the head. "Call me if you need anything."

"I will."

"I'll be back soon."

"Come right away if you see smoke rising in the sky."

"Promise."

He went downstairs. As he entered the living room, he heard laughter. Amy sat next to Claire, watching intently as Nicole's sister carefully signed the story in the picture book on her lap. Her movements were studied, but she got all the words right. When his daughter signed the word *good*, Claire laughed again.

"You're a good teacher," she said slowly.

Amy signed, "Good student."

Claire reached out and hugged her.

Amy went easily into her arms.

Wyatt was unimpressed. Claire might be able to fool a child, but he knew better. She wasn't going to be able to suck him in so easily.

CHAPTER FOUR

The following morning Claire waited until she was sure Wyatt wasn't going to show up, then made breakfast herself and carried it upstairs. She found her sister awake, which was a surprise. Every time she'd checked on Nicole the previous day, she'd been asleep, or pretending to sleep.

"You're still here, I see," Nicole said by way of greeting.

"Are you always this crabby in the morning, or is it me bringing out the worst in you?"

"You get all the credit."

"Lucky me."

She set the tray on the nightstand. Nicole looked over the simple meal.

"Thank you," she said through obviously gritted teeth.

Claire was so proud, she could have floated. "The oatmeal is really good. I made it myself."

"Two ingredients, including water. Very impressive."

Claire refused to let her sister's sarcasm spoil her happy mood. This was her first real breakfast and it had turned out with only one try. Yay, her. Today oatmeal, tomorrow, a sandwich!

Nicole reached for the bowl. "I thought maybe you were leaving."

"No, sorry. I'm here until you're back on your feet." She thought about Jesse's unexplained absence. "Unless you want me to call Jesse and ask her to come."

"No."

"Are you sure?"

Nicole's gaze turned icy. "Jesse is not welcome here."

Okay, so there *was* a problem. Claire had already guessed as much. "When did you two stop speaking?"

"I'm not discussing this with you."

"What did she do?"

"What part of my previous statement didn't you understand? She's a born liar and a cheat. She lied to you about me wanting you here and she —" Nicole dropped her spoon back into the bowl. "Just go."

Claire assumed she meant from the bedroom rather than the house. Either way she stayed in place. "She's just a kid."

"She's twenty-two and you don't know what you're talking about."

Claire wanted to understand the problem, but she had a feeling that pushing wasn't going to help. "You need to eat something. You'll get better faster if you do."

"Motivation. That's good." She took a small taste of the oatmeal. "Brown sugar?"

"Uh-huh."

Nicole ate a little more while Claire hovered in the doorway. She wanted to go sit down, but that felt too intrusive.

The whole situation was crazy, she told herself. Why did things have to be so awkward? Although she knew the answer, she wanted it to be different. She wanted *them* to be different.

"Why aren't you on tour?" Nicole asked as she reached for her coffee. "Is that what you do with your day? Play piano for people? Won't your adoring fans miss you?"

Claire stiffened. Without wanting to, she remembered her last performance. The heat of the lights, the pressure in her ears, the murmur of the crowd and most of all, the tightness in her chest.

She'd been unable to catch her breath, and had walked out on stage, feeling as if she was going to have a heart attack and die. She'd been unable to focus on her playing. There had only been the thundering of her heart and the knowledge that she would collapse at any second.

She'd played badly because of it, she thought, recalling the humiliation. While she might play the same music over and over again, she always remembered that for her audience, this was a special event. They'd taken time from their busy lives, bought a ticket and come to see her. She owed them her best. That night she'd failed. Then she'd collapsed and had to be helped off the stage.

Shame filled her. She'd failed publicly. She'd let the panic win. Worse, she didn't know how to keep it from winning.

"I didn't mean for the question to be so hard," Nicole said.

"I'm taking a break," she murmured.

Nicole's cell phone rang. She reached for it. "Hey, Sid. What's up?" She paused, then groaned. "You have to be kidding. No, no. I understand." Her gaze settled on Claire. "No way. Are you serious? But do you remember — Fine. It's your call. I'll tell her."

Nicole hung up, then looked at Claire. "We have a problem at the bakery."

Claire thought about the tumbling bag of salt and wondered what other damage it had done. "Which is?"

"Our two morning clerks called in sick. There's no one to work the front counter. Normally I would fill in or ask Jesse, but neither of those are possible. You're going to have to do it."

"What? What do you mean?"

Nicole rolled her eyes. "What was unclear? Work the counter. Take money for goods. Don't panic. There's no actual math involved. The cash register does that for you. Just take their money and give them change. Even you can do that."

Claire didn't want to. She really didn't want to. The potential to screw up seemed huge. But Nicole needed her.

"Okay," she said. "I'll do it."

"Fine. Stay away from the back."

Fifteen minutes later, Claire had changed and was heading to her car. She walked outside only to find Jesse leaning against her rental.

"Hey, big sister. How's it going?"

"How's it going? How's it going? That's all you have to say to me? You're kidding, right?" She was both happy to see her sister and so angry she could spit. "You set me up. You lied to me. Nicole doesn't want me here. She hates me. What is up with that? And why aren't you around taking care of

81

things?"

"Nicole and I are having some issues."

"Guess what? I don't care about that. How could you lie to me?"

Jesse, tall and thin, pretty, with hair down to her waist, straightened. "I didn't lie. Nicole did have surgery and she does need you."

"But she hates me. She's not interested in reconciling and everyone she knows hates me."

"Well, that's true." Jesse actually grinned. "She tells some great stories about you."

"Great from whose perspective?"

"Anyone listening. Probably not you." Jesse sighed. "She needs help. I know she thinks I don't care about her, but I do. I didn't know who else to call. You're here and that's what matters."

Claire groaned. "It isn't what matters. I don't belong here." Not that she was leaving, but still. "Every moment is uncomfortable. And who is Wyatt? He hates me, too. Did she spend all her time telling him horrible things about me?"

"Not all, but some. Wyatt and Nicole are friends. Have been for a long time. His stepbrother, Drew, married Nicole. They, ah, just broke up a couple of weeks ago. I don't know if they're going to get back together."

Jesse crossed her arms over her chest as she spoke. Claire felt the undercurrents but didn't know what they meant.

"She never even invited me to the wedding," Claire murmured.

"Did you expect her to?"

"Of course. I would have come."

"Assuming you weren't playing for the queen that night."

Claire glared at her. "Don't you dare take any attitude with me, Jesse. Most of this is your fault."

"I'm not the one who took off and left her family behind to go be famous."

There was a bitterness in her sister's words. Claire frowned. "Is that what you think happened? That I simply decided to go off and be famous? I was six years old. I didn't get to decide anything. They decided for me." Her parents, her teacher. One day she'd been living in Seattle and the next she was on a plane to New York. "They took me away from my family and no matter how much I begged, they wouldn't let me come home."

"Poor little prodigy," Jesse said. "Is the fame too much? Are you having too much fun?"

"It's not like that."

But she didn't bother explaining. No one wanted to know the truth. Not the past or the present. No one wanted to hear about the hours spent practicing, the late nights and early mornings, the delayed flights, the grueling schedule. No one cared that after a while, all the hotels rooms looked the same and that the only way she could tell what city she was in was by looking at the newspaper on her breakfast tray. That while she'd visited some of the most amazing places in the world, she'd never seen them. There wasn't time.

"I'm a trained circus animal," she said at last. "Nothing more."

"You were the princess." Jesse's mouth twisted. "Fussed over, pampered. Wanted. Probably still are. It wasn't like that here. At least not for me."

"What do you mean?"

Jesse shrugged. "It doesn't matter."

Claire had a feeling it did matter a lot. "Why did you and Nicole fight?"

Jesse stiffened. "I don't want to talk about that."

"You'd better. It's the reason you lied to me. You dragged me all the way out here to deal with some mess you couldn't. So what happened?"

"I . . ." Jesse drew in a breath. Her expression turned defiant. "Nicole caught me in bed with her husband. She wasn't happy."

Claire opened her mouth, then closed it. Shock flooded her. "You slept with your sister's husband? You had sex with him?" It was impossible. Who did that sort of thing? "She's family."

"She would disagree with you about that. She disowned me."

Jesse sounded so calm about all of this. As if what she'd done didn't matter. Claire wanted to shake her. "Do you blame her? What were you thinking?"

"I wasn't thinking. I wasn't doing a lot of things but no one wants to hear that."

Claire glared at her. "You need a better excuse than that. Sex doesn't just happen. You didn't stumble into him and suddenly you were having sex. It requires a plan, a relationship of some kind. I can't believe it. How long were you seeing him?"

"We weren't seeing each other. I told you. It just . . . It's not . . ." Jesse straightened and walked back toward her car. "I don't want to talk about this with you."

"Ask me if I care." No wonder Nicole was upset and crabby. Her own sister and her husband. "Are you in love with him?"

"Oh, please. Give me a little credit. Besides, I have a boyfriend."

"But you slept with Drew?" None of this made sense to Claire. "Why?"

"I didn't sleep with him."

"What? Nicole walked in before you consummated the deal and that makes it okay?"

Jesse looked at her for a long time. "I know you won't believe me. Nicole didn't, either. I don't know why it happened. Why it had to happen. Maybe because I've been a screwup my whole life. This is just one more way I've made things worse."

"That's not good enough."

Jesse looked at her for a long time, then opened her car door. "Pretty funny. That's what Nicole said."

Wyatt buttoned the back of his daughter's blouse, then reached for the brush. She signed as he worked, but he pretended not to see. Amy wasn't saying anything he wanted to hear.

But when she turned to face him and put her small hands on her hips, he knew he didn't have a choice. He set down the brush and held out both hands, palms up, signing "What?"

"You know what," Amy signed in response.

He did. He didn't want to, but his daughter's message had been clear enough.

"Not a good idea," he signed back.

Which earned him the inevitable, "Why?"

Why? There were a thousand reasons, none of which he could explain to an eight-year-old.

"I want Claire," she signed, her face getting that stubborn look he dreaded.

As a rule, Nicole looked after Amy from the time she left school until Wyatt got away from his work. If he was in the office, she would come there instead, but most afternoons he was on a job site — not a place he wanted his eight-year-old hanging out.

But with Nicole recovering from surgery, babysitting was becoming a problem. Amy wanted to propose her own solution.

He didn't think telling her that Claire wasn't the babysitting type would help. Amy wouldn't know what that meant. He also couldn't get into the fact that he'd decided to avoid Claire as much as possible. The sparks between them were too dangerous, not to mention unwanted.

"I like her," Amy signed. "She's nice."

Wyatt could think of a lot of words to describe Claire and none of them included the word *nice*.

"She won't want to," he signed back. "She's busy."

Amy grinned. "She likes me."

He didn't know how to deal with that. Maybe Claire did like his kid — assuming she was capable of liking anyone but herself.

"I'm not asking for a pony," Amy signed, making him smile.

It was their private joke. Nothing was too big as long as it wasn't a pony.

He was trapped by his inability to tell his daughter the truth. That he didn't trust Claire and he wasn't a hundred percent sure he could control himself around her. How was that for a sad excuse?

"I'll talk to Nicole and Claire," he signed. "No pushing."

Amy's response was to throw herself into his arms. He pulled her against him and hugged her. Love filled him, as it always did around her.

He might have the worst luck with women, but when it came to kids, he'd been blessed with the best.

The parking lot at the bakery was jammed. Claire had to weave her way through cars just to get around to the back. She found a space by the wall and managed to pull in, although she had no idea how she was going to back out.

She walked purposefully across to the rear

door of the building and entered. "Hello?"

When there was no answer, she headed toward what she assumed was the front of the bakery. She pushed open a swinging door and entered chaos.

There were people everywhere. They filled the waiting area, pushing aside tables and looking impatient.

There were so many people, she thought, feeling a little sick to her stomach. Did they all have to come at once?

Sid spotted her. "What took you so long?" he demanded. "We're busy here."

Before she could answer, he grabbed her by the arm and pulled her into the back. He set her purse on a small desk, then reached into a box and pulled out a hairnet. "Put this on."

She took it and fumbled with it for a second, before he grabbed it and shoved it on her head. After thrusting an apron in her hands, he dragged her toward the front.

"Maggie will show you how to work the cash register. It's easy. Punch in what they buy, tell them the total. Take their money. Credit cards are even easier. Good luck."

With that he disappeared back into the bakery, leaving Claire standing there with no idea what to do.

The woman she'd seen the previous day

handed someone change, then hurried over. "Prices are on the list here." She showed Claire a laminated sheet of paper by a cash register. "Doughnuts, bagels, pastries. Don't worry about the quantity button. If they buy five, hit the key five times."

She quickly went over the basics of the machine, showed her how to work the credit card part of it, then pointed to the glowing number on the wall. "Call the next one."

That was it? Thirty seconds of training and they were done? Claire looked around, not sure what to do. She glanced back at the wall.

"Um, number one-sixty-eight?"

"Here." A well-dressed woman pushed to the front of the counter. "I need two dozen mixed bagels, the same with muffins, regular and fat-free cream cheese."

Claire went over to where the bagels sat in metal baskets. She pulled out a small brown bag, reached for a tissue and started putting one of each kind of bagel into the bag. After a couple of seconds she realized the bag wasn't going to be big enough. She pulled out a bigger one, then didn't know how to get the bagels from the first bag into the second one.

"Can you hurry?" the woman asked impatiently. "I'm running late."

"Um, sure." Not knowing what else to do, Claire dumped the bagels into the second bag and continued filling the bag. When she got to ten, she'd gone through all the bagels, so she started back at the top of the case, trying not to bump into Maggie and the other man working.

She took the bagels to the woman. "I'm sorry. What else did you want?"

The woman looked at her like she was an idiot. "Cream cheese. Regular and fat-free. And two dozen muffins. Quickly."

Claire turned, not sure where the cream cheese was. Maggie thrust two containers into her hands.

"Thanks," Claire murmured, then went to get the muffins.

When she'd gathered everything, she went to the cash register. Her customer handed her a credit card. Claire stared at it, then the machine.

"Dear God, could you go slower?" the woman muttered.

Claire's chest began to tighten. She ignored the pressure.

"I'm sorry," Claire said with a smile. "I've never done this before."

"I never would have guessed."

Maggie came over and took the credit card. "I'll ring this up. You go to the next customer."

Claire nodded and looked at the number reader. "One seventy-four."

Two teenagers in uniforms stepped forward. "A cherry-cheese Danish and a medium coffee. Leave lots of room for milk, please," the first girl said.

"Sure." Claire drew in deep breaths, but that didn't make the pain go away. The tightness only increased until it made her ears ring.

She moved around Maggie and stood in front of the display case. "Which one?" she asked the teenager.

"The one with the cherry and cheese on it," the girl said and pointed. "Hello. That one."

Claire reached for a tissue and pulled it from the case. She handed it to the girl, then went to get coffee.

There were four dispensers standing in a row. She took a cup and managed to fill it nearly full. When she carried it back to the teenager, the girl stared at her.

"Medium, not small and real coffee, not decaf. What's wrong with you?"

Claire looked at the cup, then back at the stacks of them. At the same time she saw a little sign above the dispenser she'd used saying Decaf.

The chest pain got worse. She couldn't breathe. No matter how much air she sucked in, it wasn't going into her lungs. She was going to pass out and then she was going to die.

"I can't —" she gasped, and set the coffee on the counter. "I can't."

"What's wrong?" the girl asked. "Are you having a fit? Is she having a fit? Can I have my coffee first?"

There was a buzzing in her ears. Claire staggered back. She leaned against the wall.

Maggie hurried over. "What is wrong with you?"

"Can't . . . breathe. Panic . . . attack."

"You're worse than Nicole said. Just get out of here. Go. You're scaring the customers."

It was just like what had happened the last time she'd been on stage, only no one rushed to help her. She wasn't urged to lie down or sip water. It was as if she didn't exist.

As she leaned against the wall and struggled for breath, she watched customer after customer be served, then leave. They went on with their lives. They had lives. What did she have?

She sank into a crouch, still gasping. Tears burned in her eyes. This wasn't what she wanted, she thought grimly. She wanted to be more than a crazy person with mutant hands. She wanted to be strong and capable. She wanted to be normal. But how?

She tried telling herself that despite how she felt, she really was breathing. Otherwise she would already be dead. Panic attacks were just a sensation. They were a biological response but they weren't about anything.

What she wanted to do was curl up in a ball until it was over. Instead, she forced herself to stand. After taking in two slow, deep breaths, she walked back to the counter and called out the next number.

A man stepped forward. "A dozen doughnuts," he said. "They're for the secretaries in my office, so lots of chocolate."

She nodded and reached for a box. After collecting twelve doughnuts, mostly chocolate, she went to the cash register and looked at the card. There was a single price for a dozen.

"Five-fifty," she said.

He handed her a ten.

Claire put that into the cash register, made change and handed it over. The man smiled at her.

"Thanks."

"You're welcome."

She checked the next number and called it out. Her chest still ached and she couldn't catch her breath, but she kept going. Working carefully, trying to smile and give each customer what he or she wanted.

One customer turned into two. Two turned into five. Eventually the bakery cleared out. When they were finally alone, Maggie looked at her.

"You all right?"

Claire nodded. "Sorry about the panic attack. It happens sometimes."

All the time, lately, but she didn't want to admit that.

"You didn't give up," Maggie said. "That's something. And you helped. So thanks for that."

"You're welcome."

"You can go. We'll be slow from now until lunch. By then Tiff will be here."

Claire nodded and walked into the back of the bakery. After removing the apron and hairnet, she collected her purse and walked to her car.

She started the engine and leaned back in the seat. She was exhausted. A quick glance at the clock told her less than two hours had passed since she'd arrived, which didn't seem possible. She felt as if she'd been working days.

Her cell phone rang. Claire pulled it out and glanced at the screen. Lisa again. Nothing good would come from that call. She turned off the phone and shoved it in her purse.

No doubt Nicole would have something snippy to say about her panic attack, but Claire refused to care. She'd managed to work through it and come out the other side. It was, for her, the first victory in a long time and nothing was going to take that away from her.

CHAPTER FIVE

Claire heated the last of the takeout Wyatt had brought over. As she waited for the microwave to do its thing, she placed her hands on the counter and closed her eyes. Without even willing them to, her fingers moved against the cool granite. In her mind, she played notes and heard music. The sound filled her until her body seemed to rise up and float.

The microwave dinged, dropping her back into this reality — the one where she didn't play piano anymore, didn't go to classes or teach or fit in that world.

She missed playing. Crazy, considering the fact that she could barely look at the damn instrument without having a panic attack. Maybe it wasn't the piano she missed as much as the sense of getting lost in music, of losing herself in the richness of the sound. Plus, practice and play were her life. It was like quitting smoking — even without the physical addiction, she still had all the behaviors in place.

She glanced at the stairs leading to the basement. While she didn't want to go back down there, she should take care of the piano. Her mental problems weren't the instrument's fault.

After checking on Nicole's dinner, she found a phone book and looked up piano tuners. She called three places before finding a guy who would come out this week and tune the piano. That done, she put the plate on a tray, along with a pot of herbal tea and some bread, then carried everything upstairs.

Nicole's door stood open. Claire entered and smiled at her sister. "I thought you might be getting hungry, so I brought a little more than last night. How are you feeling?"

Nicole lay on top of the covers. Sometime during the day, she'd changed into different sweat pants and a new T-shirt. Thick socks covered her feet. The color had returned to her face.

"I'm fine," her sister said.

"Good."

Claire set down the tray. "This is the last of the takeout. I'll get something else for tomorrow."

"Are you cooking?" Nicole asked.

"Uh, no. I was thinking maybe Chinese."

Nicole didn't say anything, which left Claire feeling as if she'd failed again. She didn't know how to cook. When was she supposed to find the time?

She told herself that she didn't have to apologize to anyone for her life, but couldn't shake the feeling that she was once again being judged and found wanting.

Nicole slid the tray onto her lap, then looked up. "Thank you for helping out in the bakery this morning. They were swamped."

Claire stepped forward eagerly. "I couldn't believe how many people were there. It was a huge crowd. Everything went so fast. It was difficult to figure out how to use the cash register, but by the end of the morning rush, I sort of knew what I was doing."

She'd come through and that was what mattered, she told herself. Every challenge met made her stronger.

"I heard you had some kind of fit," Nicole said sounding more curious than concerned. "Are you on medication?"

Claire felt herself blushing. She forced herself to continue to stand there. "I had a panic attack, but I worked through it."

"Don't expect an award for showing up," Nicole muttered.

Claire's embarrassment shifted to annoyance. "Did I ask for an award? Did I ask for anything at all? My recollection of recent events is a phone call from Jesse asking me to come home because you needed help. I dropped everything and flew out the next morning, showed up here to do exactly that — take care of you. I've brought you meals and snacks, helped you to the bathroom, carried in whatever you've asked for, helped out at the bakery and in return you're nothing but mean and sarcastic. What is wrong with you?"

Nicole dropped her fork onto the tray. "Wrong with me? You're the one who totally screwed up. You think I should be grateful that you brought your oh-so-special self to the peasant world for a few days? You think that makes up for anything?"

"All your labels, not mine." Claire's voice rose. "As for finally showing up, I've been trying to connect with you for years. I send letters and e-mails. I leave messages. You never get back to me. Ever. I've asked you to join me on tour. I've asked to come home. The answer is always the same. No. Or more accurately — go to hell."

"Why would I want to spend time with you? You're nothing but an egotistic, selfish, mother-murdering princess."

And I hate you.

Nicole didn't say those last words, but she didn't have to.

Claire stared at her sister for a long time, not sure what accusation to take on first. "You don't know me," she said in a low voice. "You haven't known me for over twenty years."

"Whose fault is that?"

"Not mine." Claire drew in a breath. "I didn't kill her. We were driving together. It was late and rainy and another car came out of nowhere. It hit us on her side. We were trapped and she was dying and there was nothing I could do."

Claire closed her eyes against the nightmare of memories. The coldness of the night, the way the rain dripped into the shattered car, the sound of her mother's moans as she died.

"I lost her, too," Claire whispered, looking at her sister. "She was all I had and I lost her, too."

"Do you think I care?" Nicole yelled. "I don't. She went away. She went away because of you and she was all *I* had. She left and I had to take care of everything here. I was twelve when she left. I was twelve when I figured out she would rather be with you than with me or Jesse or Dad. She was just gone and I had to do everything. Take care of Jesse and the house and help out at the bakery. Then she was dead. Do you know what it was like after that? Do you?"

Claire remembered the funeral. How she'd stood with Lisa rather than her family because they were strangers to her. How she'd wanted to cry, but there were no tears left.

She remembered wanting to be with Nicole, her twin. How she'd longed to have her father say it was time for her to come home. Stay home. Instead Lisa had explained about Claire's schedule and concert dates and that she was very mature for her age and capable of handling her life without a guardian or chaperone around. Her father had agreed.

Ten-year-old Jesse had been a stranger to her and Nicole had been distant and angry. The way she still was.

"Go back to your fancy life," her sister told her now. "Go back to your stupid piano and your hotels. Go back to where you don't have to earn everything you get. I don't want you here. I've never wanted you here. Do you know why?"

Claire stood her ground, sensing her sister had to say it and it was Claire's job to take it all in.

Nicole's blue eyes burned with white-hot rage. "Because every night after her death, I prayed God would turn back time and make it you instead of her. I still wish that."

Claire sat on the bed in the guest room and let the tears come. They rolled down her cheeks, one after the other, washing away nothing, simply seeping from the great open wound inside of her.

She'd known about Nicole's anger and resentment, but she'd never thought her sister wished she was dead.

The situation was hopeless, she thought grimly. She'd come home for nothing. No one wanted her and she had nowhere else to go.

She covered her face with her hands and cried for a few more minutes, then sniffed and realized she couldn't feel sorry for herself forever. But maybe the rest of the night would be acceptable.

She stood and walked over to her suitcase. A small photo album lay at the bottom. She carried it back to the bed and sat down.

There were only a dozen or so pictures inside, all of them taken before she'd left Seattle when she was six. She and Nicole laughing. She and Nicole on a pony. Their identical Halloween costumes, when they'd both been Dorothy from the Wizard of Oz. One photo showed them in bed together, sleeping, curled up like kittens.

Claire touched the cold, flat surface, remembering and wishing, knowing neither would change what time and distance had destroyed.

After washing her face, she grabbed a box of tissues and set it by the bed, then changed into an oversize T-shirt she'd bought in London — one with a huge head shot of Prince William on the front — and crawled into bed. She knew she wouldn't sleep, but curling up would make the whimpering easier.

She flipped channels on the small television on the dresser. As the pictures flashed in front of her, she wondered if she and Nicole could ever make peace with the past and each other, or were they forever destined to be strangers. She wasn't going to give up but she was also only half the equation.

And what about Jesse? Claire thought about their conversation from that morning. How could Jesse have violated Nicole's trust like that? Had she really slept with Drew? Could it have been a misunderstanding? If not, reconciling those two was going to be a nearly impossible task. Not that she was making great progress herself. Honestly, her personal life sure put her professional troubles in perspective.

Claire's eyes closed. She felt herself drifting off and welcomed the escape of sleep. What seemed like a few seconds later — although it could have been a couple of hours — she heard a *creak* on the stairs. She stirred and heard it again.

Just footsteps, she told herself, prepared to roll over. Then she sat up. Nicole couldn't use the stairs and Jesse was too slight to make that much noise. The possibility of Wyatt flashed through her brain, but the steps sounded too stealthy . . . as if the person climbing was trying not to make noise.

Claire got out of bed and crept over to her door. She cracked it and glanced out. Sure enough, a strange man stood on the landing, staring at Nicole's door.

He was only a few inches taller than her and not all that big. Instinctively, she glanced around for a weapon. The only thing she saw was a pair of high-heeled shoes. She grabbed one and quietly eased into the hall.

The man crossed to Nicole's door and opened it. Claire didn't stop to think, she charged, jumping onto his back and hitting him with the heel of the shoe. The guy shrieked, then stumbled into Nicole's room, all the while yelling at her to get off.

"Call 911," Claire screamed as she and the guy went down.

She braced herself for the impact. Fortunately he crashed into the hardwood floor, and she only landed on him. While he was still gasping for breath, she dropped the shoe, grabbed his right wrist with both hands and pulled it against his back, up high, near his shoulder blades. He yelled in pain. At the same time, she planted her foot on the back of his neck and pressed down as hard as she could.

The man swore loudly. "I'm fucking bleeding. Goddammit, Nicole, what the hell is going on here?"

"Call 911," Claire repeated. "I can't hold him much longer."

Nicole sat up and stared at them. "Claire, I have to say, you've really impressed me. When did you learn to do that?"

Claire felt her strength fading. "I took martial arts classes off-season for a couple of years. Plus, I've seen my bodyguards at work."

"You have bodyguards?"

Talk about the wrong thing to say, she thought with a sigh. "Not all the time. Not in New York, but sometimes in Europe. Fans can be aggressive."

"Nicole!"

The shout came from the guy. Claire looked at him, then at her sister. "He knows you?"

"Apparently. You can let him go. That's Drew. My husband."

Her . . . "What?" Claire released the guy's wrist and stepped off his neck. "Drew?" The cheating bastard who slept with his wife's sister?

The man in question rose slowly and glared at her. "Who the hell are you?"

He seemed good-looking enough, she thought absently, if one ignored the deep, oozing gouge in his cheek and the second one just under his ear. The wounds gave the phrase "killer high heels" a whole new meaning.

She ignored him and picked up her shoe. "I'll be down the hall if you need me."

Nicole looked at her. "Thank you."

"No problem."

Claire left Nicole's door open, then retreated to the guest room. As she shut her door, she heard Drew's impatient repeated question, "Who the hell is she?" but couldn't hear Nicole's response.

Feeling proud of herself and empowered,

Claire sank onto the bed and grinned. She'd done good. Maybe she should start working out and get stronger. Maybe take up martial arts again. She could be a dangerous killing machine. She looked down at her long, tapered fingers — a part of the freak hands she was supposed to protect at all costs. Maybe not.

She turned her attention to the television when what she really wanted to do was listen at the door. But that would be rude. She did her best to get interested in a show on HGTV only to jump when Drew started yelling.

"You're taking this all wrong."

"How am I taking it wrong?" Nicole demanded, just as loud as Drew. "Are you saying you just slipped on the carpet and ended up having sex? She's my sister, you bastard. My baby sister. If you had to whore around, at least keep it out of the family."

"Look, I know it's bad, but it's not what you think."

"Saying it didn't mean anything is not going to help you."

"I'm not saying that. It's just I want you to know I'm sorry for how much this is hurting you." His voice dropped.

Claire muted the television and tiptoed to her door. When she still couldn't hear anything, she opened it a tiny bit.

"I never wanted to hurt you," Drew said.

Claire frowned. She was willing to admit she knew nothing about men and women and the complications of their relationships, but it seemed to her Drew was apologizing for the wrong thing. The problem wasn't that he'd hurt Nicole. The problem was he'd had sex with her sister.

Nicole seemed to agree with her. There was a loud crash, followed by a "Get out, you slimy bastard. Get out!"

Claire opened her door wider. If she had to, she was prepared to escort Drew out of the house. She wondered how he'd gotten in, then wondered if he still had a key. She would have to talk to Nicole about changing the locks. Before she could decide if she wanted to interfere, she heard more footsteps on the stairs. Who now?

Wyatt couldn't believe Drew had been stupid enough to show up here. There were some relationships that couldn't be fixed and his marriage to Nicole was one of them. There was no recovering from sleeping with Jesse. He couldn't figure out if Drew was too optimistic or just too stupid to know that for himself.

He climbed the stairs, only to come to a halt near the top when he saw Claire standing on the landing. She was speaking — at least he figured she was. Her lips were moving and there was probably sound, but he couldn't hear it. Not when every cell in his body had spun around to get a look at her wearing a baggy T-shirt and — he swore and prayed at the same time — nothing else.

Her face was washed clean of any makeup, her hair hung long and straight. She was barely covered to the tops of her thighs and he would bet every penny he had that she wasn't wearing a bra.

"He just showed up. I didn't know who he was, so I jumped him. I don't think the punctures are really deep. I don't actually care about him, but someone should look at those just in case. He could get an infection."

He had no idea what she was talking about.

She took a step toward him. Yup, no bra. Worse, he could see the outline of her nipples pressing against the soft cotton.

Panties, he told himself. She had to be wearing panties. So that was something, right?

It wasn't enough as he imagined her in silk and lace and nothing else. He rubbed the bridge of his nose. Why her? That's all he wanted to know. He accepted that he had lousy taste in women, but why her? Why not someone reasonably intelligent and compassionate? Or just a regular person. Not the ice princess.

He moved past her and walked into Nicole's bedroom. Ignoring his stepbrother, he asked, "You okay?"

Nicole shook her head. "Get him out of here."

"Sure." Wyatt glanced at Drew. "You shouldn't have come. You —"

He stared at the deep puncture wounds on Drew's cheek and neck. "What happened?"

"Claire attacked him," Nicole said. She sniffed, then gave both a sob and a laugh. "It was pretty impressive actually. She jumped him from behind and started hitting him with a shoe. They both went down. She got him in some kind of armlock, then stood with her foot on the back of his neck. I guess they take interesting classes at music school."

Claire had attacked Drew to protect her sister? Who would have thought.

"She got me by surprise," Drew said defensively. "I've been drinking. My reflexes aren't working right."

Wyatt couldn't help grinning. "You were taken down by a girl?"

"Shut up."

"I'd say make me, but we both know that's not going to happen. I doubt Claire weighs a hundred and forty pounds. Jeez, Drew, talk about embarrassing." He grabbed his brother by the arm. "Come on. I'm taking you home. You can sleep it off."

Drew pulled free of him. "I'm not leaving. I belong here. With Nicole. I love her."

"You have a funny way of showing it," Wyatt muttered. "Come on. Don't make me get Claire to beat you up again."

"Get off me. At least I was willing to fight for my woman."

Wyatt ignored the dig. Shanna hadn't been worth fighting for. "If you'd been faithful in the first place, you wouldn't have to fight."

Drew glared at him, then stalked out into the hall. Wyatt watched to make sure he didn't go into Claire's room, then turned back to Nicole.

"You okay? One of his buddies told me he was drinking a lot tonight and talking about how much he missed you. He thought it was just talk, but I went by Drew's house to make sure he got home and he wasn't there. I came by and saw his truck in front."

Nicole sagged back against the pillows. "I'm fine. He's an idiot and he won't even apologize for what he did. He's sorry he got caught, but I don't think he cares that he had sex with Jesse." Tears filled her eyes. "I just can't believe it happened."

Wyatt sat down next to her. "I know. He's too stupid to live."

She nodded. "I don't love him anymore. I can't. But it still hurts." She wiped her face with a tissue. "Thanks for coming by."

"It sounds like the situation was under control."

Nicole gave him a shaky smile. "She was an animal. I was impressed."

"Drew will be humiliated for weeks. That should be worth something."

"It is."

He patted her arm, then stood. "I'll make sure he gets home in one piece."

"Okay."

"See you in the morning."

He braced himself for the impact of seeing Claire again. She still hovered in the hallway, looking five kinds of sexy and practically naked. She was probably one of those women who claimed she had no idea what she did to a man, prancing around like that.

He hated the wanting that rushed through him, the heat and the need that made him feel primal and hungry. She was completely the wrong woman — not that he would ever be the right man.

Claire glanced past Wyatt toward her sister. She wished she and Nicole were talking so she could comfort her and maybe make what was a bad situation a little better.

"I need to talk to you," he said, sounding almost angry.

She squared her shoulders. "I'm not sorry I hurt Drew."

"Neither am I."

"Oh. Okay. I thought you were mad at me or something."

"I'm not mad."

He stared at something over the top of her head. She turned but couldn't see what had captured his attention.

"It's about Amy," he said. "My daughter."

She folded her arms across her chest. "I know who Amy is."

"Nicole looks after her a couple of days a week. After school. Just until I can get away from work. But with Nicole laid up and recovering, that hasn't been possible. I work construction, so Amy can't always be with me. Job sites aren't safe."

Claire had no idea what he was talking about. Maybe he wanted her to drive Amy to her new babysitter.

"She likes you," he said, sounding unhappy with the fact. "Would you be willing to watch her? It won't be for long. A week or so. I'll pay you."

Claire blinked. Amy liked her? A happy warmth filled her body. "Really? She said she would like me to be her sitter?"

"Go figure," he grumbled.

Amy liked her! Claire wanted to do a little happy dance right there on the landing. Finally, someone around here enjoyed her company.

"I like her, too," she told Wyatt. "Of course I'll look after her. I'd be delighted. Just tell me when and where and I'll be there. You don't have to pay me. I'm happy to help."

"Don't make this more than it is."

"I won't."

"You're grinning. It's weird."

"I'm excited. It'll give me a chance to learn sign language."

"There's nothing to be excited about. She's a kid. You watch her. End of story."

Maybe for him, but this was the first positive thing to happen to her since she'd moved to Seattle.

"Starting tomorrow?" she asked.

He sighed heavily. "I'm going to regret this, aren't I?"

She held her happy dance inside. "Not even for a minute. Thank you, Wyatt."

He grumbled something and left. Claire twirled to her room, went inside and fell on the bed.

This was a sign, she told herself. Things were turning around. Everything was going to work out great.

Chapter Six

Claire walked into the bakery at four-thirty the next morning. Sid saw her and started shaking his head.

"No."

She ignored that. "I'm here to work."

"We can't afford your help."

"I did fine yesterday."

"You had a breakdown."

Claire didn't want to think about that. "I had a panic attack and I handled it. I helped out when you were in trouble. You owe me."

"That's crap."

She put her hands on her hips. "It's true and you know it. Plus, I'm Nicole's sister. This is a family bakery. I'm family. Put me to work."

He glared at her. "Why do you want to be here?"

She thought of the line from *An Officer and A Gentleman*. Richard Gere's impassioned cry that he had nowhere else to go.

"It's important. I'm offering you free labor. Why is that a problem?"

"Because two days ago, you ruined a batch of French bread. You're a pain in the ass."

She winced. "The salt thing wasn't totally my fault."

Sid glared at her.

She held up her hands. "Not that I won't accept my responsibility in the situation. Look, I'm just asking to help out. There must be something I can do."

Despite the loud noise from the mixers and the hum of the ovens, she would swear she could hear his snort of impatience. Still, he didn't dismiss her again. Instead he yelled, "Phil, the princess is back."

Phil, a tall, thin man, stuck his head out from behind a stack of racks. "Tell her to stay away from me."

"I was thinking she could do the sprinkles."

"What?"

Sid jabbed his finger at her. "Don't screw up."

"Words to live by. I won't. I swear."

Sid looked unconvinced as he walked away.

Claire turned to Phil and gave him her best smile. He glowered. "Come on."

She trailed after him, weaving through

118

narrow walkways, avoiding contact with any equipment. They came to a stop in front of a slow-moving conveyor belt.

"The sprinkle attachment is broken," Phil said as he handed her a hairnet and gloves. "You're going to put on sprinkles by hand. Not too many, not too few. You got that, Goldilocks?"

She nodded, wishing she knew how many were the right amount.

"That's what you're wearing?" he asked.

She glanced down at her black wool slacks and knit sweater, then nodded.

He muttered something, passed her what looked like a giant salt shaker, then hit a button on the conveyor belt so it started moving again.

Chocolate-covered doughnuts inched toward her.

"Sprinkle," Phil said.

She hated that she wasn't dressed right and found his disapproving attention unnerving. Worse, when she upended the shaker over the first doughnut, about a pound of sprinkles tumbled out.

"Just great," he muttered.

"I'll get it," she said, trying not to sound defensive.

"It's sprinkles. There shouldn't be a learning curve." With that, he left.

Claire quickly learned the right angle for the shaker and began to cover all the doughnuts evenly. Chocolate iced changed to white iced and she kept sprinkling. When her right arm got tired, she switched to her left, then back.

Thirty minutes later, both her arms burned and trembled, but she didn't stop until Phil reappeared and switched off the conveyor belt.

"Muffins on trays," he said by way of explanation and started walking.

She put down the sprinkler shaker and followed him.

They stopped in front of racks and racks of huge, warm, steaming muffins. Her mouth began to water.

Phil pointed from the muffins to big empty trays that would fit in the display case. "Keep the same kind on the same tray. Fill the trays. Got that?"

She nodded and went to work.

After muffin duty, she dumped dozens and dozens of bagels into bins. At six-thirty, she ducked out of the bakery and drove back to the house. She made coffee, then carried it upstairs with two fresh muffins.

Nicole was still asleep. Claire crept into the room, put everything on her nightstand, then tiptoed out. She was back at the bakery by seven-fifteen and put to work shoving loaves of bread into plastic bags.

Nicole woke and rolled over. It took her a second to realize the smell of coffee wasn't just her imagination, and that next to the carafe was a plate with fresh muffins. Muffins that could only have come from the bakery.

It was barely seven-thirty, which meant Claire had gotten up early, driven to the bakery, picked up the muffins and driven back. Perhaps not a big deal for anyone else, but for the piano princess? Actual work?

Nicole sat up slowly, holding in a groan as the movement pulled at her incision. She ached, which was how she started each day lately. She knew she was healing, but the process was a whole lot longer than she wanted it to be. There were —

Memories from the previous night crashed in on her. The fight with Claire, what she, Nicole, had yelled at her, Drew showing up, Claire attacking him.

Her sister had been possessed, leaping on his back and swinging that high heel like a knife. She'd managed to wrestle Drew to the ground, which was damned impressive. Claire had protected her, even after everything that had been said.

Nicole reached for the carafe and poured herself a cup of coffee, then sipped the hot liquid.

Claire was like one of those puppies that just kept coming after you, no matter how many times you told it to go away. Except Claire wasn't a puppy and Nicole hadn't told her to go away — she'd told her she wished she were dead.

"A pretty horrible thing to say," she murmured to herself. Worse, she'd meant it at the time. Not yesterday, but twelve years ago, when their mother had died, she'd really wanted Claire to take her place.

It shouldn't have been like that, she thought sadly. It should have been different. She and Claire had been so close when they were little. Like most twins, they knew what the other one was thinking. They'd been there for each other. Then one day Claire left and Nicole had felt as though someone had cut off her arm.

She'd spent weeks crying, wandering from room to room thinking that maybe if she kept looking hard enough, she would find her sister. But Claire had been really gone — probably lapping up her new princess life, she thought bitterly.

Familiar anger filled her — resentment for all Claire had experienced, annoyance that she, Nicole, cared. Genuine rage for being stuck behind to take care of everything.

Then she sipped the coffee again, coffee Claire had made and brought. Okay, maybe it wasn't the beginning of world peace, but Claire was making an effort. She could have left the first time Nicole told her to. But she hadn't. She'd hung in and kept trying.

With anyone else, she would have assumed that had to mean something. But with Claire . . . Nicole couldn't figure out if all this was a game or not. But maybe, just maybe, it was time to stop assuming the worst.

Shortly after noon, Claire climbed the stairs. She knocked on Nicole's open door, then stepped in.

"How are you feeling?" she asked.

"A little better."

"Good."

"Thanks for bringing me the coffee and the muffins. They were good."

Claire beamed. "You're welcome. I was happy to do it."

About a thousand sarcastic comments exploded in Nicole's brain. They were coming so fast, she would have trouble picking one. She remembered what had happened yesterday, what she'd said and what Claire had done and vowed to try not to be such a bitch.

"You got up early."

Claire eased into the chair by the bed. "I was at the bakery at four-thirty. Sid nearly had a heart attack. I promised I wouldn't screw up. I told him I just wanted to help. He didn't believe me at first, but then he put me to work. I did the sprinkles and sorted bagels and that kind of stuff."

Idiot work, Nicole thought. Where the new kid always started. "Kid" being the key word.

"Why would you do that?" she asked. "Get up that early, go down there and do the crappy jobs?"

Claire frowned. "Because this is a family business and you can't go there yourself. I know I can't fill in for you specifically, but I can free up someone else to do what's important."

The words made sense, but in this context they were way confusing. "You're a famous concert pianist. You probably make millions a year. Why do you care about the bakery?"

Claire stared at her as if she wasn't all that bright. "You're my sister. Of course I care."

After everything that had happened. After all that had been said. For the first time in a long time . . . maybe ever . . . Nicole felt very, very small.

"Look, I —" She pressed her lips together. Apologizing wasn't her best skill. "About last night. What I said." She sighed. "I'm sorry."

Claire nodded. "I know. I'm sure I'd say the same thing in your position."

Somehow Nicole doubted that.

"It's okay," Claire added.

Nicole didn't believe that, either. But she'd apologized and now she would try to be nicer.

"The bakery is really interesting," Claire said. "Everything happens so fast. All those products. Sid made me stay away from the chocolate cake, but I saw a few of them coming out of the oven."

"The famous Keyes Chocolate cake," Nicole grumbled. "It's a moneymaker."

The recipe had been a family secret for generations, and a local Seattle favorite. In the 1980s, a local politician looking to make a good impression had delivered one to President Reagan. It had been served at a White House dinner where the president had declared it better than jelly beans.

Three years ago, Nicole had received a call from one of Oprah's producers, saying the cake would be featured on the show. Nicole had hired a company to handle the influx of calls, braced her employees for eighteen-hour shifts and flown to Chicago with high expectations.

Oprah had been lovely and had gushed about the cake for all of eight seconds, before shifting the conversation to Claire and a performance the talk show queen had seen just weeks before. There had been a brief flurry of orders, followed by nothing.

"I don't know how you do it," Claire said earnestly. "Run the business. It's a lot of work. How do you know how many dough-nuts and bagels to make, and what kind? All those people working for you must be tough, too. I only have to deal with Lisa and sometimes that's a problem."

"We know what sells," Nicole said, ignoring the need to snap at her. "We have years of history to look at."

"But you run a very successful business."

Nicole shrugged. "I've been doing it for years. I started helping out when I was a kid. By the time I was in high school, I was handling most of it. I took over everything a couple of years later."

Her father had never been interested in the bakery. He'd done it out of obligation. But Nicole actually enjoyed her work.

"I couldn't have done it," Claire said. "I don't have any business sense."

126

"You don't have any practice," Nicole pointed out. "Things would have been different if you'd stayed."

Claire bit her lip. "I'm sorry I left."

Nicole had the sense of being sucked into a conversation she didn't want to have. "You were six," she said grudgingly. "It's not like you had a choice."

"But you got stuck with everything here. The bakery, being on your own, Jesse."

"I screwed up that last one for sure," Nicole muttered, trying not to fall into the painful combination of betrayal, anger and hurt that always filled her when she thought about Jesse and Drew.

"I'm sorry about that."

"How'd you find out?" Nicole couldn't imagine Wyatt talking about it.

"Jesse told me. She stopped by a couple of days ago. She's the one who called me to ask me to come help out." Claire's mouth twisted. "I don't understand how she could have done that."

"Me, either," Nicole said, hating that she wanted to ask how Jesse was. Did she actually miss her? After what she'd done? Impossible. "Let's change the subject."

"Okay. Wyatt asked me to look after Amy."

"Have you done any babysitting?"

"No. Is it hard?"

Nicole thought of a dozen snippy comments, each more hurtful than the one before. Instead she smiled. "I guess it could be with another kid, but not with Amy. She's a sweetie. I'm sure you two will get along great."

Claire waited by the bus stop as Amy waved to her friends, then climbed down.

"How was your day?" Claire signed, then took the girl's backpack.

"Good," Amy signed back, then said, "You've been practicing."

"Some. I'm trying." Claire motioned to her rental car. The plan was for her to pick up Amy, then take her back to Nicole's house. She paused by the passenger side door.

"I need to go shopping," she said, speaking slowly and facing Amy so the girl could read her lips. "I need different clothes. Maybe jeans."

Amy signed something Claire didn't recognize.

"Casual," the girl said.

"Right. I need a cookbook, too." She finger spelled *cook* and then signed *book*. "Something really easy. Do you want to come with me or go to Nicole's?"

Amy pointed at her. "Shopping."

128

Claire smiled. "They grow up so fast."

Twenty minutes later, they were at Alderwood Mall. Claire had already called Nicole to say they would be a while. After parking, she and Amy headed for Macy's.

"You need jeans," Amy said as she signed.

Claire fingered her wool slacks. More than jeans. She needed a whole wardrobe that wasn't expensive and difficult to take care of. Cashmere was nice, but not every minute of every day.

Once they were inside, Amy took charge. Claire tried not to be upset about the fact that an eight-year-old knew more about shopping than her. The truth was, she rarely shopped. Lisa, her manager, brought a selection of clothes to Claire's apartment or her hotel room if they were on the road, Claire tried them on and kept the ones she liked.

She wore classic styles from expensive designers. Her performing clothes were mostly long black dresses . . . variations on a theme. She didn't own jeans or T-shirts or a sweatshirt. Which was all about to change.

Amy led her to a table of jeans in different colors. Claire picked dark blue and black, then followed the girl to racks of shirts and knit tops. Some were plain, but others had embellishments — printing, or appliquéd flowers. Even small rhinestones. She grabbed a jean jacket, a couple of pairs of dressier jeans, sweatshirts, casual sweaters and a couple of white cotton blouses.

Amy picked up T-shirts, a halter top in bright pink and a couple of lacy tunic tops Claire wasn't sure about. Then they made their way to the dressing room.

Thirty minutes later, she had a casual wardrobe filled with easy-care cotton and fun colors. She bought jeans with flowers sewn on the back pockets and skimpy T-shirts that fit snugly enough to both make her nervous and make her feel good about herself.

She bought blouses and a couple of sweatshirts, along with a few sweaters. Nothing in black, nothing she couldn't wash. The five bags they dragged back to the car had cost less than the last designer blouse and skirt she'd bought only two months ago.

Amy helped her stow the bags in the trunk. Claire pushed it shut.

"That was fun," she said, then signed, "Thank you."

"You're welcome," Amy said. "Bookstore now."

They stopped for ice cream first, at the Cold Stone Creamery, then sat in the sun at a metal table to eat their snack.

"How was school?" Claire asked.

"Good," Amy signed, then switched to voice. "We practice speaking," she said slowly. "Practice every day."

"Can you hear anything?" Claire asked.

"Tone. Not words."

"What if I yell really loud?"

Amy giggled, then signed, "I'm deaf."

Claire couldn't imagine not hearing. Memories of music she'd played filled her head, making her ache to be at the keyboard again. Her fingers curled into her palms. How could she both love and hate playing at the same time? No matter how she filled her day, the nagging sense of needing to practice haunted her. Yet the thought of sitting down at a piano made her chest tighten with the first whispers of a panic attack.

"Were you always deaf?" Claire asked.

Amy nodded, then moved her hands, signing what Claire assumed was *born*.

"I'm lucky," the girl continued, both signing and speaking. "I can hear a little. Some don't."

"Do you feel sound?" Claire asked, hitting her chest with the palm of her hand. "In your body?"

"Music. I feel music."

She wondered if Amy would be able to feel her play. If putting her hands on the

131

piano would produce enough vibration. Would she be able to tell the difference between notes? Would she recognize the difference in pieces? Would a concerto feel differently than a Broadway show tune?

She was about to suggest they experiment when she remembered that she didn't play anymore. She'd just been panicking a minute before. Why was it so easy to forget she wasn't that person anymore?

They finished their ice cream and went to the bookstore. Amy helped her pick out a couple of basic cookbooks.

"Now I can cook dinner," Claire said.

Amy nodded and flipped through the book. She pointed to a meat loaf recipe.

Claire read the list of ingredients. It didn't look hard.

"For tonight?" she asked.

Amy nodded.

The recipe suggested mashed potatoes and carrots. Under vegetables she actually found a recipe for mashed potatoes and a chart that told her how long to steam carrots. It was a miracle.

"Grocery store?" she asked Amy.

The girl smiled at her. "I know where."

They made their way to a grocery store, with Amy giving great directions. Claire chuckled as she wondered who was babysitting whom.

They gathered potatoes, carrots, an onion, found the hamburger, although Claire was momentarily stumped by the different kinds. She bought the one that cost the most and hoped it was right.

"Your daughter is so pretty," an older woman said as she walked past them. "She has your eyes."

The comment surprised Claire, but she smiled. "Thank you. She looks a lot like her dad."

"I'm sure he's a handsome man."

Claire thought about the last time she'd seen Wyatt. He'd been on the landing, in Nicole's house. As usual, he'd been frustrated by her. She wasn't sure why she pushed all his buttons; she certainly wasn't trying.

"He's pretty cute," she admitted.

The woman smiled and moved on.

Amy touched Claire's arm. "What did she say?"

"She thought you were my daughter. She said we had the same eyes."

Amy studied her for a second, then raised her hand, fingers together, thumb across her palm. "Blue," she said, wiggling her hand back and forth.

Claire repeated the sign. They did both

have blue eyes, and they were blond, she thought. Amy was lucky — her beautiful color was natural while Claire's required a touch-up and highlights every four weeks.

"My mom is gone," Amy said. "She moved away."

"I'm sorry," Claire signed.

Amy shrugged, then looked at the list, as if it didn't matter.

They continued their shopping. Claire found herself wondering about Amy's mom. Who could have left this child behind? Who could have left family?

That's what Claire wanted while she was here — to reconnect with Nicole and Jesse. To belong somewhere. She also wanted — hoped — she could find someone of her own to love. A man who would care about her, love her, want to marry her. What she couldn't decide was whether or not she had a manageable goal or a stupid dream that was never going to come true.

They made it back to the house by four-thirty. Amy helped Claire unload the car, then she dashed up the stairs to visit with Nicole. Claire set all the food they'd bought on the counter, turned on the oven and opened the recipe book. As the meat loaf took nearly an hour to cook, she would start with that.

She combined and measured and stirred until she had everything mixed together, then dumped it into a loaf pan and smoothed the top. She slid the meat loaf into the preheated oven and set the timer.

The potatoes were next, she thought as she pulled out the bottle of red wine she'd bought. Then the carrots. She'd even bought a little bag of brown gravy mix.

She was making dinner by herself. Something she'd never done in her life. This, after working at the bakery nearly eight hours, babysitting Amy, hitting the mall and going grocery shopping. It had been a regular day. Totally normal.

She found a corkscrew and opened the bottle. After pouring herself a glass, she held it up, as if toasting herself.

"To fitting in," she whispered. "And being just like everyone else."

CHAPTER SEVEN

Wyatt let himself into the house. He was later than he'd expected to be, having spent the last two hours explaining why adding a window at this point in the construction wasn't going to be as easy as they made it look on the home improvement channel. He was tired, he was pissed off and the last thing he wanted was to see Claire.

It wasn't that he didn't appreciate her help with Amy. He did. Nicole's unexpected surgery had illustrated that he depended on his friend too much for babysitting. He needed a couple of backup plans. Claire had filled in during an emergency, which was great, but now he had to see her. And seeing her meant wanting her.

He didn't know what combination of her chemistry and his made him so attracted to her, but there it was. An annoying need to claim her whenever they were together and way too much time spent fantasizing about

136

her naked, wet and begging when they weren't. It was worse than being a teenager again. Back then, his desire had been vague, due to his lack of experience. But now he was very specific with what he wanted and he could imagine it in high-definition detail.

He walked into the living room and saw Claire and Amy sitting next to each other on the sofa. Claire signed something and Amy laughed, then shook her head. Claire finger spelled *mutant.* Amy laughed again, then looked up and saw him.

She jumped to her feet and ran toward him. He caught her and pulled her up into his arms.

"Hey, baby girl," he said. "How's the best part of my day?"

They hugged, then he put her down and she began signing frantically. He watched carefully to follow the conversation.

"You got an A on your math test? Good for you. Uh-huh. Tacos for lunch sound good. The mall?" He glanced at Claire, then back at his daughter. "Yes, we can talk about new jeans."

He signed as he spoke, watching the light in his daughter's eyes, both pleased and grateful that she was so happy, so normal. He'd been terrified to be a single parent — sure he was going to screw up completely.

But maybe not.

He watched as she told about meat loaf and cookbooks and how Nicole had moved to a chair, then Amy dashed off to tell Nicole that he was here. Which left him alone with Claire and unable to ignore her much longer.

"Thanks for looking after her," he said.

She smiled. "She's wonderful. I had a great time. She's a lot of fun to be with. So sweet and friendly. She's very patient with my lousy signing."

Claire moved her head as she spoke. Her long, blond hair fell over her shoulders, catching the light, making him think about burying his hands in that hair, of feeling the silky strands against his skin as she bent over him, took him in her mouth and — He swore silently and pushed the erotic image from his mind.

"You're getting better at signing," he said, hoping she didn't notice his sudden erection. He took a couple of steps to the left so he was partially concealed by a club chair. "What is mutant?"

"Oh." She looked at the floor, then back at him. "We were talking about my hands. They're large, with long fingers. Freak hands, really. It's good for playing the piano, though. I have a great range. Years ago, serious pianists would cut the tendons between their fingers to give themselves a greater range."

"Nothing is worth that."

"You'd be amazed what some people will do to be the best. It's a serious business with a lot on the line."

It was just playing the piano, he thought. How serious could it be?

"I bought a cookbook," Claire said, changing the subject. "My very first meat loaf is in the oven. I'm not much of a cook, so this is a big deal for me."

"Cooking isn't that hard. You'll get it."

"We'll see. When I went to use the oven, it was pretty complicated. There were three choices. Regular bake, convection bake and pure convection."

"When Nicole remodeled, she had a convection oven put in. It cooks faster and hotter, with a fan circulating the heat. You get more even results. In a regular oven, you can't stack cookie sheets and expect everything to cook evenly. In a convection oven, you can. You have to change the temperature and the cooking time if you're using a conventional recipe and a convection oven."

"How?"

"I don't have a clue. Our oven is regular,

so I bake the old-fashioned way. There are cookbooks that can help with that."

"Maybe I'll give it another week of practice before I head into that world. It's a little complicated for me." She tilted her head slightly. "You really use the oven?"

His arousal had eased, so he moved around the chair and sat down. "I bake a mean brownie. My chocolate cookies are okay, but that's because there's a recipe on the chocolate chip bag. I can bake a cake, although I usually order them from Nicole and I've never tried pie."

"Impressive," she said. "A renaissance man."

"A single father. Shanna left when Amy was three months old."

He'd been beyond terrified. Being a dad had been scary enough, but being both parents had been unimaginable. He'd barely slept the first year. Between reading everything he could get his hands on, dragging Amy to the pediatrician if she so much as sighed too heavily and grilling mothers for information, he'd driven everyone crazy. But they'd survived and once Amy started walking and signing, things had gotten easier. At least she could tell him what was wrong.

"How could your wife do that?" Claire asked, her eyes darkening with confusion.

"Leave her child? A baby is a miracle and Amy is so amazing."

"It was Shanna's choice to go," he said, not trying to hide his anger. He'd never missed the woman, but Amy needed her mother. "She doesn't come back and visit. Amy deals." Because she had to.

"I'm sorry," Claire said. "She's missing out. Amy is a wonder. I can't believe how well she talks."

"She goes to a special school for deaf children. In addition to signing, they focus on speech and lipreading. It was hard for her at first, but she's getting it. But there's some controversy in the deaf community about the practice."

"Lipreading?"

"And speaking. A large portion of the deaf community believes they have a viable culture that should be respected. That they aren't handicapped, just different, and that they shouldn't have to learn to communicate the way hearing people do. But I worry about Amy's life when she's older. All her family is from the hearing world, so she's going to have to fit into it some way. I want to make that as easy for her as possible. Learning to speak so people outside the deaf community can understand her is part of that."

He stopped talking. "Sorry. I get carried away."

"Don't apologize. She's your daughter. Of course you care. It's just all so interesting. Thank you for trusting me with her."

"I'm the one who should be thanking you."

They stared at each other. Tension filled the room. The wanting returned and with it, Wyatt's temper. Rather than walk around with a hard-on, or snap at someone who didn't deserve it, he stood.

"I'm going to grab Amy so we can get home."

"I'll go get her."

He watched Claire walk out of the room.

She moved with an easy, graceful stride, he thought, then wanted to hit himself in the head. He had it bad. More than bad. He was also going to have to find a way to get over it and her. She might not be as awful as he'd first thought, but there was no way he was getting involved with her. She was a complication he didn't need, even if she was a woman he desperately wanted.

Nicole shifted in the chair. Sitting up was the next step in her healing. She had muscles that had to be retrained. So far she was making excellent progress, although it felt incredibly slow to her. The pain was less, she wasn't as tired and the doctor had pulled out the stitches the day before — a wildly painful moment she didn't want to have repeated. She should be pleased.

Yet what she felt was restless. She hated that the bakery was doing so well without her. Logically she knew her business could survive without her for a couple of weeks, but emotionally she hated that everything hadn't fallen apart.

The phone rang and she grabbed it. "Hello?"

"It's me."

Nicole recognized Jesse's voice and hung up.

The phone rang again. Nicole picked it up. "Go to hell," she said, her voice low and angry.

"Wait. You have to talk to me."

"Actually, I don't."

Jesse began to cry. "I want to know how you're doing."

Nicole was unmoved by the tears. Jesse could turn it on like a faucet when it suited her.

"I'm recovering from the surgery, if that's what you're asking. Of course, having my heart ripped out by my sister and my husband is going to take longer to fix, so I don't have an update on that."

Jesse winced. "You're still mad."

"Um, yes. You must be stunned to realize I haven't gotten over the fact that after everything I've done for you, how I've supported you, taken care of you, tried to do everything I could to make your life better, you still wanted to stab me in the back. I'll give you credit, you did a hell of a job."

She refused to actually feel any of the emotions swirling inside her. Better to stay in her head, be sarcastic, because anything else would rip her open so far, she would never recover.

"You hate me," Jesse said with a sob.

"With every fiber of my being." Nicole hung up.

Her heart pounded in her chest and she hurt all over.

She hated this . . . all of this. Hated what Jesse had done, hated Drew, hated her body for betraying her and hated herself for giving a damn about her baby sister.

Nicole turned her attention back to her book. She wasn't actually reading the words, but she was willing to pretend. It was better than facing the emotional devastation of her life.

The house was silent and she was alone. Solitude pressed down on her, stealing her breath. She closed her eyes against the pain, but that didn't stop the tears from running down her cheeks.

Claire parked in front of Wyatt's house. As she took in the two-story building, the big windows and wrap-around porch, she tried to tell herself she was excited about spending time with Amy, nothing more. That the weird sensations flitting in and out of her body didn't have anything to do with seeing Wyatt.

He'd called an hour ago and asked her if she could watch Amy while he ran off to an unexpected meeting. She'd agreed, then had been surprised to find herself looking forward to seeing him.

"It's only for a few minutes," she told herself as she locked the car and walked up the path. "Then he'll be gone and I won't have to think about him."

She wasn't sure why he was on her mind at all. Okay, yeah, he was good-looking, in a rough, manly sort of way. She liked how he was with his daughter and how he'd gotten over judging her based on all the stuff Nicole had said. But it was more than that.

Right now, standing on his porch, she felt a flutter in her stomach. It was almost like the nerves she felt before she performed, but different. There was a different level of excitement. Something that —

The front door opened and Wyatt motioned for her to enter.

"That was fast," he said. "Thanks for doing this. I would have dropped Amy off, but it's her bedtime in an hour and I don't like to mess up her schedule on a school night. I have this client who's driving me crazy. I'd tell her to forget it, but I took the job, so I'm going to get it done right. Damn work ethic. It gets me in trouble every time."

He was smiling as he spoke. There was humor in his dark brown eyes. She found herself staring into them, as if she could . . . What? Get lost there? How weird was that?

"She's fed and she doesn't get much homework yet, so that's not anything you have to deal with." He glanced at his watch. "Let her watch TV another thirty minutes, then she can get ready for bed. She'll get changed and brush her teeth by herself. Maybe you could read a story with her, if that's not too much trouble."

"I would love to," she said honestly. Spending time with Amy was easy. She'd always wanted kids and being around Wyatt's daughter helped fill that empty part of her.

"Great. Thanks. I really owe you."

He was smiling again. Had he always been so tall? He was much taller than her, and more muscled than most of the men she knew. He also dressed differently, wearing jeans and a plaid shirt rather than a suit or anything designer.

"Claire?"

"Hmm?"

"You okay?"

She blinked and looked away. "Sorry. I was thinking about something. I'm fine. Go meet with your client. I'll take care of Amy."

"Thanks."

He touched her arm. It was nothing — a light brush of his fingers. But she felt the contact all the way down to her toes. It made her want to lean in to him and . . . And . . .

Then he was gone. Before she could even figure out what she wanted. A kiss? What would a kiss with him be like? He was probably the kind of guy who liked to be in charge, which was okay with her. It wasn't as if she had a ton of experience and someone needed to know what he or she was doing. Better him than her.

She heard running footsteps on the hardwood, turned and saw Amy racing toward her.

"Hi!" she said, then braced for impact as

Amy threw herself into her arms.

"You're here," Amy said, looking up at her and smiling. "I'm glad."

"Me, too. Your dad left instructions."

Amy wrinkled her nose.

Claire laughed. "Hey, they're not bad. You can watch TV until you have to get ready for bed. Then we'll read a story together. I think that sounds like fun."

Amy signed, "Okay," then asked, "Do you want to see my room?"

"Sure."

The eight-year-old took her hand and led her through the house.

Claire had a first impression of large rooms filled with light. Hardwood floors stretched throughout the house. She saw a big dining room, a study that she would guess Wyatt used for working at home, a huge kitchen, a downstairs bath and a media room that had more equipment than she'd ever seen at a theater.

A wide curving staircase led to the second story. Amy's room was the first bedroom on the left — a bright, open space with a window seat, a bed covered with pillows and stuffed animals, a child-size desk and a big bookshelf.

The walls were pale lavender, the comforter a floral fabric of various shades of purple. A big dark purple rug covered most of the hardwood floor.

Claire turned in a slow circle. "Hmm. I wonder what your favorite color is."

Amy laughed, then took her hand and pulled her onto the window seat.

Claire was shown favorite dolls and stuffed bears, several board games and a dozen or so books that all looked well-read. Then Amy opened her nightstand drawer and pulled out a framed picture.

"My mom," she said, handing it to Claire.

Claire wasn't all that excited about seeing the former Mrs. Wyatt, but didn't know how to politely decline. So she took the picture and braced herself for someone extraordinary.

Shanna Knight was beautiful. A stunning blond with short, layered hair and a smile that could sell toothpaste. She had pretty features, a perfect mouth and a gleam of mischief in her eyes. No wonder Wyatt had fallen for her. But why had he let her go?

"She's very pretty," Claire said.

Amy took back the picture. "She's in Thailand."

Claire couldn't have heard that right. "Where?"

Amy finger spelled the word. It was Thailand.

"What is she doing there?"

Amy shrugged. "I don't know. She left when I was a baby. Daddy says it's not because I'm deaf, but maybe it is."

Amy both spoke and signed, so Claire wasn't sure she understood everything the girl said, but she caught most of it.

What was she supposed to say? That it was all right? It wasn't. She couldn't imagine someone simply abandoning her husband and newborn daughter, yet that is what had happened. Even if Shanna and Wyatt had come to hate each other, wouldn't the other woman still want to be closer to her child?

It was a sad situation. Families shouldn't be torn apart. She knew that from firsthand experience.

"Nicole said her mom died," Amy said. "Your mom, too?"

Claire nodded. "Nicole and I are twins."

Amy's eyes widened. She signed, "For real?"

"Uh-huh. Fraternal." Claire spelled the word slowly. "We don't look alike, but we were born on the same day."

"I want to be a twin," Amy said with a grin. Her smile faded. "Or have a brother or sister."

Claire wondered if Wyatt was seeing anyone. At the thought of another woman,

150

she felt instantly edgy. "Your dad could get married again."

Amy frowned as if she didn't understand the word, then clasped her hands together in front of her. "Married?"

"Sure. People marry," Claire made the sign, "again."

Amy wrinkled her nose. "Daddy does not have girlfriends."

Wyatt didn't date? Why was that? Had he been so crushed by losing his wife? Claire didn't want that to be the reason. Not that there was any really great reason for a man to stay single for all these years. Of course it was possible he saw women that Amy didn't know about. He could be seeing a dozen right now.

Something else she didn't want to think about.

"You could date him," Amy said.

Claire opened her mouth, then closed it.

"Do you like Daddy?"

"He's, um, very nice."

Claire was grateful when that seemed to be the right answer. Amy put the picture of the beautiful Shanna back in her drawer, then took Claire's hand.

"Come on," she signed.

Claire followed her back downstairs, into a big living room with floor-to-ceiling windows. But what got her attention wasn't the view or the well-decorated space or the fact that this was obviously one of those rooms people had but never used except when special company came over. What had her heart thudding faster and faster and her chest tightening was the black upright piano in the corner.

Amy signed something that was probably a version of "play it" or "can you play it." Claire didn't respond. Instead she moved closer to the piano, staring at it with a combination of fear and longing.

She hadn't played in nearly four weeks. Not since that disastrous performance where she'd panicked and had been unable to breathe. Where the world had been reduced to her fear and the certain knowledge that whatever talent she had was lost forever.

She touched the smooth surface, then pulled back her hand. Even without sitting at the keys, she could imagine the music. The sound would fill the living room and spill out into the rest of the house. It would grow and bend and surround until it was inside of her, causing her blood to pump and her heart to beat.

She ached to hear the sound, to breathe in the music. She didn't need sheet music, she knew so much by heart.

There were symphonies inside of her. Movements and choral pieces, light opera, show tunes, concertos. Millions of notes. She could look at a page and know how it was going to sound. She could hear everything without even playing, but she missed the feel of the keys, the music that was able to flow through her.

Blessed and cursed, she thought, trembling as she placed her hand on the shiny black surface. This was her life and without it, she was nothing. At least that's what she'd always been taught. She was here to find out differently.

She thought of the dozen or so messages from her manager. Lisa was nothing if not persistent. But Claire had ignored every one of them. She didn't want to get sucked back into that world. Oh, but she missed the music.

Amy gave her a little shove toward the bench, then walked over and stood with her hands on top of the piano.

"Play," she said.

Claire took another step toward the bench. Immediately she found it difficult to breathe. Her chest tightened until she was sure she was going to have a heart attack. She would die right here, in Wyatt's living room, scarring his child for life. She couldn't do that. She should just walk away.

Instead she forced herself to take that last step, to sit on the bench, to open the cover and stare down at the keys.

She was breathing hard, sucking in air that never seemed to fill her lungs. She shook so much, she couldn't possibly play. Without wanting to, she remembered the looks of horror and disappointment as people had gathered around her. They'd issued a statement saying she'd collapsed from overwork. Not that she had been afraid. Not that she might be crazy.

Because she knew the panic was all in her head. That she was doing it to herself. If she couldn't fix that, wasn't she, by definition, insane?

"Play," Amy said again.

Claire nodded slowly. Ignoring the fear and the way her chest seemed to be collapsing on itself, ignoring the trembling and the knowledge that she had lost this forever, she put her fingers on the keys.

Something simple, she told herself. Something for a child.

She began to play one of Bach's lullabies. The melody flowed from her with an ease that astonished her. She remembered every note and never stumbled. Music filled the room, surrounding them. Amy stood, her eyes closed, her hands pressing hard on the piano.

Tears burned in Claire's eyes. She'd missed this, she thought sadly. Had missed playing. Even when she hated it more than anything, the piano was a part of who she was.

She played and played, losing herself in the sound, safe with her audience of one — a child who could only feel the music and who couldn't hear a single note.

CHAPTER EIGHT

Claire hovered by the oven, practically dancing with impatience as the timer counted down the last few seconds. When it dinged, she opened the oven and pulled out the roasting pan.

At first glance, everything *looked* all right. The chicken was golden-brown without being burned. The rosemary she'd put in the cavity smelled great.

She set the pan on the hot pads she'd already put in place, then pushed the meat thermometer into the breast. It read "done for poultry." Next she used a knife to break the skin by the leg and stared at the juices pouring out. They were clear. At least they looked clear to her, but as this was her first chicken, she couldn't be sure.

The last, and most important test involved actually cutting into the chicken. Claire braced herself for disappointment, then peeled back the skin and sliced into the breast.

It was cooked, but still juicy. She took a bite. Perfect!

"I did it," she hummed to herself. "I did it. Yay me."

Her first chicken ever. She'd managed to buy it and clean it and bake it and have it turn out. Amazing.

She opened the second oven and pulled out a casserole dish of scalloped potatoes. She wasn't going to take as much credit for those because they'd come from a box. Still, they looked good. Last, she checked on the steaming green beans.

When everything was ready, she got out a plate for Nicole. But before she could fill it, she heard a noise in the hallway. She looked up and saw her sister slowly walking into the kitchen.

"I got tired of living in one room," Nicole said as she pressed one hand to her midsection and made her way to the table. "I'm going to eat down here, if that's all right."

"Of course it is. How were the stairs?"

"Challenging. I'll be very slow going back up. Dinner smells good."

Claire was both proud and nervous. "I baked a chicken."

"Impressive."

Claire looked at her, not sure if the comment was really a compliment or something else. Nicole gave her a brief smile.

"I mean it. You said you didn't know how to cook. Now you're making dinner every night. You didn't have to do that. So thank you."

"You're welcome."

She hurried to set the table, then put the food out. Nicole sat in one of the chairs and continued to press her hand against her stomach.

"Do you want a painkiller?" Claire asked.

"No, I'm cutting back. I'll be fine. It'll get better in a minute."

Claire served both of them, then took her seat.

She'd gotten used to taking Nicole her dinner, sometimes eating with her, sometimes not. But this was different — being in the kitchen like regular people. She wasn't sure what to say.

"I brought home a couple of slices of chocolate cake," she said. "I'm not ready to try baking."

"One of the advantages of owning a bakery," Nicole told her. "You never have to worry about that kind of thing."

Claire nodded and cut into her chicken. Silence stretched between them. She wished they had wine with the dinner. Getting buzzed might help with the tension she felt. Not that she was a big drinker. One glass and she was happy — two and she was on the road to loopy. She struggled frantically to find a topic of conversation.

"It's been nice being in one place," she said. "I really like Seattle. Do you enjoy living here?"

Nicole stared at her for a second. "It's my home. I've never lived anywhere else. I don't have much to compare it to."

"Oh. Right. I guess New York is my home, although I don't spend a lot of time there. I have an apartment. It was difficult to find one that would accommodate a piano and still leave room to walk around. Moving day was a nightmare. The piano barely fit in the service elevator, so that took hours. I don't think I can ever move. It would be too much trauma."

Nicole speared a couple of green beans. "I was in New York a few years ago. I went with Drew. We saw a couple of plays and went shopping. I don't know if I would want to live in a city that big."

Claire kept chewing because it would be rude to spit out the chicken, but the flavor was gone and when she finally swallowed, she was afraid it was going to get stuck in her throat and choke her.

Nicole had come to New York and never called? Claire supposed she shouldn't be surprised, but she was. Surprised and hurt and feeling more alone than ever.

"Was, um, this before or after you got married?"

"Before. Sort of a prewedding trip."

"Sounds nice."

"It was before I figured out what a jerk he was, so we had a good time. All men are idiots."

Claire nodded in sympathy, when in truth she didn't have a whole lot of experience with men. Certainly not enough to make that judgment. Wyatt didn't seem like an idiot. Besides, she was still caught up in the fact that her sister had come to New York and not contacted her. Of course, Nicole hadn't invited her to the wedding, either.

"A lot of the men on tour sleep around," Claire said. "It's kind of their thing. They find a new woman in every city. I was lucky — I grew up on tour, so I watched it all while I was too young for them to be interested in me. When I was older, I'd already learned my lesson. Of course a lot of the women sleep around, too. There's plenty of sex in orchestras."

Not for her, she thought glumly. Sex was

something she seemed to avoid, or it avoided her. She'd never quite figured out which.

"How nice for you," Nicole murmured.

"Most people think orchestral musicians are nerdy or boring, but that's not true. They love to party."

"Was that how it was for you?" Nicole asked. "Sleep all day, party all night?"

"No. I had practice and lessons and meetings and interviews. I never got into the party circuit. I did get to go to some celebrity events, though. I met George Clooney a couple of times. He was nice. And Richard Gere, who really plays piano. We played together one night."

"How thrilling," Nicole said, glaring at her. "This may come as a surprise, but I don't need you reminding me how much more exciting your life is than mine. I'm totally clear on that."

"What? That's not what I meant."

"Isn't it? You certainly take every opportunity to talk about how wonderful things are with you. A New York apartment big enough for a piano. Hanging out with George Clooney and Richard Gere. Fabulous you."

Claire didn't know what to say. She'd only been trying to fill awkward conversation space. "You seem to really enjoy thinking the worst about me," she said at last. "I was trying to figure out something for us to talk about. Something we wouldn't fight about. I guess I picked wrong."

"You did. Do you think this is working? You pretending to be a real person? It's not."

Claire put down her fork. "I am a real person."

"You can't even do laundry."

"Is that the definition of a real person?"

She didn't bother pointing out that, thanks to Amy and the instruction book, she could now wash clothes, just like everyone else.

This was so unfair, she thought. She felt trapped. It wasn't as if she could lash out at her sister. Well, she could, but pointing out that Nicole couldn't bring an entire concert hall to its feet in screaming applause wasn't going to draw them closer.

"We live different lives," she said instead. "That doesn't have to be a bad thing."

"So speaks the woman with the perfect life."

Claire thought of all the time she'd spent alone. All the nights she went to bed so lonely, she ached. "It wasn't perfect."

"Oh, poor little rich girl. Was the fame too much for you?" Nicole dropped her fork

162

onto her plate. "At least you weren't stuck here, with a baby sister to raise and parents who only wanted to talk about their famous daughter. I hated you for taking Mom away, but I hated her more, because she wanted to go."

Nicole paused and swallowed, before continuing. "When Grandma came home, saying it was too much work and she couldn't travel with you anymore, Mom jumped at the chance to take her place. She wanted to go and see all those other cities. She wanted to be with you."

Claire didn't know what to say. She'd been grateful to have her mother with her. A piece of home was always welcome. She'd never thought about the family left behind.

"I didn't know."

"You didn't bother to know. While you were off running around with other rich, famous people, I was stuck here. I started looking after Jesse the day she was born. When Mom left, she became my primary responsibility. I was twelve. Grandma was in a nursing home and Dad never knew what to do with us kids. As I got older, I went to work in the bakery, as well. I never had time to do the stuff I wanted to because there was always Jesse to worry about, or my shift at the bakery. I was an adult by the time I was fourteen. Everything I wanted was stolen from me by you."

Claire had taken more than enough. She pushed back the chair and stood. "Poor Nicole, stuck home with her family. While you were going to school and making friends, I was alone. Alone with a tutor, alone in a practice room, alone in a hotel room. I never met anyone my age. I lived out of suitcases. I never saw the cities we visited. I was either studying or practicing or getting ready for a concert or sleeping. That was *my* life."

"At least you had Mom with you. Until you killed her."

"Stop saying that," Claire yelled. "I lost her, too, you know. She was my only link to my family. I was trapped in the car with her and I couldn't do anything while she died. Do you know what that's like? You had Dad and Jesse and I had no one. She died and the hospital sent me back to the hotel. Do you know what my manager said? That I had to play anyway, because the event was sold out and people would be disappointed. What did I know? I played. The night my mother died, I played onstage because there wasn't anyone around to say it was okay to grieve."

She shoved in the chair. "Apparently our

164

father had a long talk with my manager and together they decided I was mature enough to continue on my own, without a chaperone or guardian. That's right. I was sixteen and I'd just lost my mother and they cut me loose. My job was to follow the rules and I did because the rules were all I had. I don't expect you to get any of this. God forbid you should see anyone's side but your own. Being famous which, by the way, I'm not, is a lot less interesting than you think. I'm going to guess being a professional victim also gets really tiring, as well."

With that, she turned and walked out of the kitchen. She was pleased that she made it all the way to her bedroom before giving in to tears and collapsing on the floor in a puddle of pain and grief. She pulled her knees to her chest, trying to comfort herself, as she always did. Coming home hadn't mattered at all. She was still very much alone.

Her pity party continued for about ten minutes. Then she stood and went into the bathroom to wash her face.

"You knew this wouldn't be easy," she told her reflection. "Are you just going to give up?"

She reminded herself she'd never been a quitter, and that there were a lot worse things in life than fighting with her sister. So what if she'd had the fantasy of returning to Seattle and finding her family excited to welcome her back? It was going to take a little more work — that was all. She was good at working hard.

She crossed to the dresser where she'd unpacked her clothes and opened the top drawer. Under her bras and panties was a slim journal. She wasn't the diary type, but she did keep lists of goals and read them every day. That helped her stay focused. Her current list included — connect with family, start dating, have sex, fall in love, be normal.

The last one was going to be the hardest. Or maybe they all were. Have sex? Who was she kidding? She'd managed to go twenty-eight years without finding a single man interested in seeing her naked.

She sank onto the bed. It wasn't that she didn't want to have sex. She did. She'd had boyfriends, but time and distance had always been a problem. She'd never been anywhere long enough to form a really close bond. She knew better than to hook up with any of the guys in the orchestra. They were either married, total dogs or gay. She'd wanted her first time to be with someone special. The thing was, if she'd known how long it was going to take to find that certain guy, she might have been a whole lot less picky.

As she closed the book, she thought about Wyatt. He seemed like a good choice. She liked him, liked how he cared about people. He was amazing with his daughter and a good friend to Nicole. But she wasn't sure he liked her very much. That could be a problem. But he was letting her watch Amy, so maybe he was liking her a little?

Too many questions and not enough answers.

Claire stood and paced the length of the room, which wasn't very satisfying. After a couple of seconds, she went out the door and down the stairs. Ignoring Nicole, who was still in the kitchen, she took the second flight to the basement and closed the door behind her.

The studio was as it had always been, with the piano in the center of the room. She'd had it tuned, maybe because she'd known it would come to this.

The need to play swelled up inside of her. She'd managed to ignore the urge for a while, but playing for Amy had changed things. It was as if a wall had broken down and let everything spill out.

Life was messy, she thought, but music

was calm and sure and beautiful.

She sat in front of the piano and lightly touched the keys. The sound was good. It would take a few more tunings to get it right, but she wasn't in a place where she could be picky.

She closed her eyes and let the need grow inside of her. She didn't have to ask what she wanted to play. That would come to her. She put her fingers on the keys and began.

Wyatt knocked on Nicole's back door and let himself in. He'd braced himself to deal with Claire, but instead found Nicole standing at the counter.

"Look at you," he said. "You made it downstairs by yourself."

"I know. I'm practically ready to run a marathon. How are you?"

"Good. I wanted to check on you."

"I'm fine."

She didn't look at him as she spoke, instead dumping the contents of what looked like her dinner into the sink. She put on the garbage disposal and ran water until the drain was clear.

"Not hungry?" he asked.

"I was. I just . . ." She sighed. "Claire and I had a fight. Nothing like family discord to blow my appetite. The last two years Jesse was in high school, I lost ten pounds using the little-known 'I'm too sick to my stomach to eat because my personal life sucks' diet. If I wrote a how-to book about it, I could make millions." She looked at him. "How does it go so wrong so fast? This wasn't what I wanted. I came downstairs specifically to have dinner with Claire so we could talk. Instead, we end up fighting. I don't get it."

Wyatt was careful not to say anything. He loved Nicole like a sister, but she could be a handful. From what he'd seen, Claire was a lot more even tempered. Not that he would admit to that, even if tortured.

"She's been gone a long time. You're dealing with a lot," he said instead. "Take things slow."

"I guess."

She turned to him, stepped into his arms and buried her head in his shoulder.

"Do you think I'm a good person?" she asked.

"Of course! Why?" He rubbed her back.

"It's possible I'm the biggest bitch on the planet."

"No way."

"You weren't here."

"I didn't have to be. I know you. You're not a bitch. You're difficult and stubborn, but not mean."

"Gee, thanks."

"You're welcome."

He put his arms around her and held her close. She closed her eyes. He paused, hoping to feel something . . . anything. A flicker. A spark. Even an ember would be welcome. There was nothing.

The fire only happened with Claire, he thought grimly. Just his luck.

"My life sucks," she muttered as she pulled back and sank into the chair. "And I just made it worse."

He took the seat across from hers. "I doubt that."

"Stop defending me. I don't deserve it. I was mean to Claire."

He didn't say anything. He'd learned a long time ago that when a woman wanted to talk, it was best to stay out of the way and listen.

"She made dinner," Nicole continued. "She cooked a chicken. It was really good. We were getting along, but then she started talking about George Clooney. She's met him. She's met all kinds of stars and famous people and hearing about them really pissed me off. I hate that her life has been so great. She spends all her time going from city to city, playing the piano. Oooh, there's a tough job. She talked about the guys in the orchestra, how they like to party every night. Of course she claimed she didn't party. Her life was just so hard. I suppose fitting in that extra massage would be a real problem. And counting her money. That has to take days and days."

Nicole stopped talking and looked at Wyatt. "You want to change your opinion about me now?"

"No. But I do want to know why she pushes all your buttons."

Nicole hesitated. "It just makes me so angry. She got everything. She's the one our parents talked about all the time. They were so proud. She was the star and I was stuck home taking care of everything. I hate her."

"No, you don't."

Nicole narrowed her gaze. "I don't like it when you're reasonable. Have I mentioned that?"

"Once or twice. You don't hate your sister. You don't know her well enough to feel much of anything. You hate what happened to you because of her life and it's easier to say you hate her than blame your parents or circumstances."

"Have you been watching *Oprah*?"

"You're saying a guy can't be insightful?"

"Pretty much."

"I've known you a while now. It's a lot easier for me to see what's going on in your life than it is for you."

"I guess, but I like it better when I'm the deep one in our relationship. I just . . ." She shrugged. "I feel guilty. I hate that I feel guilty. I know she's fine." She looked at Wyatt. "Tell me she's fine."

"Want me to go check on her?"

"Please. She's downstairs."

"In the basement?"

"In the studio."

Wyatt got up and headed for the basement stairs. He'd forgotten about the enclosed soundproof room built for Claire to practice. She'd gone away when she'd been six or seven, which meant it hadn't gotten a whole lot of use. As he stepped in the basement, he frowned as he realized Claire had been a couple of years younger than Amy was now when she'd gone off with her grandmother. She must have missed her family a lot.

Especially Nicole, he thought. They were twins.

He knew Nicole had a lot of issues and he didn't blame her for any of them. She'd had it tough, looking after Jesse, working in the bakery. She'd been the responsible one. But what had Claire been?

He opened the door to the studio and was immediately caught up in the beauty of the music. He didn't know anything about classical songs or concertos or whatever it was she was playing — only that the piece was incredibly rich and almost . . . sad.

The piano was situated such that Claire's back was to him. She swayed as she played, her long, blond hair moving with her, catching the light. She either hadn't heard the door or didn't care that he was there. He would guess the former.

She seemed to be almost in a trance of some kind. As if the music transformed her.

He backed out the way he'd come and returned to the kitchen.

Nicole looked at him. "How is she?"

"Fine. Playing the piano." He walked to the refrigerator, pulled out a beer, then joined her at the table. "Why isn't she on tour? Isn't that what she does?"

"I don't know. I guess. Maybe she's on vacation."

"Her time off just happened to be when you needed surgery?"

Nicole scowled. "Don't try to make me feel guilty about her being here."

"I'm not."

"You're saying she might have had plans, but she dropped them to be with me."

"I don't know. That's why I asked." He knew Jesse had called Claire and that she'd shown up the next day. Had it just been good timing or had she had to cancel events to be here?

"I would guess she probably books up weeks at a time. Is there a concert season?" Nicole asked. "A better time to hear Mozart?"

"You're asking the wrong person."

"I know. It's just I hadn't thought of that. What you said. About her being here when she might have other stuff to do." Nicole didn't sound happy about the fact.

"Does it change anything?"

"Maybe." She paused. "I'm sure she's on vacation," Nicole said firmly.

"If you say so."

"You don't agree?"

"You're not going to get the answer you want regardless. Either she walked away from prior commitments to take care of you or she took her vacation time to come look after you. It's hard to make her the bad guy in this."

"Give me time," Nicole muttered. "I can work the problem. Besides, it's not as if I hate her. You were right about that."

He took a drink of the beer.

"I don't hate her. I don't like her." Nicole

174

sighed. "Say something."

"You're doing all the talking."

"Have I mentioned how annoying you are?"

"More than once."

"What do you think about her?" Nicole asked.

The question caught him off guard. Before he could stop himself, he remembered the last time he'd touched her. How deep the fire had burned. Then he pushed away anything close to an erotic image and shrugged. "I don't."

Nicole stared at him. "You are so lying. You like her."

He suddenly wanted to squirm in his seat. "I don't know her."

Nicole's gaze narrowed. "You think she's hot. Oh, my God. You're attracted to her."

"It's just chemical. It doesn't mean anything."

"You want to sleep with her? That's so not fair. You don't want to sleep with me."

"We've been over that material already."

"But Claire is a pain in the ass, Wyatt. You can't like her more than me." She covered her face with her hands. "I'm whining. How horrible is that?"

"You're allowed to feel what you feel."

She dropped her hands. "Don't you dare

be sensitive and understanding over this. Besides, she's my sister, which puts me in the weird position of telling you to back off."

He looked at her over the beer bottle. "Because she matters to you?"

"No. Maybe. I don't know. Just don't do anything rash."

"You have my word on that."

He wasn't going to do anything at all. Wanting and doing were worlds apart and he had no plans to make an awkward situation any more difficult than it already was.

CHAPTER NINE

"Come in," Amy signed before getting out of the car. "Come in."

Claire hesitated, looking at the two-story house, then back at the girl next to her. She didn't mind going into the house or spending extra time with Amy. What made her hesitate was the big truck parked in the driveway. Wyatt was home and as much as Claire wanted to see him, the thought of seeing him made her feel oddly nervous. Still, she nodded and got out of the car.

They walked up the main path. The front door opened before they could knock and Amy flew toward her father. He caught her hard against him and laughed as he spun her in a circle.

"How's my best girl?" he asked, looking at her as he spoke so she could read his lips.

"Good," Amy signed, then looked at her and spoke. "Claire's driving is getting better."

Claire laughed. "Gee, thanks for the compliment. I've been practicing. The freeway still doesn't make me happy, but I can manage. And my GPS barely yells at me at all."

"Come on in," Wyatt said. He put down his daughter and held open the front door.

Claire walked into the house. She'd been here several times. There was no reason to be nervous. Yet her stomach kept clenching and her skin felt funny. Sort of tingly and tight.

Maybe all this was because she'd been looking over her to-do list and had thought Wyatt would be a great candidate for the "have sex" item.

She looked at him now, from under her lashes, appreciating the way his broad shoulders stretched his shirt. He was strong. What would it be like to have someone to lean on? Someone dependable who could handle anything? Not that his strength was any reason she would want to sleep with him. Or maybe it was. She certainly wasn't an expert.

Amy signed that she was going to her room, then disappeared down the hallway. Wyatt watched her go, then turned to Claire.

"I really appreciate you looking after her."

"I'm happy to do it. She's a lot of fun and

very patient with my signing."

"She's happy you want to learn."

Claire frowned. "Why wouldn't I? It's how she communicates."

"A lot of people won't take the trouble."

"Why?"

"I don't know." He shoved his hands into his jeans pockets and looked at her. "We never discussed me paying you for your time. We should."

"I don't want to be paid," she told him. "I don't want to talk about money." When he didn't look convinced, she added, "We're family. Sort of."

He nodded. "Almost related until Nicole heals enough to get a divorce lawyer. I can't believe how Drew screwed that up."

She couldn't, either. Who did that kind of thing? She remembered her attack. "Is he okay? Is there still a puncture in his face?"

"Do you care?"

She considered the question. "Not really."

Wyatt grinned. "Now you sound like your sister."

"She's rubbing off on me." Which might be a good thing, Claire thought. Nicole wouldn't have let Lisa push her around. Nicole would have told her exactly what she could do with her stupid, demanding schedule and then she would have walked.

"You're looking fierce about something," Wyatt said. "What are you thinking about?"

"My manager. I'm wishing I was more like Nicole so I could tell her off."

"Is that what you want to do?"

"Sometimes. Right now I'm avoiding her calls. Not the best way to handle the situation."

He led the way into the kitchen. The room was large and bright, like most of the others in the house. The cabinets looked relatively new. There were granite countertops and stainless steel appliances.

Impressive, she thought, remembering he knew how to cook. Talk about the perfect man. Except, if he was so perfect, why wasn't he married or at least with someone. *Was* he with someone?

"Want something to drink?" he asked.

"Anything diet."

He looked at her. "Do I look like a guy who drinks diet?"

The tingles were back. "Not really."

"Good. But I keep some around for Nicole." He got a soda out of the refrigerator, collected a glass, filled it with ice and set it in front of her. "So why don't you tell her off yourself?"

"Lisa? I don't know. I never have. I should. It's different now. I'm not a kid anymore."

The problem was that she still *felt* like a kid. As if she had to ask for permission.

"Is she why you're not playing?" he asked.

She stared at him. "What do you mean?"

"You're not playing the piano," he said. "Shouldn't you be? Isn't that what you do?"

Not anymore, she thought sadly, remembering the previous evening when she'd managed to lose herself in music. She'd played for hours, until she was trembling with exhaustion and soaked with sweat. She'd played and played, wanting the music to heal everything. Unfortunately the complications in her life were such that playing was only a distraction, albeit a satisfying one.

"I don't have any current tour dates," she said. "It's close to summer. The season winds down during the late spring. Everything starts back up in the fall."

Wyatt pulled a beer out of the refrigerator and took the chair across from hers. "You didn't cancel anything to look after Nicole?"

"No. Would it have been better if I had?"

"I don't know. We were talking about it last night. I dropped by to check on her."

He'd been at the house? Claire fought a sense of loss for having missed the visit.

"I would have canceled dates to be here,"

she said. "Not that Nicole would believe that."

"She can be tough."

"Is that what we're calling it?"

He smiled. "You're more alike than either of you realize."

Because they were twins. There was a connection. At least there had been.

"How does it work?" he asked. "Do you just play out of New York? Are you with an orchestra? I don't know anything about what you do."

It was a simple question that might have been brought on by casual interest. Nothing more. Yet she felt both flustered and pressured.

"I, um, usually book for individual nights. I can do a series in a city, as well. I've played with different orchestras in the past. For a season or part of a season. But I —" Her chest tightened and not because Wyatt was so good-looking. "I'm not playing anymore. I can't."

"You're a little young to retire."

"I haven't retired. I just . . ." She didn't want to tell him, didn't want him to be ashamed of her. Yet she couldn't seem to hold in the words. "I can't play. I have panic attacks."

He looked at her as if he didn't understand

the words.

"They started last year," she said in a rush. "I was so tired. I wanted a break and I was looking forward to doing nothing for a few weeks. But Lisa wanted to book me on a special summer tour. I got upset and sort of faked a panic attack. She totally backed off. I know it was wrong. I know the mature thing to do was tell her the truth, right? I'm an adult. It's my life, but it's just not that easy."

She grasped the glass in both hands and stared at the contents. It was better than looking at him.

"I faked a couple more attacks, just to get her off my back. But then one day an attack happened on its own and I couldn't control it. I guess I'd gotten so good at faking them that they became real. They got worse and worse and now they control me. I barely got through the final week of my schedule and I collapsed at my last performance."

She ducked her head as shame rushed through her. She felt the heat on her cheeks. As much as she tried to forget what had happened, she relived the experience over and over again.

"I'm so ashamed. I don't know what to do. I've been to a therapist, who has tried to help. I know in my head that as long as I believe this is the only way I can get power, I can't get better. But I don't know how to change how I feel. And what if I can't play again? This is all I know. It's who I am. What will I be without that?"

Wyatt regretted bringing up the subject of her playing more than he could say. Now he was faced with an obviously upset Claire and he had no idea what to do or tell her. This was completely foreign to him — not just female and emotional, but nothing he'd ever experienced.

"Maybe, uh, if you saw, you know, someone else," he mumbled. "Another therapist."

"I guess I could try. I just don't know."

She looked small and broken, which made him feel like crap. In typical guy-speak, he wanted to tell her to ignore the problem and it would eventually go away. But he knew that wouldn't help.

"I hate feeling helpless," she said. "Weak."

Weak he could handle, he thought with relief. He was strong and tough. He could protect her. He could offer to . . .

He put on the mental brakes and did a one-eighty. Protect her? Where had that come from? He didn't want to protect any female, except for Amy. And maybe Nicole because she was his friend. But not romantically. He didn't get involved — ever.

Sex was fine. He liked sex, looked forward to it. He understood it. But caring, feeling and anything else emotional? No way. He knew the disaster that could result. He came from a long line of men who totally screwed up when it came to women. Drew and his ex-wife were only the latest illustrations.

"To be honest," Claire said, "Jesse's call came at a perfect time. Not that I wouldn't have come no matter what. I would have. But I'm kind of hiding out from my manager and Nicole's surgery gave me the perfect reason to disappear. Is that terrible?"

He thought about how she'd totally accepted his daughter, learning sign language and listening patiently as Amy slowly worked to speak clearly. He thought about how she'd kept showing up with Nicole, despite her sister's ill temper. He remembered her sitting at the piano, playing as if it was as important to her as breathing. How her gift and abilities had stunned him.

"It's not terrible," he said. "Everyone needs a place to go when things get hard."

"According to Nicole, they're not hard for me at all."

"She doesn't know everything."

"She thinks she does."

"She's wrong," he said, staring into her blue eyes. There was something there, a hint of sadness, but something else. Something he couldn't place. Interest? Passion?

Talk about projecting what he wanted to see.

Still, he found himself wanting to hold her. To put his arms around her and be the rock she needed for a while. Of course there was also a part of him that wanted to drag her close and kiss her until they were both breathless.

Claire smiled. "Thanks for listening. It helped."

"Good. Want to stay for dinner?"

The invitation had come from nowhere. He was rewarded by a slow smile that heated his blood.

"I'd love to."

Nicole told herself she wasn't actually watching the clock. What did she care if Claire was taking a long time to return Amy. It wasn't as if she was worried or even cared. Claire was nothing to her.

Still, as the clock in the great room ticked along, she found herself getting nervous and thinking about accidents and car jackings.

"You're being stupid," she muttered to herself. "If something bad had happened, you would have heard by now."

Just then, someone knocked on the front door.

Nicole pushed herself into a standing position and started toward the door. She wasn't moving very quickly and the person knocked again before she could get there.

"I'm coming," she yelled, annoyance sliding over worry. "Hang on a sec."

Expecting to see a uniformed police officer or sheriff, she could only stare at the well-dressed older woman standing in front of her.

"Who are you?" the other woman asked coldly.

"No one who is going to answer that question," Nicole told her. "You must have the wrong house."

"Is Claire Keyes here?"

Nicole hesitated a second before saying, "Not at the moment."

"But this is where she disappeared to?" Her dark gaze moved over Nicole before dismissing her. Her red lips thinned. "You're the sister, I presume."

Nicole felt no need to confirm or deny. "Who are you?"

"Lisa Whitney. I'm Claire's manager."

With that, the other woman swept into the house. Nicole didn't think she'd healed enough to physically throw the other woman out, so she closed the door and followed her into the great room.

Lisa shrugged out of her tailored coat, revealing a slim body, quality clothing in neutral colors and a handbag with a designer label. Nicole's idea of high fashion was a cashmere blend twin set, so she didn't recognize the shoes, but would guess they cost as much as a decent used car. Lisa's short brown hair was expertly styled, her makeup suited her face and the gold earrings, watch and necklace were probably real and 18 karat. Nicole pretty much hated her on sight.

Lisa draped her coat over the back of a chair and looked around. "She's really staying here?" The tone of the question implied this place wouldn't be much better than sleeping in a car.

"In my house, you mean? Yes. She's staying here."

"I see. What about practice? I don't see a piano. Is she taking classes?"

"Not that it's your business, but there's a piano downstairs."

Lisa looked at her. "Everything about Claire is my business. How much is she practicing? Four hours a day works best. She can get by on three and much more than five doesn't help anyone." She paused

188

expectantly.

Nicole didn't know what to say. Until last night, she hadn't been sure Claire was playing at all. She told herself she didn't owe her intruder anything.

"I have no idea," she said. "I don't keep track of her."

"You should. Is she eating well? Getting enough sleep?"

"Claire is twenty-eight. She's capable of getting herself food and putting herself to bed." Jeez, no wonder her sister was totally useless. She'd never been allowed to be a real person.

Lisa glared at her. "Claire isn't like the rest of us. She is a gifted artist. If she isn't watched, she'll work herself into the ground. She needs rest. A lot of rest. The last few years have been grueling. There seemed to be a window of opportunity. We had to take advantage of that." She hesitated over her next words. "Claire said it was too much, but I knew what was possible. Now she's at the top. We must do everything we can to keep her there."

Nicole wasn't clear on who this Lisa person was, but she knew she didn't like her.

"There is no 'we' in this."

Lisa ignored that and walked the length of

the room. "Do you know if she looked at the schedule I sent? It should have arrived today."

Nicole thought about the FedEx package in the kitchen. "No, she hasn't seen it."

"She can study it tonight. We need to get going if we're going to confirm for this fall. It's already so late, but there were openings. There's so much for her to do. Learn new music, schedule fittings and media events. Publicity is a large part of what we do. There's the travel to set up. It's only thirty concert dates in four months, but still. Preparations must be made."

Thirty concerts in four months? Nicole did the math. That was about a concert every four or five days. If they weren't in the same city, that meant travel to and from. Add in the four hours of practice Lisa seemed to require, along with fittings, interviews and who knows what else, it made for a busy day.

Was that really Claire's life? Constant travel and practice, with the possibly evil Lisa watching over everything?

Nicole remembered Claire telling her that her life was more difficult than it seemed. Not that Nicole was impressed or felt bad or anything. It was still a lot easier than living in the real world.

Lisa crossed to the front window and stared out. "Has she said anything about the recordings?"

"No." What recordings?

"She's been invited to be on several CDs. I know she'll accept the ones for charity. She always does." Lisa seemed annoyed by that fact. "But some of the others would be helpful, too."

Recording sessions in addition to everything else? It made Nicole tired hearing about it.

"At least she gets to see all those cities she travels to," Nicole said, more to herself than to Lisa.

Lisa turned to look at her. "It's not her job to see the cities. It's her job to practice and play and give interviews. Of course she would rather run away. I don't know how I let things get so out of hand."

Lisa walked back to the chair and picked up her coat. "I will not simply stand around waiting for her. Please tell her she can call me on my cell. And that I'm not leaving Seattle until we get this disaster straightened out."

Nicole didn't know what the disaster was and she didn't want to know. Fortunately, Lisa was no longer her problem. She listened to the familiar sound of a car in the driveway.

"Tell her yourself," she said. "She just got home."

"I'm back," Claire called as she walked into the kitchen. "Sorry I'm late. Wyatt asked me to join them for dinner, which turned out to be KFC. It's their one fast-food night a week and Amy picked. Have you eaten there? It's really —"

She walked into the living room, saw Lisa standing next to Nicole and instantly wished she hadn't had that extra chicken leg.

"Hello, Claire," Lisa said coolly. "Tell me you didn't actually eat fried chicken."

Lisa had always had the ability to make her feel small and stupid. An apology hovered on her tongue, but she bit it back. She was a grown-up and if she wanted to eat fast food, she would. It was her right.

"Yes, I did. It was delicious."

Lisa pressed her lips together. "What about the diet I gave you? It's nutritionally balanced, with a strong emphasis on soy."

Nicole made a gagging sound, then held up both her hands, palms out. "Sorry. She just showed up. I didn't know what to do."

"It's okay," Claire said. She couldn't hide from Lisa forever. Although it was a lovely daydream.

Lisa ignored the exchange. "I can't begin to tell you how disappointed I am in you, Claire. Disappearing like that, with no warning. Just a voice mail to tell me you were gone. You've been ignoring my calls. Did you think that would work? That I would just go away?"

Claire squared her shoulders and lifted her chin. "I had a family emergency," she said, then prayed Nicole wouldn't pipe in with a stinging comment about how Claire wasn't exactly welcome here.

Fortunately, for once her sister was silent.

Lisa's gaze flickered over Nicole, then returned to her. "Everything seems to be fine on that front. I assume you're returning to New York shortly?"

"I am not."

"What about the fall schedule? It's already half the dates it should be. If you are not out there, people will forget who you are. Brilliance isn't enough. You know that. You know how easily everything can be lost."

It was a message Claire had been hearing for years. She'd once heard a university professor complaining about the "publish or perish" rule. For Claire it was "perform or perish."

"I can't take anything on right now," she said firmly. "I have no idea when I'll be returning to any kind of schedule."

Lisa's eyes widened. "You don't mean that. You can't."

Claire wanted to ask if she remembered what had happened the last time she'd gone on stage. How she'd collapsed and humiliated herself. How the panic had won. But she was too aware of Nicole listening and too ashamed to tell her sister the truth.

"There are people depending on you," Lisa continued. "You are an industry. People's livelihoods are at stake."

Another line Claire had heard dozens of times. Couldn't Lisa get some new material?

"Mostly yours," she snapped. "If you want to resign as my manager, I don't have a problem with that."

Lisa took a step back. "No. That's not what I mean." She cleared her throat. "Claire, dear. I had no idea you were so upset. Of course you must have time with your family. I shouldn't push you."

It was amazing how Lisa could play both sides of good cop, bad cop and never miss a step.

Claire hated this. Hated having to disappoint people, hating not being able to play. But that's where she was right now — trapped with a talent she couldn't use. She was bone tired and not willing to get back onto the treadmill that was her life. She was tired of making decisions based on what everyone else wanted. What about what she wanted?

An excellent question, if only she had an answer.

"It doesn't matter if you push me," she said. "I'm not changing my mind. I'm here until Nicole is better. I might stay longer, I don't know. I'm not willing to make any commitments for the fall or any other time. I won't be pushed. So you need to just back the hell off."

Lisa stared at her for a long time. "All right. I can see you're not ready to come home. That's fine. I'll wait. You know how to find me."

Claire nodded but didn't speak. She stayed where she was until Lisa had left, then collapsed onto the sofa and covered her face with her hands.

"Impressive," Nicole said. "You really stood up to her."

"I did, didn't I?" Claire dropped her hands to her lap. "I'm shaking."

"That'll pass. She's really your manager?"

"Has been since I was twelve."

"She's scary."

"Tell me about it. But she's also the best.

195

There are a lot of talented musicians out there who haven't had half the opportunities I have."

Nicole settled into a chair across from the sofa. "She talked about your concert dates, the practice, fittings, media interviews. Is that a regular day?"

Claire leaned back against the sofa and closed her eyes. "Pretty much. There isn't a lot of free time. Sometimes I feel like those hamsters in a cage, running on a wheel. You go and go, but you don't get anywhere and the view never changes. I will say it's gotten easier. I know a lot of the music. When I was younger, I had to learn everything. That was a nightmare."

She paused, then braced herself for the sarcastic attack to follow. Nicole wasn't one to walk away from a good comeback.

But her sister only said, "It sounds tough."

Claire opened her eyes. "Are you feeling all right? Do you have a fever?"

Nicole shifted in her seat. "No. I'm fine. It's possible that after talking to Lisa I've come to see that maybe your life isn't as princessy as I'd first thought. That there might be actual work involved."

"Oh, really." Claire sat up and smiled. "Which would mean you're . . ."

"What?"

"You know. Say it. If you're not right, you're . . ."

Nicole shook her head. "Forget it. We're not going there. I'm saying I might have been misinformed. That's as good as you're getting."

"Wrong," Claire told her. "The word you're looking for is *wrong*."

"Never. So you stayed to have dinner with Wyatt?"

"Uh-huh. We went out. Amy's great. I really like her a lot."

"How do you feel about Wyatt?"

Claire had the sudden sense of stepping into dangerous territory. "He's a great dad. Patient and caring. Those two obviously love each other."

Nicole studied her for a long time. "They do. Amy's his world."

"I can really tell. He, uh, isn't seeing anyone, is he?"

Nicole stood. "Why do you care?"

"I don't. I just wondered. He's really nice and it seems like he would have remarried again."

Nicole's expression hardened. The temperature in the room dropped about twenty degrees. "I can't believe it," she yelled. "You're attracted to him? No way. You are so not dating him. You can just forget it.

197

He's my friend. *Mine.* Do you hear me? It's bad enough that Jesse slept with Drew. There is no way in hell you're going to sleep with Wyatt." With fists clenched, Nicole made an abrupt about-face and left the room.

CHAPTER TEN

Claire had never been on a construction site before. She got out of her car and looked for the trailer Wyatt had described. She saw it off to one side, but instead of heading directly toward it, she paused to look at what was going on.

The huge space had been cleared of most of the trees, although there were still several in what she guessed would be backyards. A few of the houses were already framed, while others were little more than stakes pushed into dirt. Big, loud equipment dug out foundations and moved soil.

She'd never thought about all the effort that went in to building a house. Or several houses. It looked complicated, and almost miraculous. How could someone create a house from nothing? How did anyone know what to do first, then second and so on until it was finished? Who figured all that stuff out?

Not a question she was going to get answered just standing here, she reminded herself and walked toward the trailer.

She was about halfway there, when a tall, thin man with a mustache stopped her.

"Aren't you the prettiest thing I've seen all morning," he said with a smile. "I'm Spike. Who are you?"

Spike? She'd never met anyone called Spike before. She took in the tattoos on his arm, his University of Washington T-shirt and the big smile that seemed to welcome her. She appreciated his friendliness.

"I'm Claire. I'm looking after Wyatt's daughter. He forgot to sign a permission slip so I brought it by."

Spike looked her over. "You're one of those fancy nannies?"

That sounded a whole lot better than an out-of-work, panic-filled piano player. "Sort of."

"It's nice to meet you, Claire."

"You, too."

"I haven't seen you around here before."

"I've just started looking after Amy. I'm new to Seattle."

"Need someone to show you around?"

Was this flirting? Was he flirting? She wished she knew more about men and women and how they interacted with each other. She didn't want to say the wrong thing or feel stupid.

"I have a GPS system," she told him. "I'm doing okay."

Spike chuckled. "You're doing better than that, darlin'."

Oh, my. Not sure how to respond, she smiled. "I, ah, need to get this to Wyatt, then back to the school. It was nice to meet you."

"You, too. We could get a drink sometime."

She froze in the act of taking a step. Had Spike just asked her out?

She turned back to him. Would it be a date? A real, live date? "That would be nice," she said, and continued toward the trailer.

Okay, so she wasn't desperately interested in Spike. At least going out with him would be practice, so she could do a better job when she met someone she really liked. Besides, he seemed nice enough. Maybe she was judging him too quickly.

As she approached the trailer, the door flung open. Wyatt stood in the opening, glowering at her.

"Why were you talking to Spike?" he demanded.

"What? I don't know. We were just chatting."

"It looked like more than that."

"You're right. We were planning our elopement. We're going to have to wait until his day off."

Wyatt stepped back and motioned for her to enter the trailer. "You're not good at sarcasm."

"Give me time, I'll get better."

He stared at her; his dark eyes seemed to see into her soul. "Did he ask you out?"

Why was Wyatt acting like this? "He mentioned getting a drink."

Wyatt closed the door behind her. The trailer wasn't huge and most of the space was filled with desks and filing cabinets. Blueprints had been pinned up on the wall, showing the different floor plans. At least she thought that's what they were.

Wyatt stood close enough that she had to tilt her head back to meet his gaze. He didn't look happy.

"You don't want to date Spike," he told her.

Which was true, but she hated being told that by him. "Because you say so?"

"Because he's only been out of prison a couple of months. He's a good worker, but he was convicted for assault. He's on probation now."

Claire swallowed. Prison? As in incarceration? Okay, then. "I'm sure everyone deserves a second chance," she said primly, suddenly relieved she hadn't given Spike her phone number. Not that he'd asked.

"He's also married."

"What? Are you serious? Married?"

That was so unfair, she thought, suddenly furious. Not that she was all that interested in dating Spike, but married? At this rate she was never going to have a relationship, never going to have sex. She was a freak on too many levels, she thought as she stared at her hands. Why couldn't she be normal, like other people?

"You sound upset," Wyatt told her. "Is his wife going to get in the way of your plans?"

"Don't be mean," she said, suddenly feeling defeated. "I'm not interested in Spike, which you probably could have guessed. I don't care that he's married, it's just . . ."

This was so her life, she thought sadly. Where had she gone wrong? How was she going to make things different?

"It's just what?" he asked.

She shrugged. "He was interested. Maybe. That was nice."

"You enjoy ex-convicts coming on to you?"

"Of course not. It's just no one ever asks me out. Even for a drink. I managed to go through life with men looking the other way."

She braced herself for his scorn, or maybe an explanation of what was wrong with her.

Instead he folded his arms over his chest. "Yeah, right."

"It's true. I don't date. Ever. I'm rarely home. I don't travel with an orchestra so I don't meet a lot of guys there. Besides, most of them are total players or gay. The good ones are already married. Anyway, when I'm on the road, I'm going from event to event. I don't have time to meet anyone let alone form a relationship. The person I see the most is Lisa, my manager, and believe me, she's *not* my type."

He stared at her, not speaking. She sighed.

"I'm not making this up," she said. "If I do manage to meet someone seminice or normal, he's usually completely intimidated by me. It's the fame or the money or whatever, I'm not sure. But it's terrible. It's not like I'm not trying, you know. I want to meet a great guy. I want to be involved." She glanced toward the door. "Maybe not with Spike."

"You think?"

She glared at him. "You're not taking me seriously, are you?"

"Not really."

"That is just so typical. You criticize me all you want, but do you try to see my side of things? Do you care about —"

She was still talking when Wyatt moved in, put both hands on her face, leaned down and kissed her.

The feel of his lips on hers was so startling that she said, "What are you —"

"Be quiet."

It seemed like really good advice.

His mouth was firm, yet amazingly gentle. Warm, too, she thought as her eyes fluttered closed. He kept the kiss light, but not soft. As if he was giving her all the time she needed to get used to what he was doing.

He tilted his head, bringing more of his lips in contact with hers. He brushed back and forth, exploring, teasing. His kiss seemed to steal her breath and make her brain fuzzy.

Heat blossomed between them. Heat and need and a strong desire to be as close to him as possible.

She raised her hands, not exactly sure what to do with them, then rested her fingertips on his shoulders. He dropped his hands to her waist and pulled her against him until they were touching everywhere.

It was better than she could have imagined. He was strong and hard and totally male. He smelled good, too. Clean and masculine with a hint of something out-doorsy.

He touched the tip of his tongue to her bottom lip. Even she was able to recognize the request for what it was and parted for him. He eased into her mouth, exploring as he went. Everywhere he touched, she felt tingles.

His tongue brushed against hers, which made her whole body clench. She met him stroke for stroke, melting on the inside, wrapping her arms around his neck to keep from sinking to the floor.

He held her against him. Her breasts flat-tened against his chest. When he moved his hands up and down her back, she wished she could feel his touch on her bare skin.

They kissed again and again. Individual cells deep inside of her began to whimper. When he broke the kiss, she nearly cried out in protest.

Fortunately, he wasn't done with her. He pressed his mouth to her jawline, then down her neck. He moved to her ear, where he sucked on her lobe before licking the sensi-tive skin just beneath. She shivered and her breasts swelled, as did that place between her legs. She wanted and needed and was prepared to beg.

Finally Wyatt straightened and looked at her. She saw fire in his eyes. Thank God she wasn't the only one affected.

She wanted him to kiss her again. She wanted whatever he was offering.

"We should go out," he said.

"On a d-date?" she stammered.

He nodded.

A real date? The two of them? Her insides quivered at the thought.

"That would be great," she said, hoping she wasn't as flushed as she felt. "You're not seeing anyone, are you?"

"I wouldn't have asked you out if I was. Or kissed you. Just for the record, Nicole and I have never gone out."

She hadn't asked but it was good to know. "I'd like to go out with you," she said. More than like. Especially if there was going to be more kissing.

"Friday? Amy's spending the night with a friend."

"Sounds great."

"I'll pick you up at seven."

"I'll be ready."

Wow. So that's what it was like to be asked out. She should do this more often.

She started to leave, then remembered the permission slip and pulled it out of her pocket. He signed it and she left. Technically, she walked to her car, but it felt a whole lot more like floating.

She was going on a date! With Wyatt. Now all she had to do was figure out how to tell Nicole.

"These are amazing," Claire said as she grabbed another onion ring. "I've never tasted anything this good. Ever."

Jesse picked up her burger. "See. Not everything good happens in New York."

"I never thought it did," Claire said as she looked around at the colorful interior of Kidd Valley, the burger place where Jesse had suggested they meet. "I may have to have these flown in for my next concert." She took another bite of the onion ring, chewed and swallowed. "I've never made any crazy food demands. I could start with these."

"They won't travel well."

"You're right. Which is seriously disappointing." Claire licked her fingers. "So what's going on?"

"Nothing." Jesse didn't look at her. "I just wanted to say hi."

Claire thought there might be another reason for Jesse's call suggesting they get together. "Are you doing all right?"

"I guess. I'm keeping busy and, ah, stuff.

Nicole's still mad, huh?"

"I'm the wrong person to ask. We're not exactly sharing bondy moments."

From Claire's perspective, they'd been avoiding each other since the fight about Wyatt. Which was going to create a really big problem. She had found someone she wanted to go out with. He wasn't married, involved with anyone else, or a convicted felon. So Nicole was going to have to get over her hissy fit and accept the relationship, such as it was. At least that was the plan.

"But she's okay," Jesse said. "She's getting better, right?"

"She's moving around better. I think she's going back to the bakery next week."

"But she's still mad at me?"

Jesse looked miserable. Claire wished she had better news to tell her.

"You slept with her husband. That's going to take some time for her to get over." Worse, Nicole had walked in on them. She had a clear visual of the betrayal. That couldn't be easy.

"I didn't sleep with him," Jesse said as she slumped in her seat. "It's not what she thinks." She held up her hand. "Don't say it. My shirt was off, so I must have been having sex with him. I'm bad, he's bad."

Jesse shook her head.

Claire fought frustration. Why couldn't Jesse understand that the fact that Nicole had interrupted and kept things from going all the way didn't make the situation right? The intent was there. The semi-nakedness was there.

"I have a boyfriend," Jesse said. "Matt. I love him. I would never hurt him. But then I found a ring. An engagement ring. Matt wants to marry me."

What? A boyfriend? And she'd screwed around with Nicole's husband? "That's great, but if you love Matt what were you doing with Drew?"

"I can't explain it. We always talked. Drew listened when Nicole wouldn't. I was freaked about the ring because I never thought anyone would love me like that. I didn't know what to do. Drew was there and then he was touching me. I don't know. Maybe I deserved it."

Now Claire was confused. "Deserved what?"

"Drew. Maybe I deserved what happened."

"Sex with your sister's husband as punishment?" Nicole was right, Claire thought, getting annoyed. Jesse didn't take responsibility for anything.

Nicole had every right to feel hurt. She'd raised Jesse, been there for her, had loved her and cared for her. In return, her sister had violated her trust in her own home.

"I want to take it back," Jesse admitted. "Seriously, if I could go back to that night, I'd walk away. I never wanted to hurt Nicole or anyone else."

Jesse looked painfully young as she spoke. And wounded. Claire was unimpressed.

"Where are you staying?" she asked, deciding to change the subject rather than fight.

"I was with a friend. Now I have a place in the University district. You can get rent really cheap in the summer, when most of the students are leaving."

"Are you working?"

Jesse shifted in her seat. "Um, I'm doing some Internet stuff. Nothing big. I have to earn a living, right? I'm allowed to do that."

"No one's saying you don't," Claire said, not clear on what Jesse's temper was about. "What were you doing before this all happened?"

"Taking business classes at a community college. Working in the bakery. It's half mine. Did she tell you that? My half is in a trust fund until I'm twenty-five. I want her to buy me out but she won't. Why do what

I want? She's such a bitch."

"Maybe if you hadn't been with Drew, she would be more willing to listen."

"Oh, sure. Take her side."

Claire stared at her. "Do you understand that you did something incredibly wrong? How much you hurt Nicole?"

"What about how she hurt me?" Jesse pushed away her lunch. "You don't care, either. I'm not all to blame here. It's like the bakery. Nicole is the only one who gets to be right. Only she gets to be in charge. I had some ideas for these brownies based on the chocolate cake recipe. I'd been playing with different ingredients. Nicole wasn't all that interested, but I knew if I found the right way to make them, she would be blown away. I wanted to make something of my own. Something special."

"You could still be working on that."

Jesse shook her head. "It takes money to buy ingredients."

"Do you need money? Are you broke?"

"I'm okay."

Claire reached for her handbag. "I don't have a checkbook. I pay for everything with my credit cards, but I have some cash. Do you want it? I can get more if you need it."

Jesse stared at her for a long time. "Why would you give me money?"

"Because you need it." Because Jesse was her sister and despite everything, Claire wanted her to be okay.

"There's something wrong with you."

Claire had known that for a while. She'd just hoped it wasn't visible to everyone else.

"Not the point. Yes or no on the cash."

"No for now. I may have to change my mind."

"Just let me know."

"I will." They seemed to have reached a temporary truce. Jesse picked up her burger again. "Are you getting along any better with Nicole?"

"I was until I asked about dating Wyatt."

Jesse nearly choked. "How did that go?"

"Not well. But it doesn't matter. I'm going to stand up to her and date who I want to date."

Jesse looked surprised. "Good luck with that."

"It's not as if *they're* dating."

"Uh-huh."

"She doesn't want him, but she doesn't want anyone else to have him. That's not fair."

"I agree."

"So it's not really a problem."

"Are you trying to convince me or yourself?" Jesse asked, reaching for her burger again.

"Both. How am I doing?"

"I'm totally with you. Sorry I'm going to miss the show."

Claire had a feeling she wasn't talking about the date, but instead her telling Nicole *about* the date.

"I don't know what to wear," she said. "Out with Wyatt. I don't, um, really date a lot."

"Where are you guys going? Did he say?"

Claire shook her head. "I have no idea."

"Probably dinner out. Maybe a movie. Wear something nice but not too dressy. Seattle isn't New York. Maybe some really nice jeans with a silk blouse and a blazer. You want to look hot but not slutty. Interested without being desperate."

"How are dressy jeans different from regular jeans?"

Jesse sighed. "You're hopeless."

"I know."

After Claire drove back to the house, she sat in the car giving herself a pep talk.

"I am strong," she told her reflection in the rearview mirror. "I am empowered. I am an adult. I am a good person. I appreciate myself. I'm going to go in there and tell

Nicole what's going on. I am strong and brave and I will not be intimidated by anyone. Especially her."

She sucked in a breath, then marched into the house. She found Nicole standing in the kitchen.

"Good," she said forcefully. "I want to talk to you."

Nicole only raised her eyebrows.

Claire refused to be intimidated. "Look. I respect who you are and all of your relationships. I know Wyatt is your friend. I'm not trying to change that."

"You couldn't."

Claire felt a little of her strength fading away, but she kept her mind focused. "That's not what I meant. The thing is you're not interested in dating him and I am. I don't know what your problem is. If you think I'm not good enough for him or what, but you're just going to have to get over it."

"You're going out," Nicole said, sounding tired.

"Yes, we are. He asked and I accepted. You can fight and pout and protest, but you can't change what's going to happen. Besides, it would be wrong of you to suggest otherwise."

Nicole stared at her. "Anything else?"

215

"Yes. Several things. I'm sorry for what happened to you. I'm sorry that Drew slept with Jesse. I'm sorry your own sister betrayed you. I'm sorry you got stuck working in the bakery and you think you were cheated out of your life. I'm sorry you lost your mom. But I lost out, too."

Nicole started to speak, but Claire held up her hand.

"I'm not done. It happened to me, too. And you've never once considered that. You've totally blown me off and dismissed any feelings I might have had. I've spent the past ten years trying to connect with you. You've ignored my phone calls, my letters, everything. Yet when Jesse called, I dropped everything to be here with you."

"According to what I hear, there wasn't much to drop."

Claire ignored that. "There was enough and that's not the point. You're my sister and I wanted to be here for you. It wouldn't have mattered what I'd had on my schedule. I still would have shown up, because you needed me. Because you matter to me."

Claire fought a sudden wave of emotion. "When we were five, you went to a birthday party and I couldn't go because I had to practice. I cried and cried, but my teacher didn't care. You got the chicken pox and they tried to keep me away from you because they didn't want me getting sick, either. But I just wanted to be with you. I crawled into bed with you that night and I got sick, too. Because you're my sister."

"You already said that," Nicole murmured.

"You don't seem to remember it very much. So here's the thing. I'm not going away this time. We're going to figure out how to have a relationship and I'm not leaving until we do. It would help if you acted human once in a while and showed a little gratitude. You could even be friendly. But whatever you decide, you need to get off my ass because you weren't the only one who didn't get to make a lot of choices about her life."

"You're really pissing me off," Nicole said.

"Ask me if I care."

They stood there, staring at each. Claire didn't know what to think, she only knew she wasn't backing down.

"Fine," Nicole grumbled, staring at the floor. "Date Wyatt. I don't care."

"Really?"

Her sister nodded. "And thank you for coming. You didn't have to do that."

Claire grinned. She felt lighter and happier. "You would have been totally screwed without me."

"Don't push it."

"I still have scars from the chicken pox. You so owe me."

Nicole smiled slowly. "Yeah, maybe I do."

CHAPTER ELEVEN

"Mixed two dozen bagels," the man in the suit said, pausing his cell phone conversation long enough to place the order, then saying, "I need those numbers by the time I walk in the door. Numbers, not excuses."

Claire collected the bagels, rang up the order and handed him his bag. "Number ninety-eight," she yelled.

"Two glazed doughnuts and a large coffee with extra room for milk."

"Got it."

She moved quickly and efficiently, getting the doughnuts, then pouring the coffee. She took the money, made change and called out for the next customer.

A well-dressed woman approached the counter. "I want to order a custom cake," she said. "I'm in a hurry."

"No problem," Claire told her as she moved to the counter off to the side. She pulled out the special order book and took a sheet. "What are you looking for?"

"The Keyes cake," the woman said. "But with custard filling, not chocolate."

Claire smiled. "I'm sorry but we don't make changes on the Keyes cake. We have other chocolate cakes we can customize any way you like, but the Keyes cake recipe is a tradition we don't mess with."

"Excuse me, but I'm the customer. Your job is to give me exactly what I want. I've told you what I want, now do it."

Claire allowed herself a moment of visualizing the hostile customer covered in frosting and being attacked by flying sprinkles, then she smiled again.

"There are a few things in life that shouldn't be changed. You wouldn't want the *Mona Lisa* to suddenly become a nurse or have someone put a hula skirt on the Statue of Liberty."

"You can't possibly be comparing your ridiculous cake with either of those."

"Have you had the Keyes cake before?"

The woman sniffed. "It's just a cake."

"I'll take that as a no. It's beyond wonderful. Trust me. My family spent sixty years getting that cake recipe right. So which would you rather have? An honest-to-goodness legend, or one of our other cakes made to your exact specifications? Or you

220

could get one of each and have a taste test. It might be fun for your guests."

"I suppose that's a possibility."

"It would be a great ending for the evening."

The woman hesitated, then ordered a regular chocolate cake, with the custard filling and the special Keyes chocolate cake. When she'd paid and left, Phil looked at her.

"She's been here before, that woman. She's not easy. You did good."

Simple words, Claire thought, a sense of pride swelling inside of her. "Thanks."

"I didn't think you'd make it, but you didn't give up. That's something."

Claire grinned. "You've made my week."

It was only when she'd moved on to the next customer that she realized she'd never once thought about panicking. She'd done what needed to be done. It was a great feeling and one she wanted to have again.

"Maybe," Nicole said, as she leaned back on Claire's bed. "Are you really going to wear jeans on your date?"

Claire didn't mention they had been Jesse's idea. "I thought my other clothes were too dressy. These have a dark wash and I'm wearing them with high-heeled boots."

"Very fashion forward," Nicole said as she shoved another pillow behind her head. "But Wyatt knows you're all Park Avenue. He'll dress up and you'll feel funny in jeans. What about those white wool slacks. Those are really nice."

"He's seen them."

"With what?"

"A white sweater. Well, ivory. Technically the outfit is ivory."

Nicole rolled her eyes. "Of course it is. Do you have a different sweater?"

Claire looked through her clothes and pulled out one that was a pale blue with threads of light silver shot through it. "I never wear this one," she said, half to herself, "even though I really like it. Maybe with pearls."

"Earrings maybe, but not a strand of pearls. That's too old lady. The color will be great with your hair and your eyes."

She held the sweater up to herself and looked in the mirror. Honestly she didn't see any difference, but she was willing to be wrong.

"Okay. I'll wear this sweater with the ivory slacks. I have pretty silver heels and a great bag."

Nicole wrinkled her nose. "That goes without saying. All your stuff is great. You must really like shopping."

Claire wondered if they were about to get into dangerous territory. "Not really. Lisa buys stuff and I either keep it or not. I don't really have time to go to stores."

She braced herself for a sarcastic comment but Nicole only nodded. "From what she said, your days did seem full. Is that your real hair color?"

Claire fingered a strand. "I get highlights."

"Maybe I should do that. My hair seems really dull and boring compared with your forty-seven colors."

"It's about five different highlights," she admitted. "It takes forever, but the different shades make it easier as it grows out. No obvious roots."

"A plus when you're traveling."

Claire nodded slowly, looking for sarcasm in her sister's comment, but not finding any. "It helps."

Nicole stood. "I should let you get dressed. Wyatt will be here soon and I don't want you to keep him waiting. Under the circumstances, it would be too weird for me to make polite conversation."

Knowing she was probably asking for trouble, Claire said, "Thanks for all your help and advice."

Nicole shrugged. "Just trying not to be

the Bitch Queen of the Western World."

"You're doing a great job."

"Gee, thanks."

When Nicole had left, Claire plugged in her electric curlers. She wasn't going for some fabulous style, just a little body in her hair. She curled it, applied light makeup, then dressed, fussed with her hair and shrieked when she glanced at her watch and saw Wyatt was due any second. As she opened her bedroom door, she heard Nicole yell, "Get your skinny ass down here. He's pulling up and I will not act like your mother."

"I'm ready," Claire called back and hurried toward the front door.

"You're on time," Wyatt said by way of greeting. "I wasn't expecting that."

"Oh. Okay." Were women usually late for dates? Nicole hadn't said anything. "Did you, ah, want to come in?" As she spoke, she glanced over her shoulder and saw Nicole shaking her head and motioning for them to leave. "Or we could just go. That might be better."

"Sure."

She grabbed her purse and went outside. Even with her wearing high heels, he was still a lot taller. And bigger. He was also dressed differently. A dress shirt and dark slacks replaced the jeans and plaid shirts he usually wore. He looked nice. Was she allowed to say that to a guy?

They approached his truck. He opened the passenger door and waited for her to move inside. As she brushed past him, she was jolted by awareness and a massive case of nerves.

"Do you eat meat?" he asked. "I couldn't remember if I'd ever seen you eat any. You're not a vegetarian, are you?"

She laughed. "No. I eat meat."

"Good. We're going to a terrific steak place. Buchanans. It's one of my favorites. They have great food."

"Sounds perfect."

They talked about Amy and the bakery on the drive to the restaurant. Wyatt pulled up in front of the valet sign and handed over the keys, then came around and opened her door. Once they were inside, he told the hostess they had reservations.

Claire liked that he'd planned their evening together. She also liked the restaurant. It was intimate, all rich woods and leather booths. It was atmospheric without being dark, and elegant without being intimidating.

They were shown to a booth in the corner. After they'd slid onto their seats, the hostess put their menus on the table, along with the wine list, then left.

"You look good," Wyatt said.

Claire paused in the act of reaching for her menu. "Ah, thank you." She felt heat on her cheeks and was grateful for the subtle lighting. "Thanks for asking me out. This is really fun."

"Don't you want to wait until the evening is over to decide that?"

She smiled. "I don't have to."

He raised one eyebrow. "Are you flirting with me?"

"Maybe a little."

"Good."

The blush turned into a glow.

Wyatt didn't need to look at the menu. He'd been to Buchanan's enough times to know what he liked. But he enjoyed watching Claire study the selections. She looked intense, as if her decision had consequences.

He still hadn't decided if asking her out had been smart or not. He was attracted to her, she was single and sexy as hell. Dating made sense.

Except she was Nicole's sister and no one he would normally meet, let alone get involved with. A few minutes on the Internet had produced more information on Claire Keyes than he'd expected. She was

226

famous, revered and adored on every continent she'd visited. Critics loved her, fans worshipped her and she'd had multiple bestselling CDs. He was a guy who built houses in Seattle. What was wrong with this picture?

"Would you like to order a bottle of wine?" he asked, refusing to talk himself out of the evening before it had even begun.

"That would be great. Do you —"

Just then a man in a tux walked over to their table. "Good evening. I am Marcellin, your sommelier. I heard you mention wine and my ears perked up. May I offer some assistance?"

He had a French accent that sounded so perfect, Wyatt wondered if it was fake. Before he could decide whether or not to use Marcellin's services, Claire began speaking to him. In French.

They chatted for a few minutes, before Marcellin excused himself. Claire turned to Wyatt.

"Sorry. I got carried away."

"No problem. You two know each other?"

She smiled. "I'm into wine, so I was asking about their wine list."

"You speak French."

Her eyes widened as if she hadn't realized she'd slipped into the other language. "Um, a little."

It sounded like more than a little to him.

"Sometimes I would listen to language CDs on flights. It helps pass the time. Then I get to practice when I'm in that country."

"So it's more than French."

"I speak Italian, a little German. I tried Mandarin, but I so don't have the ear." She shifted in her seat as if she was uncomfortable. "It's not a big deal. Anyway, the wine list is very impressive. A lot of good Washington wines. I like to try local when I'm somewhere, both food and wine. I always order a glass of something regional with my room service dinner."

"Room service? You're not out partying every night?"

"Not even close. After a performance, I'm usually exhausted. I go back to the hotel where I eat something light, try to unwind, then go to bed. Occasionally there are dinners with patrons. Those aren't as fun as they sound. I have to be totally on, which is its own kind of tiring."

He knew nothing about her or her world, he thought. A few articles on the Internet and Nicole's dismissive comments hadn't prepared him for Claire. As she talked about life on tour, he realized he'd asked a world-famous pianist to be his babysitter.

"Who are you?" he asked, without meaning to speak the question aloud.

"What?"

"You don't belong here. In the real world."

"But I like the real world. That other place isn't very fun."

He couldn't begin to understand her life. What it would be like to go from city to city, performing at a level only a handful of people could reach.

"I want to fit in," she added. "I'm trying to be like everyone else."

"Don't lower your standards."

"I don't think I'm better. I'm just different. I want to be less different."

She was beautiful, he thought absently. When had she gotten so beautiful? Amy said she looked like Barbie. He was willing to admit she had the long blond hair and even longer legs, but there was little about her that reminded him of a girl's toy. She was all woman and he liked that. He liked her. When had she stopped being the evil ice princess?

"Why don't you order the wine," he said. "Go crazy. We'll both try something new."

She smiled with obvious delight. "Are you sure? I can be very free with money."

"I'm good."

Marcellin returned and they had a lengthy

229

discussion in French about different wines. Claire flipped pages in the wine book and pointed. Finally they agreed on a local boutique winery he'd never heard of. The waiter appeared and they ordered their dinner. When they were finally alone, she leaned toward him and smiled.

"Did I already thank you for asking me out?"

There was something about that smile — an invitation that made him want to lean close and kiss her. He'd liked kissing Claire. He wouldn't mind doing a lot more. But a nagging voice in the back of his mind reminded him that he had to make sure they were playing by the same rules.

"You did."

The wine arrived. They went through the ceremony of tasting and approving. When the sommelier had left, Wyatt asked, "Has Drew been back to the house?"

"Not that I know of. I still can't decide if I feel badly about hurting him or not."

"Don't bother. He's healing. Pain and suffering might help his character."

"He's your stepbrother?"

"One of many."

She raised her eyebrows. "Big family?"

"One that's constantly changing. I come from a long line of men who screw up relationships. Most of my uncles haven't been married and the few that have are going for the land speed record for divorces. My dad recently remarried. It's his fifth. Drew's my stepbrother from two or three marriages ago. I can't remember which one."

Claire looked a little startled. "What about your mom?"

"She found someone decent. They've been together about twenty-five years. But not my dad. I give this one six months." He leaned toward her. "The problem with him is he keeps trying. He thinks he's something he's not — a man capable of choosing the right woman."

"It could happen."

"Not likely. We have screwed up relationship biology. I wasn't going to get married. Figured I'd try to stop the train wreck before it happened."

"You married Shanna."

"She got pregnant. I didn't have a choice."

Claire tilted her head. "Actually you did. You could have not married her and still been a part of Amy's life."

"Marriage seemed to be the right thing to do. At the time."

"Because you do the right thing."

Somehow the conversation wasn't going

in the direction he wanted. "I'm not the hero here."

"Why not? Shanna's the one who left. Was it right after Amy was born?"

"Within a couple of months, after we confirmed she couldn't hear. I didn't mind being a single father. I guess I half expected Shanna to bolt, what with my family history." He met her gaze and held it. "You're missing the point, Claire. I don't do relationships. I'm glad we're going out and I'm having a good time, but that's all this is to me. Casual fun. Sex would be good, but I don't get involved. I don't do serious."

He shrugged. "I might be putting all this out there for nothing. I don't know if you're interested. But if you are, I want to be clear about what I'm willing to do and not do."

Her blue eyes widened. "You want to have sex with me?" Her voice was low and breathless.

"Is that all you got from what I said?"

"No, I got the rest of it. You're warning me off, for my own good. I totally understand that. But you really want to sleep with me?"

"Why is that a surprise?"

Because no one ever wanted to, Claire thought, lacing her fingers together tightly in her lap so she wouldn't give in to the need to clap her hands in delight. Wyatt wanted her. Her!

He was a pretty macho, good-looking guy. He could probably have anyone he wanted and he wanted her! Could this day get any better?

She wanted to ask him to repeat the statement again, maybe with a few details thrown in. Like when he'd decided she was sexy and did he plan to make his move anytime soon? But she found herself feeling nervous and shy and went for a safer topic.

"I'm not surprised, exactly. Tell me about Amy's hearing loss. She was born with it?"

"That's the theory. She has a small amount of hearing in one ear and almost none in the other. Hearing aids help, but they're far from perfect. Even with all the medical advances."

"Like what?"

"They can tune digital hearing aids to the specific hearing loss. Whether it's high tones or low tones."

"What about other treatments? Could she get a cochlear implant?"

"It's possible." He sipped his wine. "The current surgeries require the inner ear to be destroyed for the implant. Which means if some better technology comes up, it can't be used. There's a lot of debate in the deaf community about them."

She hadn't known that. "You decided not to go in that direction?"

"For now. Amy hasn't pushed. I want something better. I want her to hear." He shrugged. "A very unpopular opinion and one I wouldn't say to a lot of people. For some, being deaf isn't considered a handicap. It simply . . . is. Like height. I don't agree. I want my daughter to have every advantage. I'm not convinced the implant gives her that."

"You have a lot to deal with."

"Amy has more."

He was a good dad, she thought happily. A good man. Not that she had a huge frame of reference, but she didn't think she was wrong about Wyatt.

"Spike was asking about you."

She looked up and met his gaze. There was humor in his eyes.

"Very funny," she told him. "I'm not interested in Spike."

"You were."

Not in the way he meant. She was excited that someone had asked her out. "I don't meet a lot of men like him in my travels."

"There's a surprise. You probably don't meet a lot of guys like me, either."

"No, I don't," she said slowly, thinking

that was a real pity. Guys like Wyatt were worth knowing.

Dinner passed in a blur of great conversation and laughter. Before Claire realized it, they were back at Nicole's house, walking to the front door.

Claire told herself not to be nervous. That the end of the evening was no big deal. Sure, Wyatt would probably kiss her and she would probably like it. Kissing at the end of a date was an age-old tradition.

But she'd never been on a real date before. Not one that involved a guy picking her up where she lived and then driving her home. She'd gone out in foreign cities, meeting at a restaurant or joining a group. Nothing about her life was the least bit traditional.

They reached the front porch. Claire did her best not to look as tense as she felt. She also avoided pressing a hand to her suddenly writhing stomach.

"I had a really great time," she murmured, finding it difficult to look into Wyatt's dark eyes. "Thanks for dinner."

"You're welcome." He raised his hand to her face and lightly touched her cheek. "I can't figure you out."

"Is that a good thing or a bad thing?"

"I'll have to let you know."

Then he leaned in and kissed her.

His mouth was sure against hers, claiming her with a confidence that took her breath away. There was no wondering, no indecision, just flesh on flesh, breath mingling and her heart pounding about a million beats a minute.

She put one hand on his shoulder, while he cupped her face with both hands. He held her as though she was precious, which made her want to give him whatever he asked for.

He didn't deepen the kiss, probably because they were standing on Nicole's porch, in view of the neighbors. Not that she cared, but he might. Then he drew back just enough to lean his forehead against hers.

"You're going to be a lot of trouble, aren't you?" he asked.

"I'm actually very easy to get along with."

"Sure."

He kissed her again, then he was gone. Claire sighed, then floated into the house.

Nicole sat in the great room, watching TV. When she saw Claire, she muted the sound.

"I see I don't have to ask how things went," she said. "You had a great time."

Claire crossed the room and sank onto the edge of the large, sectional sofa. "I did. He's wonderful. We went to Buchanans.

Have you been there?"

"Yes. It's expensive. He was trying to impress you."

"Really?" Wyatt wanting to impress *her?*

"Why are you surprised?" Nicole asked.

"I just am. Are you mad?"

"No. One of us should have a decent love life and that one is obviously not going to be me. So, come on. Details. I want details."

Claire curled up and pulled a pillow against her chest. "It was great. We talked and laughed. He's easy to be with." She grinned. "He wants to have sex with me."

Nicole winced. "I need to have a talk with that man."

"Why?" It was amazing news.

"Because saying that is just plain tacky. And you're my sister."

"No, it's fine."

"Uh-huh. Just be careful. Wyatt doesn't do relationships."

"He said that."

"At least he was honest. How do you feel about this?"

Claire considered the question. "I like him. I just hope he was telling the truth about the sex."

Nicole laughed. "He's a guy. Why would he lie about that?"

As if Claire knew the answer to that. "So

he wasn't being polite?"

"On what planet are men polite about sex? Is it different in the music world?"

"Not exactly. At least I don't think so. I really don't have a lot of experience with . . . you know."

Nicole frowned. "I don't know."

"Um, well, men." Claire held the pillow in front of her face, then dropped it. "I've never done that. Been with one."

She felt herself blushing and wanted to crawl in a hole. Unfortunately she couldn't escape the truth so easily.

Nicole's mouth dropped open as her eyes widened. "You're kidding. You're a virgin?"

"Sort of."

"It's really a yes or no question. Claire, you're twenty-eight."

"I know. I didn't mean for it to happen. It just did. I never dated much. I couldn't get away from my schedule. I never met anyone and when I did, Lisa was always prepared to make sure things didn't get too interesting. God forbid I should meet a man and stop playing the piano. I was busy and while I wanted a relationship, it just got more and more difficult to schedule anyone in. Then one day I realized I was in my twenties and I'd become a freak."

"You're not a freak," Nicole told her.

"You're . . . you're . . . sexually challenged."

"Oh, yeah, *that* sounds better."

"It's not a horrible thing."

"It is for me. It makes me feel like I'm not real. That I'm only part of a person."

"It's amazing," Nicole murmured. "You're so beautiful and successful. I would think you'd have men hanging all over you."

"I wish. I seem to scare them off. Not Wyatt, though. So when he said he wanted to have sex with me, I thought maybe it would finally happen."

Nicole swore. "He doesn't know, does he?"

"No, and you're not going to tell him."

"I wouldn't know where to start. A virgin. Wow."

Claire grimaced. "Stop saying that."

"Sure. I'm sorry. I'm just —"

"Shocked."

"A little, but not in a bad way. Look, I don't have personal experience, but I'm sure Wyatt is great in bed. If you don't tell him, he won't know to go slowly, but I don't think that's a problem. I'm sure he's very considerate. You could hint that you don't have a lot of experience. Jeez. I almost wish I could see the look on his face when he finds out the truth."

Claire didn't know if she should appreciate Nicole's honesty or hit her in the arm.

"You're not helping."

"Again, I'm sorry. I'm just dealing with this. Here I thought you were having all the fun."

"Not that kind."

"I guess." Nicole smiled. "Got any questions?"

Claire laughed. "About a thousand."

"Fire away."

CHAPTER TWELVE

Claire pulled into the side parking lot at Amy's school, then turned off the engine. "Are you sure?" she asked, speaking directly at the girl.

Amy nodded and smiled. "I want you to meet my teacher."

There was some signing that Claire didn't catch, but she understood the major point of the conversation. Amy had mentioned her at school. Claire hoped the topic had been more about how fun she was and not about anything significant . . . like the fact that she was a concert pianist.

Claire still hadn't figured out how she was going to deal with her "other" life. Walk away completely? Until she got her panic under control, did she have a choice? People came to see her play, not have a total breakdown. While the writhing and scream-ing might have some minor interest the first time around, it would quickly get boring.

None of which had anything to do with Amy.

"I'd love to meet your teacher," Claire told the girl.

Amy led the way through the bright and open school. There were wide corridors and skylights. Big signs reminded students that hearing aids were required to be worn in classrooms. That and the students signing with each other were the only indications this school was different from any other Claire had been in.

Amy led the way to the main office where she asked the woman behind the desk to get her teacher.

"They have a meeting every Tuesday," Amy said, speaking slowly. "They should be done now."

A meeting? As in more than one person in a room?

Claire told herself not to worry. That Amy would call her teacher over, they'd be introduced and it would be over in a matter of seconds. No biggie. But couldn't Wyatt have asked her to take Amy to school on a nonmeeting day?

A dozen or so adults filed out of a room behind the main counter. Amy waved and began signing at the speed of light. Her proficiency reminded Claire that her signing still had a way to go before it even got close to being basic.

A woman in her midthirties walked toward them. "Hi," she said as she signed. "Amy, it's good to see you. Who did you bring with you today?"

"My friend, Claire," Amy said. "This is my teacher, Mrs. Olive."

Claire smiled. "Hi. Nice to meet you. I've been looking after Amy while visiting my sister."

"I heard about Nicole's surgery," Mrs. Olive said as she signed. "How is she doing?"

"Better," Claire signed, feeling awkward and slow. She was really going to have to get better at the whole deaf communication thing.

Amy tugged on her teacher's sleeve. "Claire plays piano. She played for me. It was beautiful."

Mrs. Olive looked at Claire. "That's great. A lot of hearing people assume the deaf can't appreciate music, but that's not true. There are a lot of . . ." She blinked. "Oh my gosh! Are you? You couldn't be. Are you Claire Keyes?"

Claire stifled a groan as she nodded.

"I have a couple of your CDs. I love your music. I saw you on PBS. I can't believe it."

She turned to the other teachers still in the area. "Sarah, you'll never guess. This is Claire Keyes, the famous pianist."

The other women hurried over and introduced themselves. Claire found herself answering questions.

"Yes, I do travel all over the world," she admitted. "It's a lot more work than you'd think."

"Still," one of them said. "You're so lucky. Have you really played with those singers? The three tenors?"

Claire nodded. "They're charming men."

"I can't believe this. A world-famous musician — at our school!"

The crowd increased. Claire grabbed Amy's hand to keep her close. Mrs. Olive continued to sign the conversation so the girl could follow. She seemed to be doing it unconsciously.

An older woman joined them. "I'm Mrs. Freeman, the principal. What a pleasure, Ms. Keyes."

Claire shook hands with her. "The pleasure is mine."

Mrs. Freeman touched Amy's head. "She's one of our favorite students. So smart and motivated."

Claire smiled at Wyatt's daughter. "She's pretty special," she said.

Amy beamed.

"We've all heard about you," Mrs. Freeman continued. "But we didn't understand exactly who you were. Would it be too much to ask you to play for us?"

Too much? Those weren't the words Claire would have used. Bone-chillingly horrible was a better choice.

"I know you're on vacation," the principal continued. "It's just most of us will never have the opportunity to hear you play live."

They weren't alone, Claire thought, fighting the need to throw up. Until she conquered her fears, no one was going to hear her play live ever again.

"I, ah . . ."

She looked at all the teachers staring at her. They were so excited and hopeful.

"H-how many people are we talking about?" Claire asked cautiously.

"Just a few of the teachers and some students."

She could handle the students, she thought. It was the adults that made her nervous.

She wanted to tell them no. She wanted to bolt for the car and never look back. She wanted to not be afraid anymore.

It was the last one that got her attention. Not being afraid would be a miracle. She knew she'd made some progress — she could now work at the bakery without having a panic attack. She'd conquered driving. But did any of it matter if she couldn't play the piano?

"Only a few people," she said reluctantly. "I'm ah, resting, and I don't want to have to deal with a large crowd."

Mrs. Freeman clapped her hands together. "Of course. How wonderful. Absolutely. Shall we say two-thirty this afternoon? In our music room. There's seating in there for about thirty."

Claire nodded. "Sure. I'll be back."

She crouched down and smiled at Amy. "I guess I'll see you later."

Amy nodded, then hugged her. Claire hugged her back, feeling an uncomfortable combination of affection and terror.

Nicole went up the stairs without holding on to the railing but mostly dragging herself. Progress, she thought. At least she was making progress. She wasn't supposed to go back to work for another couple of weeks but she could probably pop into the bakery on Thursday or Friday.

She missed her life. While she appreciated that the surgery had gotten rid of the pain in her stomach, it hadn't done anything for the pain in her heart. That still burned hot, like a fresh wound.

"Don't think about it," she told herself aloud, wishing she'd asked Claire to stop at the grocery store and pick up a movie. Anything that could be a distraction. Because the alternative was to sit in the house missing and hating Drew and Jesse in equal measures.

She heard Claire's car in the driveway. Seconds later her sister burst into the house. She was pale and wild-eyed.

"I have to play," she said as she headed for the stairs. "I have to play. I said yes. What was I thinking? I can't do this. It's too soon. I'm never going to get better. I should just face it. I can work in retail, right? Like the bakery. Do people make much doing that?"

Claire raced up to the second floor and dashed into her room. Nicole followed her. By the time she'd made it to the landing, she could see Claire kneeling on the floor flipping through what looked like hundreds and hundreds of pages of sheet music. Who traveled with sheet music?

"What are you talking about?" she asked

Claire glanced up at her. "Amy's school. She told her teacher I play piano. She put it together with my name. The principal asked me to play for a few of the teachers. Today."

She flipped through dozens of pages, looking at them once and flinging them over her shoulder. One fluttered to Nicole's feet.

She looked at it, at what looked like thousands of notes. How could anyone make sense of that?

"What's the big deal?" Nicole asked. "You play all the time."

Claire sat back on her heels. "Wyatt didn't tell you?"

"Didn't tell me what?"

Claire rolled onto her butt, then dropped her head to her hands. She hated having to confess the truth to her überpractical, confident sister. "I've been having panic attacks when I play. It started a few years ago. I faked a panic attack to get Lisa off my back. But somehow I lost control and instead of me controlling them, they're controlling me."

"Panic attacks? Like what you had at the bakery?"

Claire nodded. "Only worse than that. I collapsed the last time I performed. They practically had to carry me off stage. It was horrible." She shook off the memory.

"Is that why you wanted to come here?"

"What? No. It's why I didn't have to cancel performances to come here."

"Okay. So what happens now? Are you in therapy or something?"

"I have been. I know what's wrong, I just don't know how to fix it." She squeezed her eyes shut. "Music is who I am. It's my life. I've been so empty without playing. I've tried to enjoy my time off, but the truth is I miss playing. Last night instead of reliving my date with Wyatt, I found myself imagining Mozart. I lay there in bed, playing the piece in my head."

"Not anything I would do," Nicole muttered. "Do you want to go back to playing?"

Claire looked at her. "Every minute of every day. But I'm terrified. Worse, I doubt myself." She put her hand on her chest. There was a feeling of tightness. Adrenaline poured through her body. "I can't breathe."

Nicole crossed the floor and sank down on the bed. "Of course you can. Take a breath and focus. In, out. In, out. You can breathe."

"It doesn't . . ." She gasped. "It doesn't feel like it."

"That doesn't matter. You can breathe. You're talking. You're not turning blue."

"Okay. Okay. You're right. I'm fine." Claire's eyes filled with tears as she tried to convince herself. "It doesn't feel fine. What if I can't do it? What if I can't go back?"

"I'd probably give you a job in the bakery. I hear you're terrific on the cash register."

Claire started to laugh. Nicole joined her. They laughed and then Claire was crying.

"I hate this," she admitted, wiping her face and wishing her emotional weakness involved getting hives or throwing up. Anything but this awful sense of dread and panic. "I feel so weak and stupid. I want to be able to do what I love."

"Look, we're talking about a bunch of regular people," Nicole said. "Teachers can't afford to go to the symphony every week. They won't know if you're playing well or not. They'll just be excited to see you. You'll be the biggest star they've ever seen."

Claire wiped her face. "They have CDs. They'll know if I mess up."

"Oh. Yeah. Good point. But you're playing on some school piano. My point is they're not going to judge you."

"Probably not to my face."

"Does the rest of it matter? Do you think the people who pay to hear you play aren't being critical."

Claire winced. "I so didn't need to think about that."

"Have you played for anyone since you've been here?"

"Amy. She stood with her hands on the

250

piano, feeling the vibrations."

"And you were okay with that."

Claire rolled her eyes. "She's deaf."

"I know. You didn't answer the question."

"I was fine with it."

"Then have Amy stand where she stood before and play for her. Ignore the rest of those bitches."

Claire's mouth twitched. "They're really nice women."

"Probably, but for the purposes of this conversation, they're bitches."

Claire nodded, trying to be brave. Knowing she was going to be emotionally eviscerated, she pushed up to her knees, slid over to the bed and put her arms around Nicole.

"I've missed you so much," she breathed, holding her tight. "Please don't hate me anymore. I can't stand it."

Nicole hesitated, then hugged her back. "I don't hate you," she said, hugging Claire back for the first time in over twenty years. "I couldn't."

"But you tried."

"Okay, yes. I put a lot of effort into it."

"You need to stop."

"I will."

Claire straightened. "Promise?"

Nicole smiled. "I promise."

Claire had trouble finding parking at the school that afternoon, which was weird. There had been a ton of spaces that morning. Not sure what was causing the problem, she finally found a spot by the far fence and turned in.

The sense of pending disaster hovered just at the edge of her consciousness. She could feel it and taste it, but she refused to acknowledge it. Maybe she would totally freak out and start frothing at the mouth. Maybe she would get through with scary foam. Either way, she was going to play the piano because that was what she'd been born to do. And because it would make Amy happy.

She collected the music she'd chosen and walked into the school. After finding her way to the main desk, she smiled at the receptionist.

"Hi. I'm Claire Keyes. Could you direct me to the music room?"

The woman stood up. "Oh, you're here. Everyone will be so excited. Principal Freeman asked me to take you to the auditorium."

Claire swallowed. "Excuse me. I'm playing in the music room."

The other woman laughed. "Not anymore. Word got out and we're full to capacity. A lot of the parents came to hear you play. You're totally famous."

The woman kept talking, but Claire couldn't hear the words. She couldn't hear anything except a loud buzzing sound.

"H-how many people?" she asked.

"About four hundred."

Dear God. The room spun and dipped. The buzzing got worse, as did the pressure on her chest. She was going to die, right here at Amy's school.

"I know it's more than you were expecting, but how could we tell people no? This is a once-in-a-lifetime opportunity. To hear someone of your caliber play live."

If the panic didn't ease, they were going to hear her play dead.

This wasn't possible. She couldn't do it. She wouldn't. She didn't owe them anything. What did they think, that they deserved to hear her for free? She earned thousands of dollars for each . . .

She sighed. It wasn't about the money. It was about excuses. That was the bottom line. Either she did what she'd promised to or she weaseled out.

Claire clutched her music to her chest.

"Would you please show me where I'm going to play?"

"Sure. I'm Molly, by the way."

"Nice to meet you, Molly."

They walked down a long corridor and stopped in front of several sets of double doors. Claire could already hear the crowd inside.

"I need to go in the stage entrance," she said. Maybe not seeing the crowd would help.

"Not a problem."

Molly took her around the side. The space might be smaller than most venues she played, but the controlled mess of props and cables was very much the same. The contrast between what the audience saw and the chaos behind the scenes was oddly comforting.

"Anything else?" Molly asked.

Claire nodded. "If you could please make sure the curtains are closed and have Amy Knight join me?"

"Right away."

When she was alone, Claire practiced the breathing she'd been taught. She pictured herself in a safe bubble and when that didn't work, tried to imagine a field of flowers. She paced, she stretched, she studied her music, then she put it down when she heard foot-steps.

Amy ran toward her. "You're here," she signed.

"I know. I'm going to play the piano for a lot of people. Would it be okay if you stood like you did before?"

Amy nodded, then signed, "Why?"

"I'm scared," Claire admitted. "Having you nearby makes me not so scared."

"I'll protect you," Amy said.

Easy words, but oddly enough, Claire believed her.

"Have you ever heard her play live before?" Wyatt asked as he and Nicole walked down the hallway of Amy's school.

"No. I've listened to a couple of CDs, but that's it. Talk about weird. She's my sister. Shouldn't I have been to at least one perfor-mance?"

"You didn't have any contact with her," he told her. "Why would you go?"

"Don't try to finesse this with logic. I can't believe how long we've been apart." She waited while he pulled open one of the auditorium doors. "I wouldn't have gone to New York to take care of her. I would have let her figure it out herself."

He tugged on a strand of her hair. "Expect

me to judge you for that?"

"Maybe. I'm judging myself. I've been nothing but mean to her and yet she still showed up. She leads with her heart."

"I know."

They stepped into the auditorium. Amy's teacher, Mrs. Olive had promised to saved them seats, otherwise they wouldn't have had a chance of finding a place to sit. Wyatt had heard that some of the parents were coming, but he hadn't expected a standing-room-only crowd.

"I've never seen it like this," Nicole said.

People were moving around and talking excitedly. They'd dropped whatever they were doing to come see Claire play the piano. He felt a sense of pride for her and what she was able to do.

"I hope she's going to be able to pull this off," Nicole murmured. "She was pretty freaked before."

"She told you?" Wyatt asked. "About . . ." He didn't want to say too much in case Claire hadn't said anything to her sister.

"The panic attacks? She told me this morning, when she was digging through her sheet music and about to fall over the edge. We talked, she seemed better, but I don't know if she's going to make it. She was really upset."

"What she does can't be easy."

Nicole smiled. "So you like her now."

"Uh-huh."

"I take it the date went well."

"Didn't you get all the details from Claire?"

"A few. But now I can hear the man's perspective."

"I don't think so."

Amy's teacher waved them over. "Isn't this amazing? I'm beyond excited. Imagine being able to hear Claire Keyes in person. You must be so proud."

"I am," Nicole murmured.

They settled into their seats. Heavy black drapes covered the stage.

"Are you proud?" he asked quietly. "Of Claire?"

"Yes, and it surprises me, too. I guess I've stopped resenting her. I know this hasn't come easy for her. She's worked her butt off to get where she is now. I just hope she'll be all right."

"She'll make it through," he said. Claire didn't have a choice. There were a couple of hundred people with expectations. He had a hard time accepting she would be comfortable letting them down.

"Do you really believe that?"

"I'm going on faith. It's all I have."

"It was easier when I didn't like her," Nicole muttered. "Now I have to be all worried and concerned. Before I would have been happy she was suffering."

"You're always looking at the bright side."

"Shh. I'm ignoring you and sending calm, healing thoughts to my sister."

A few minutes later, the principal stepped onto the stage. She had a handheld microphone and asked for quiet.

"We have an unexpected pleasure this afternoon," she said when the crowd had stilled. "Claire Keyes is going to play for us."

Everyone clapped. Mrs. Freeman waited for silence before continuing. "Most of you already know Claire's story. When she was three years old, she walked over to a piano and began to play. She'd never seen the instrument before, had received no instruction of any kind. She was a true child prodigy. But unlike those who peak early, Claire only improved as she grew up. She studied, she played, she traveled the world, sharing her gift. Today she will share that gift with us. Claire Keyes."

"I hope she doesn't fall on her ass," Nicole whispered.

Wyatt privately agreed.

The drapes parted showing a piano in the

center of the stage. Nicole crossed her fingers when Claire appeared, holding Amy's hand. They moved to the piano. Claire took her seat on the bench without looking at anyone, while Amy stood next to the piano, her hands on top of it, as if prepared to feel the music.

Wyatt could see tension in Claire's back. There was something about the set of her head that told him she was having trouble breathing.

He swore silently, wanting to do something, anything, to fix the problem. But it didn't require anything from him. Claire was truly on her own.

She spread out her music. Wyatt stared at the pages, at the small black dots that meant something to her. How could anyone get that right? How could she possibly —

Claire put her hands on the keys and began to play. Music filled the auditorium, the notes sure and strong and more beautiful than anything Wyatt had heard since the night he'd listened to her practice. Amy looked out and smiled at them.

She was doing it, he thought with relief. Claire was doing it.

Wyatt watched over the next forty minutes as the tension faded. Claire relaxed, apparently losing herself in the moment.

Nicole leaned toward him. "She's doing it."

"She's impressive."

"Break her heart and I'll beat you with a stick. Worse, I won't be your friend anymore."

Wyatt looked at her. "For real?"

She nodded. "She's my sister."

He put his arm around her. "I'm glad you finally figured that out."

Claire went for a drive after she played. She found Pike Place Market under points of interest on her GPS system and let the calm computer woman direct her to a parking garage. After walking down the hills, she crossed the street and moved toward the path offering a view of the sound.

It was sunny but breezy. The wind tugged on her sweater and blew her hair around her face. There were crowds of people everywhere, yet she felt totally alone in the best way possible.

She'd done it. Despite the fear, the pounding heart, the dry throat, she'd played and after a few minutes, the music had become everything.

She'd been horribly out of practice. Anyone with any training at all would have winced through her performance, but her audience had been kind and forgiving.

It was a start, she told herself as she stared at the water and felt life ease back into her. She wasn't going to kid herself that she was cured, but she was making the right kind of progress. Tomorrow she would practice for a couple of hours. Limber up. Let music back into her life.

She returned to her car and made her way home. When she walked into the house, excited, wanting to thank Nicole for coming, she was surprised to find her sister pacing the length of the great room, her face pale, her mouth set in a thin, angry line.

"What's wrong?" Claire asked. "Are you all right? Is someone sick?"

Nicole glared at her. "Tell me you didn't know. I swear to God, if you did, I'll . . . I don't know what, but something big and ugly."

Claire wanted to back up but she stood her ground. "Know what?"

"About Jesse. She's selling cakes on the Internet. She's set up a Web site that looks almost exactly like ours. The Web site address is damn close, too. But the difference is, instead of just giving out information like we do, she's selling the cakes."

Claire couldn't believe it. "The Keyes chocolate cake?" No way. Jesse wouldn't do that, would she? Not after sleeping with Drew. This was bad. Worse than bad.

"Yes. I can't believe it. She's even selling them for five dollars more. I'm so pissed off. I just want to find her and crush her like a bug."

"You're really angry and you should be, but we can figure this out," Claire began.

"No we can't. I knew she was a screwup. I didn't expect miracles, but this is the last betrayal. I couldn't do anything about her sleeping with Drew, but by God I can do something about this."

Claire didn't like the sound of that. "What are you going to do?"

"Press charges and have her thrown in jail, where she can rot."

CHAPTER THIRTEEN

Claire waited on an old bench by the wall until Jesse walked out. Her sister was pale and looked as if she'd been crying. Claire stood, not sure what to say or what she wanted her sister to say. When nothing came to mind, she turned and led the way to the car.

"I'm sorry," Jesse said when they were pulling out of the parking lot.

"That's the first time I've bailed anyone out of jail."

"It's the first time I've been in jail. I can't believe she had me arrested. I never thought she'd do that. She's supposed to love me."

Jesse began to cry.

Claire was torn. While she sympathized with Jesse's pain, she felt she was more comfortable siding with Nicole on this one. Jesse had crossed the line too many times.

"What did you think she would do?" Claire asked.

"Yell at me."

"You stole the recipe and you're selling Keyes cakes on the Internet. Yelling is usually reserved for things like violating curfew."

Jesse turned to look at her. She brushed away her tears. "How could I steal it if I'm a Keyes, too? Dad left half the bakery to me. Isn't that recipe half mine?"

"If that's the best excuse you've got, you're in serious trouble. Where am I taking you?"

"Home." Jesse gave her the street address, which Claire plugged into the nav system. "I don't get the big deal. I was making some money off the cakes. So what? It's not like I had a job after Nicole threw me out."

Claire couldn't believe it. "Did you expect Nicole to keep you at the bakery after what you did with Drew? Don't you take responsibility for anything?"

"I have to take care of myself. I've already told you, none of this is my fault. Nicole won't listen to me. Whatever I say isn't going to be good enough. I'm going to be punished forever. Nicole is never going to forgive me."

"That's her decision, but even if it's true, that doesn't mean it's okay for you to steal the cake and then sell it like that."

"I wasn't stealing," Jesse repeated stubbornly. "What was I supposed to do? She threw me out of my home. I had nowhere to go. I'm living in a shitty little studio apartment, renting space from a restaurant from three in the morning until ten. I bake cakes and yes, I'm selling them. Big deal. All my customers are out of state anyway. I'm not taking anything from the bakery."

"What about what you're taking from Nicole?"

Jesse looked out the side window. "Now you're taking her side in this. Figures."

"I'm not taking anyone's side. There are no sides. There's only us — three sisters who can't seem to get along."

"You and Nicole are getting along. That should be enough for you."

"I'm not taking sides," she repeated. Not exactly.

"It seems like you are. I don't care. I don't need either of you."

Claire felt both sad and frustrated. How could Jesse not see the problem with what she'd done? On the heels of sleeping with Drew, it was only making a bad situation worse.

"Why do you want to keep hurting Nicole?" Claire asked. "I thought you cared about her."

Jesse folded her arms across her chest. "I do care about her. But I don't have any other choices."

"Not much of an excuse."

Jesse turned on her. "You don't know anything about me. You don't know what I'm going through. Matt found out about the whole Drew thing and he won't listen, either. I know I screwed up before, but this is different."

It didn't sound all that different, Claire thought grimly. "I know you've made some really bad decisions and you're doing your best to avoid the consequences."

"Shut up. You don't know anything. You have everything and I have nothing. You don't have any right to come back here and tell me what to do."

Jesse opened the car door and got out. Claire stopped the engine and followed her. They hadn't even left the police parking lot. Couldn't they at least go a couple of miles before a blowup?

"Jesse, don't."

Jesse turned to her. "Don't what? Don't get in the way? Don't be a screwup? All my life I've created trouble for Nicole. I'm the reason she couldn't do what she wanted to do. I'm why she couldn't leave Seattle or go away to college or any of that stuff. You think I don't know that? You think it makes me happy?"

"Then why do you keep hurting her?"

"I'm not," Jesse screamed. "Go away. Just go away." She started walking.

"Wait. I'll take you home."

"I can take the bus. I've done it before."

Jesse pulled her coat around her and walked across the street to the bus stop. Claire returned to her car. What was she supposed to do now? She had no experience with situations like this. Should she demand Jesse get in the car? It wasn't as if she could force her.

Before she could come up with a plan, a bus pulled up and Jesse climbed on. Claire watched her go, wondering how they'd all come to this and what hope there was to ever getting it right between the three of them.

"Amy's going to spend the night with us Friday," Nicole said at breakfast the next morning. "It's time for Wyatt's annual self-flagellation."

"What are you talking about?" Claire asked.

"Every year, on the anniversary of Shanna leaving, he gets totally drunk and reminds himself why his romantic relationships never work out. It's a guy thing, because it makes no sense to me. Fortunately he doesn't want Amy to see any part of the event, so I take her and when he's sober, he comes to get her. It's become a tradition."

"Sounds like a fun girls' night," Claire said. "Why does he have to get drunk to deal with his past?"

"Not a clue."

Claire didn't think she could ask Wyatt about that kind of thing yet, though they'd been out a couple more times and each date had been better than the one before. She'd wondered why he hadn't asked her out for this weekend and now she knew why. But she didn't know how much he still cared about Shanna or why he hadn't told her about the annual night of drinking and solitude.

"You don't think he's still in love with her, do you?" she asked.

Nicole sipped her coffee. "Not even for money. That was over years ago. This is more about what he thinks about himself. He swears he comes from a long line of men who screw up relationships. Based on my brief but disastrous marriage to Drew, I'm inclined to believe him."

Claire didn't bother pointing out that Drew was only Wyatt's stepbrother.

"We'll have a good time with Amy," she said. "What about a movie fest? We could go rent some DVDs."

"Good idea. Wyatt normally takes a couple of days to get over his bender, but I think he'll surface more quickly this time." Nicole grinned. "He'll want to see you."

"Maybe," Claire said, hoping it was true.

She was intrigued by the idea of a drunk Wyatt. Didn't men want to have sex when they got drunk? She'd seen it in hundreds of movies. So far, while their dates had been fun, the physical side of the relationship hadn't progressed at all. They were kissing and kissing, but nothing else. She knew he didn't know she was still a virgin, so that wasn't the reason he was holding back. Was he just being a gentleman?

If he was, didn't that make him a nice guy? Would it be wrong of her to take advantage of him while he was drinking?

The phone rang. Nicole reached for it. While her sister was talking, Claire walked up to her room and pulled her to-do list out of her drawer.

Have sex was right there, near the top. She desperately wanted to know what it felt like to be with a man. Wyatt had flat out told her he wanted to have sex with her. She was simply considering manipulating circumstances to her advantage. Who would that hurt?

By ten that night, both Amy and Nicole were in bed. Claire had spent the afternoon trying to find something sexy to wear over to seduce Wyatt. She'd wanted to be appealing, but not obvious. There was also the issue of having to drive over to his house in whatever she chose, so lingerie was out of the question.

She'd settled on tight jeans, shoes she could slip out of and a low-cut sweater. Underneath, she had on matching bra and panties in pale pink silk.

It felt strange, dressing to seduce a man — probably because she'd never done it before. Would Wyatt be critical of her choices? Was she overthinking the process?

Unable to decide, she left her room and crept downstairs. She wrote a note and propped it against the coffeemaker, the one place Nicole was sure to look in the morning, and kept the wording vague enough that if Amy read it, as well, she wouldn't know what was going on. Then Claire went to her car and drove over to Wyatt's.

On the way, she tried to rehearse what she was going to say. Nothing sounded right.

With any luck, she wouldn't have to speak at all.

She got to his house and had just pulled in the driveway before she realized that while she was nervous, she wasn't freaked. She had butterflies in her stomach but no impending sense of doom. No panic attack.

That had to be good, she told herself as she walked up to the front door and rang the bell. At least there were still lights on. She'd been worried about waking him.

He answered fairly quickly. "Claire?"

"Hi, Wyatt."

He frowned. "Are you okay?"

"Uh-huh. I thought you might like some company." She pushed past him and walked into the house. He closed the door and followed her into the family room.

Here she could see evidence of his party for one. There was a half-empty pizza box and a bottle of Scotch on the coffee table. The glass next to it was nearly empty.

She turned around and smiled. "How are you?"

He put one hand on the counter, as if he needed help balancing. Other than that, he didn't seem drunk. Had Nicole been exaggerating or had he gotten a late start?

"I'm okay," he said. "Why are you here?"

"I told you. I thought you might want

271

company."

His eyes were slightly dilated. But she didn't know all that much about drinking. She never partied and her big indulgence was an occasional glass of wine.

"Tonight's not good for me," he told her. "I'm not at my best. You should probably go."

"You don't have to entertain me," she said. At least not in the way he would think she meant.

She walked over and put her hands on his shoulders. Now she could smell the liquor on his breath, but it wasn't icky. She leaned in and kissed him.

Wyatt responded right away, kissing her back with an intensity that delighted her. This was going to be easier than she'd hoped. Then he pulled back.

"Not a good idea," he muttered. "Not tonight. Not like this."

"It seems like a great idea to me," she murmured. "Come on, Wyatt. What's the harm?"

She kissed him again, this time brushing his bottom lip with her tongue. He put both his hands on her waist and groaned. When she leaned into him, she felt the hard planes of his body and something pressing against her belly — something she desperately hoped was an erection.

He pushed his tongue into her mouth and kissed her with enough intensity to set them both on fire. They circled and teased, even as his hands roamed over her body. He touched her back, her hips, then slid his hands down her rear and squeezed.

She arched against him, pressing against that intriguing ridge. This time he rubbed against her, making her almost totally sure he was aroused. That had to be good, didn't it? She was one step closer to being just like everyone else.

He kissed her over and over, as if he couldn't get enough of her. Without warning, he stepped away and pulled her sweater up and over her head. Then he just stared at her.

"You are so damn beautiful," he muttered. "Better than I imagined."

He'd been thinking about her? Being with her? Was that possible?

She shivered in anticipation and maybe a little from nerves. He kissed her again and at the same time, reached behind her. Suddenly her bra was loose.

Although she'd long since left her comfort zone, she let it drop to the floor. He cupped her breasts in both hands and, still kissing her, began to explore her sensitive flesh.

He brushed her nipples with his thumbs. He stroked her curves. When he broke their kiss, it was to bend down and lick her right nipple.

It was as if someone had zapped a nerve that went all the way from her breast to that place between her legs. She jumped, then grabbed him by the head to hold him in place.

"More," she breathed.

He chuckled, then obliged her. He moved between her breasts, licking, sucking, making her feel things so exquisite, she didn't know how she would survive if he stopped. Then he did stop. But before she could protest, he'd dropped to his knees and was pulling her down with him.

They were on the rug in front of the coffee table, his leg between hers, kissing, with him pressing his thigh against her center. He braced himself with his hands so he was on top of her, but not crushing her. They were both being swept away. At least that's what she tried to believe.

Claire did her best to give herself over to the experience. This was everything she'd wanted — at least that's what she told herself. But the truth was, she'd hoped for more than the floor in the family room. She wasn't exactly comfortable and she felt kind of exposed, as if anyone could walk in on them. Besides, now that he'd stopped kissing her breasts, she was able to think and that couldn't be good.

Not sure how to explain she was uncomfortable without giving away the truth, she didn't say anything. When Wyatt unfastened her jeans and tugged them off, she was okay with that. Somewhere along the way, she'd lost her shoes, which was also fine. Then he bent over her and drew her nipple into his mouth again. At the same time, he slipped his fingers between her legs and began to explore her.

While she liked what he was doing, she had the sense that everything was going too fast. The sensations were good, but she couldn't seem to get lost in them. Her stupid brain kept asking questions. Did she really want to do this right now? Here? With him drunk? They barely knew each other and —

He brushed against one spot between her thighs. A single cluster of sensation that, had she been standing, would have brought her to her knees. Her brain went totally blank.

It was as if he'd found the feel-good switch and turned it on.

He touched that place again and she

groaned. The third time she wanted to know exactly what she had to promise so that he would never ever stop.

She breathed his name. She closed her eyes and felt herself sinking into the floor. It was perfect, the way he circled and brushed and rubbed.

Teasing at first, getting close, then moving away. A single stroke, then more, deeper, faster, over and over again. Her muscles tensed. She pushed toward something . . . anything. She desperately wanted to get what all the fuss was about.

Her breathing quickened. She parted her legs, offering herself to him. Closer, she thought, pushing and tensing and hoping that —

He stopped. He actually stopped. She opened her eyes, assuming something horrible had happened to distract him. Maybe the house was on fire or something.

He gave her a quick kiss. "Can you finish with me inside of you?"

"I, ah, don't know." She wasn't sure what he was asking. When he started undressing, she got the basic idea of the question.

Oh, no. This wasn't right. She wasn't ready and it would probably be better if she just told him the truth. But how, exactly?

In the few seconds it took her to consider

her options, he managed to get naked. She had a brief impression of lean muscles and broad shoulders, then he was kneeling between her legs.

"Wyatt? We have to talk."

He mumbled something, then settled on top of her. Really on top of her. Apparently with all his weight. She couldn't breathe. Mercifully, he stopped moving. After a moment, she realized he pretty much stopped doing anything.

"Wyatt?" She shoved at his shoulder. He didn't move. "Wyatt?"

He rolled off her, onto his back. His eyes were closed and he was breathing deeply.

"Wyatt?"

Nothing, except a soft snore.

Her gaze slipped from his face down his amazing body to his erection. Or what was left of it. As she watched, it got smaller and smaller, fully illustrating how she felt inside.

He'd passed out in the middle of almost sex. Just like that. She tried to tell herself that it was because he'd been drinking, but what if it wasn't? What if it was her? Was if she was so unexciting that he'd actually preferred sleep to making love with her?

Depressed beyond anything she'd ever felt, she collected her clothes and pulled them on. While she desperately wanted to leave, to go home and hurt in private, she was worried about leaving him alone. What if he needed medical attention?

Confident the evening couldn't get any worse, she threw a blanket over him and then curled up on the sofa and wondered what was wrong with her. Why did she have to be such a freak? And was she really going to die the oldest non-nun virgin in the history of the universe? If she did, it would be just her luck.

Chapter Fourteen

Claire woke the next morning to find herself fully dressed, in an unfamiliar bed. She had a moment of wondering if she'd been abducted by aliens, only to recall the humiliating events of the previous evening. Abduction sounded a whole lot better than facing Wyatt. She could only hope he'd been drunk enough that he didn't remember anything. Of course her place in what she would guess was his guest room meant he'd awakened to find himself naked, on the family room floor, with her curled up on the sofa. She had a feeling he was going to have some questions.

She walked into the attached bathroom and found a new toothbrush and toothpaste in the medicine cabinet. After washing her face and brushing her teeth, she followed the smell of coffee to the kitchen where Wyatt, wearing only jeans, stood leaning against the counter.

They stared at each other, neither speaking. Claire didn't know if she was supposed to apologize or not.

"I didn't imagine you here," he said at last. "I'd wondered."

"I was here."

"Want to tell me why?"

She didn't know what he was thinking and couldn't read him well enough to know if he was mad. She supposed she could fake some reason but why not go with the truth?

"Nicole told me about your night of drinking and self-recrimination. I came over to take advantage of that."

"To make me feel worse about myself?"

"No, to seduce you."

One eyebrow lifted. "You think you have to wait until I'm drunk to get me into bed with you?"

She stared at her bare feet. Hmm, it seemed it was time for a pedicure. "Not exactly. I just thought it would help."

"Why was help needed?"

"You said on our first date that you wanted to sleep with me, but then you didn't do anything about it. I thought maybe you'd changed your mind."

"So you decided to play your hand, so to speak?"

"I guess." She raised her gaze to his. "Are

you mad?"

"Because you came here and tried to seduce me? No."

She exhaled. That was something.

"For the record, I was taking my time," he told her. "I knew you had a lot going on with Nicole and Jesse and everything else. I didn't want to push you. I was waiting for you to hint that you were ready." One corner of his mouth lifted. "When you hint, you do it in a big way."

He'd been waiting for her? Wasn't that just her life? Because not only hadn't she figured that out, she wouldn't begin to know how to give that kind of a hint.

"Oh," she whispered. "Okay. Thanks for telling me that."

"You're welcome." He walked toward her. "While I distinctly remember some very hot kisses and a pink bra, I don't remember us actually getting past the preliminaries."

She felt herself flush. "We sort of, um, stalled."

"Too much Scotch really kills a good time."

"Apparently."

He touched her cheek with his fingers. "Want to give me another chance?"

Her stomach tightened. "Yes. When?"

"Now."

Now? As in the morning? Did people do that sort of thing?

Questions piled on each other, but then Wyatt kissed her and she found herself not caring about the time of day.

He tasted of mint and coffee and he kissed her slowly, thoroughly, as if he'd been thinking about doing this for weeks. He moved his mouth against hers, exploring her, teasing, making her strain toward him.

She'd never been much of a morning person, which could either be biology or the fact that she'd stayed up late every night since she was six. But despite the relatively early hour, her body managed to catch on fire pretty easily. She remembered the feel of his hands on her skin, that one place he'd touched the night before, until the giant hiccup of him passing out, and she wanted to feel all that again.

But first there was the kiss, she thought dreamily, as he pulled back slightly and kissed her chin. He licked along her jaw, to a sensitive spot just below her ear. He paused there, nipped the skin, which made her gasp, then moved down her neck.

Her body erupted in goose bumps. Her breasts got all swollen and heavy feeling. She raised her hands to his shoulders to both feel his strength and to hang on, because his nibbling kisses went lower and lower until he teased at the vee of her sweater.

He tugged at the hem of it, then pulled it up over her head. He studied the pink bra she wore underneath.

"This," he murmured, "I remember."

He wrapped both arms around her and drew her close. She went willingly, wanting to feel his body against hers.

His skin was warm, his muscles hard. Even as he moved his hands up and down her back, he put his mouth on hers.

She parted for him and he swept inside. He explored, tongue on tongue, the erotic movement heating her from the inside. One of his hands slipped to her rear, cupping her. She arched against him and felt his hardness, which made her remember him naked. Her insides clenched.

Suddenly her bra was loose. He tossed it away, then pressed her close again so her breasts came in contact with his chest.

She squirmed to get closer. She wanted him to touch her there and lick her nipples the way he had before. She wanted to feel those hot, fiery sensations flickering through her. She wanted to melt.

When he stepped back, she nearly

screamed. He wasn't stopping *again,* was he?

But instead of passing out, he grabbed her hand and led her upstairs. They paused on the landing to kiss. He slid his hands up the front of her body and cupped her breasts. Using his thumb and forefingers, he brushed her nipples over and over until her breath came in gasps. He returned his attention to her mouth, kissing her deeply, tugging her along, as they made their way to his bedroom.

When they were by the bed, he reached for the button at her waistband and unfastened it. He pushed down the denim, along with her panties and she stepped out of her clothes.

She was excited and nervous at the same time. She wanted him to keep touching her, because that made everything easier. The bed was a good idea, she thought. Better than the floor.

He eased her onto the bed and knelt over her.

"You're so beautiful," he murmured as he bent down and took her right nipple in his mouth.

She wanted to thank him for the compliment, but what he was doing felt too good. The way he sucked and licked, sending darting jolts of need down her stomach to that place between her legs. She stirred restlessly, wanting more of what he'd done before. She wanted that magic touch of his.

But Wyatt seemed in no hurry to move things along. He shifted to her other breast, licking and nipping until she found it difficult to breathe. Everything felt so good. She told herself to be patient, but in truth, she wanted *more.*

When he kissed his way along her belly, she got confused. When he knelt between her thighs and gently parted her, she had a vague idea about what he was going to do and wasn't sure how she felt about it. When he gave her an openmouthed kiss on that most sensitive, erotic part of her, she knew she was going to die right there, but it would be worth it.

Nerve endings screamed in delight, then shattered. Heat pulsed through her, burning down to the soles of her feet. She'd read plenty of books that had sex in them, had seen a few X-rated movies, had told lies with a few semifriends, but she'd never in her wildest dreams imagined anything could feel like this.

He explored her, making her gasp as he brushed across that one, special place. He circled her, eased across her again, then slipped away. He moved slowly, as if figuring out what she liked, or the fifteen easiest ways to make her crazy. Then he stretched out on the bed and flicked her with the tip of his tongue.

It was better than anything she could have imagined, she thought as she lost herself in the sensation. Better and totally beyond her control. She couldn't stop herself from responding, not that she wanted to, and she couldn't seem to hold in the gasp and sighs.

She clutched at the sheets with her fingers. Tension flowed through her, making her press and push toward a yet-unseen goal. She wanted to beg him not to stop. She wanted to scream. She wanted . . . something.

Over and over, he touched her. Muscles clenched with each brush of his tongue. She arched her back, quickened her breathing, lost herself in the sensation of —

Something changed. Pressure built deep inside her body. A sense of the inevitable. It grew, rushing through her, making her cry out, making her strain. Her breath came in pants. She shuddered and pushed and —

There was a moment of nothing, almost as if she were free-falling. Then her body shuddered with the most delicious, hot, liquid sensation she'd ever experienced in her life. It was pure pleasure, rushing through her, over her, filling her until she wanted to scream. More and more, then gradually easing and ebbing. It was perfection. Better than chocolate. Better than music.

She resurfaced a few minutes later and opened her eyes. Wyatt grinned at her.

"What?" she asked, suddenly feeling self-conscious. Had she done it wrong?

"You're amazing."

Okay. That sounded nice. "Um, why?"

"You're perfectly responsive. I knew exactly what you liked. There wasn't any guessing. Thanks for that. There's nothing worse than working in silence."

She didn't have a clue as to what he was talking about. "I really liked that."

"Good. Me, too." He pushed into a kneeling position. "Touching you like that, listening to you, made me crazy. I was afraid I was going to lose it." He shifted closer and pressed against her. "That's still a possibility."

Lose what? She hated being an idiot.

She felt him pushing against her, the way he had last night. Only now the prospect didn't seem scary at all. She wanted him inside of her, showing her everything.

Tentatively, she put her hands on his

shoulders and smiled. "Do whatever makes you feel good."

Not an invitation that guaranteed control, Wyatt thought, trying to distract himself while he still could. He didn't usually have a timing problem, but there had been something about pleasing Claire that had gotten to him.

It was that damn chemistry, he reminded himself. He couldn't think straight when she was dressed. Now that he'd seen her naked and touched her all over, he was a total goner.

He pushed in slowly, giving her time to adjust to him. She was wet and swollen and still quivering from her orgasm. It was all he could do not to come right then, but he was determined to make up for his piss-poor performance from the previous night. Besides, he wanted to make it last.

He pulled back, then filled her again, waiting for her to move against him. When she didn't, he glanced down at her, trying to figure out what was wrong.

Her eyes were closed. "Claire? Are you all right?"

She opened her eyes. "Yes. I'm fine."

"Any preferences?"

She shook her head and smiled at him.

Something was wrong. He could feel it,

but he couldn't figure out what "it" was. He knew she'd climaxed before. He'd felt it, heard it and seen it. She'd flushed all over, had trembled in his embrace. He'd felt her contractions.

He pushed in again and she wrapped her arms around him.

"This," she breathed. "I want this."

It was the encouragement he'd been waiting for. He filled her over and over again, going faster, yet holding back, hoping to feel her tensing along with him, crying out her release. It wasn't there, which bothered him, but before he could stop, the pressure built until it was too much and he drove into her for the last time.

Afterward, he lay on his back, her curled up against him. He played with her hair as she rested her hand on his chest.

"That was great," she told him happily. "Perfect. Thank you."

"You're welcome."

While he appreciated the compliment, something nagged at him. Something he couldn't get his mind around.

Was it possible Claire wasn't that experienced?

Given her fame and lifestyle, he would have assumed she had lovers all over the world. But maybe she was too busy. Or

289

something. It had to be circumstances, because she was sexy as hell. But how to find out?

"I wanted to make it good for you," he began, not sure what to say next.

She laughed. "Good doesn't come close. Trust me. I've never felt anything like that in my life."

As soon as the words came out, she stiffened. He wasn't feeling too relaxed, either.

He wanted to believe she meant she'd never climaxed before, but how was that possible? She certainly hadn't been difficult to push over the edge. Women who had trouble with that usually mentioned the fact ahead of time. If Claire was up-front enough to come to his house to seduce him, she would be comfortable telling him the road home could be bumpy. But she hadn't said a word. Why?

She sat up and gave him a pained smile. "I didn't mean that exactly."

He looked at her. "What did you mean?"

"That I, um, well . . ." She swallowed. "I don't have a lot of experience with sex."

He had a cold, hard knot in his gut. "How much are we talking about?"

She pulled the sheet up to cover herself. "I was a virgin."

She kept talking but he didn't hear anything but a rushing sound. A virgin? A virgin?

Without thinking, he scrambled out of bed and pulled on his jeans. This was not happening to him. It couldn't be. A virgin? She was twenty-eight.

"How?"

She sighed. "How did it happen? How is it possible? It just is. I don't meet a lot of men, I'm not willing to be with someone interested in volume. There are a dozen reasons and they don't really matter." She raised her gaze to him. Her eyes were dark and filled with confusion. "Are you mad?"

He didn't want to hurt her. In theory he supposed he should be thrilled in some primal, macho way. He was the only sexual partner she'd ever had. In truth, what he wanted most was to bolt for freedom.

"You're mad," she said.

"No. Just confused. Why me?"

She shrugged. "I like the way you kiss."

As simple as that? A virgin?

He watched her mouth begin to tremble. He guessed that tears wouldn't be too far behind.

"Claire." He sat on the bed. "It's okay. Seriously. You surprised me — I never would have guessed that."

She perked up. "Really?"

291

He nodded. "I would have gone slower if I'd known." He wouldn't have gone at all, but she didn't need to know that.

"You didn't have to. I enjoyed everything. Especially . . . you know."

Her orgasm. Was it her first? Did he really want to know?

He didn't know what the hell he was thinking, but he knew he had to make this right between them. He leaned toward her and touched her face.

"You okay?" he asked.

She nodded and he kissed her. She kissed him back. Wanting rose up inside him, but he pushed it away. He wasn't going there again. Not until he got it all figured out.

Claire kissed him again, then got out of bed. "I should get home. Nicole is there with Amy and you probably want your daughter back." She dressed quickly, then smiled at him. "I'm okay if you are."

"I'm great."

"Good." She rose on tiptoe and kissed him again. "Thank you. For everything."

"Anytime," he said before he could stop himself.

When she was gone, he paced the length of the house, swearing loudly and wondering when the hell everything had gotten out of control. If she was a virgin, there was no way she understood what he'd meant by not getting involved. She could say she did and even believe it herself, but he was her first lover. Wouldn't that matter?

Another thought brought him to a standstill. Right there in the hall, he realized that she wasn't likely to be on any kind of birth control. He hadn't used a condom.

The potential for disaster was so huge, he wanted to put his fist through the wall. He stopped himself by thinking that broken bones wouldn't help anyone. One problem at a time.

The odds of her being pregnant were slim to none. He would do better to figure out what was going to happen between them now and how Nicole was going to skin him alive when she found out he'd slept with her virgin sister.

Claire practically floated into the house. She felt sore and squishy and better than she had in years. She should have done this sex thing a long time ago. Of course being with Wyatt had been fairly spectacular. She doubted if anyone else would measure up.

She was also impressed with how he'd handled the news about her being a virgin. He hadn't seemed that upset at all.

She parked behind Nicole's house and

walked into the kitchen. Amy wasn't there, but Nicole sat at the table.

Claire grinned, prepared to tell her what had happened, when Nicole raised her head. She looked white with fury.

"How could you?" she demanded.

Claire was stunned. They'd talked about Wyatt. Why would she —

"How could you go behind my back and bail Jesse out of jail? I wanted her there. For once I wanted there to be consequences for her actions. I'll never forgive you for this. Never!"

CHAPTER FIFTEEN

"You can't not speak to me forever," Claire said the next morning over coffee. She was stating what she *hoped* was true, rather than what she was sure of. It seemed very possible her sister could hold a grudge for a very long time.

Nicole looked up from her mug and raised her eyebrows. "Watch me."

"We have to talk about what happened."

Nicole returned her attention to the paper on the table and didn't answer.

"Oh, that's mature," Claire told her. "I know you're upset about me bailing Jesse out of jail. I agree what she did was wrong, but I can't believe you were just going to leave her there."

Nicole stood up and started to walk out of the kitchen. Claire trailed after her. "This is crazy. We're all family."

Nicole spun back to her. "We're not a family. Not by any definition I care about.

We share biology, nothing more. You have been living your life around the world, living in your bubble of being special. You don't know anything about me or my life. Speaking of which, I'm going back to it, starting today. I'll be at the bakery, running my business. Mine. Not yours. You are no longer welcome here. Not at the bakery or here in the house. If you're so hot on staying in Seattle, there are many very nice hotels. Or you could stay with Jesse, seeing as the two of you are so close."

Claire couldn't believe it. "After all we've been through, you're going to act like this?"

Nicole ignored her and walked up the stairs.

Claire didn't know what to do. It was way too soon for Nicole to return to work. But how was she supposed to stop her? Nicole wanted to prove a point. Claire already knew how stubborn her sister could be.

"This is going to be a disaster," she muttered.

"At least let me drive you," she said fifteen minutes later as Nicole walked to the single-car garage behind her house.

"No."

"You shouldn't do this. You're still recovering."

Nicole ignored her and punched in the

code that raised the garage door. She got into her small SUV and started the engine.

"You are the most stubborn, annoying person I know," Claire yelled, then returned to her car. Fine, if Nicole was going to be a complete idiot, Claire wasn't going to stop her, but she could stay close to make sure nothing bad happened.

Nicole pulled out of the garage and started down the street. Claire followed her all the way to the bakery and was relieved when they arrived.

One crisis averted and who knows how many hovering in their future.

Nicole parked and ignored Claire who pulled up next to her. They walked into the rear of the bakery, with Claire trailing behind. That gave her the perfect view of all the employees rushing over to hug Nicole.

"It's been too long," Maggie said. "I've missed you. Is it okay that you're up and here so soon? You'll take it easy, right?"

"You look good," Sid told her. "I'm glad you're back. It's not the same without you."

Phil gave her a big hug, then stepped back looking worried. "Was that too much? Did I hurt you?"

Nicole grinned at them. "It's wonderful. I've missed you guys. It's been awful, trapped at the house. I thought I'd go crazy."

Claire felt herself getting mad, which was easier to deal with than the hurt inside. She'd been there to help take care of Nicole. Didn't that count? Was her company so boring that it hadn't been able to make up for the scintillating chitchat about cupcakes and bagels?

They all talked for a few minutes, with Claire feeling as if she was standing on the outside, looking in at a place where she didn't belong.

Nicole glanced at her. "You can go now."

Something bubbled up inside Claire. Something hot and angry, that made her willing to be stubborn and difficult.

"I don't think so," she said calmly. "We're going to get this settled, once and for all."

Nicole rolled her eyes. "Whatever. We can talk in my office."

"We can talk right here," Claire told her.

Everyone scattered.

"Is humiliating me your goal?" Nicole asked. "Because you're doing a hell of a job."

"You know exactly what my goal is, however much you try to avoid it. I want us to be sisters again."

Nicole's gaze narrowed. "Sisters don't betray each other."

"Sure they do. Sisters do everything

everyone else does. It's the nature of close relationships."

"You're an expert now?"

"More than I was. You're pissed off because I bailed Jesse out of jail without talking to you first. Fine. You didn't talk to me about putting her in jail in the first place."

"It wasn't your business."

"She's my sister."

"She stole from me."

"You're still punishing her for Drew. You couldn't do anything about that, so you're looking for another way to get back at her."

"Why the hell not?" Nicole demanded. "Should I be happy about what they did together? Should it fill me with pride? She screwed up everything."

Claire got it. She finally got what was going on with Nicole.

"You're the victim," she said slowly, filling in the details as she talked. "I can't believe it. You're so tough on the surface, but underneath, you're blaming everyone else for what's going wrong. It's true you were left with all kinds of crap here, but you did an amazing job. You took care of everything. But that's not enough. I don't know if you can't accept your part, or if you're not getting enough support or what."

"Stop it!" Nicole yelled. "Don't you dare

think you can get inside my head. I don't need any amateur psychology from a poor little princess who doesn't know how to function in the real world."

"At least I'm trying to make things better. I'm not running around, blaming everyone else."

"No, you're sneaking around, hiding from your manager because you're not willing to face her like a grown-up."

That shot hurt, Claire thought, but refused to acknowledge the zing.

"I did run," she admitted, "but I also faced her. I keep showing up with you, time after time. You keep trying to get rid of me. Who's the one with the problem? Want to blame me for that? Or maybe Drew. I think a lot of this is his fault. It sure can't be yours."

Nicole glared at her for several heartbeats, then turned. "I don't need this or you. Get out. Just go away. I don't want to see you again."

She started to walk past Claire. Claire wasn't going to let her just end the conversation. She grabbed her arm. "Not so fast."

Nicole tried to pull free. Claire wasn't going to let go. They each moved toward the large vat of dough. A second too late, Claire saw the puddle of what looked like oil on the cement floor.

They stepped in it at the same time and both went sliding. Claire released her sister, but it was too late. They went down, hard on the floor.

Claire crashed into the cement butt first. The jolt of impact made her teeth ache. She sat there for a second before rolling onto her knees, then starting to stand.

As she did, she turned her head. Nicole lay on her side. Her eyes were closed and she wasn't moving.

Nicole refused to open her eyes. She didn't want to know where she was, even though it was impossible to ignore the medics working on her. Words like *transport* and *hospital* made her wince.

Reluctantly she opened her eyes and saw two guys bent over her.

"You're back," one of them said. "Do you know where you are?"

Wished that she didn't. "On the floor in my bakery. I know the day of the week and who's president, if you need that information."

"You didn't hit your head, then."

"Not on purpose."

There were two agonizing points of pain. Her incision and her knee.

"She had surgery a few weeks ago," Claire said from somewhere out of Nicole's range of vision. "She shouldn't have been here at all. It's all my fault."

There were tears in her voice, and anguish.

"We were arguing. She tried to walk away and I wouldn't let her. She slipped on the oil."

"Relax," one of the medics told her. "Your sister will be fine. The incision didn't tear, at least not on the outside. They'll check her out internally at the hospital. Her knee's pretty messed up, but that's not fatal."

He looked back at Nicole. "Ready to take a ride?"

"Not really."

"I was only asking to be polite."

They got her on a gurney. As she moved, pain shot through her leg. It was sharp enough to take her breath away. An IV dripped into her arm. She felt as if she'd been run over.

Once they were moving toward the ambulance, Claire rushed over and took her hand.

For once, she looked as bad as Nicole felt. She was crying and not in a pretty way. Her eyes were red, her mouth swollen.

"I'm sorry," she said over and over again. "I'm sorry. I didn't want anything bad to happen. I just hate that you're mad at me. I love you. You're my sister. I don't want you to die."

It was all a little dramatic, but kind of nice, in an over-the-top way. Nicole couldn't remember the last time anyone had fussed over her. No, wait. She could. When she'd come home from the hospital and Claire had been waiting to take care of her. Claire, who led with her heart and not her head. Claire, who was holding her hand as if she was never going to let go.

"I'm not going to die," Nicole told her. "And I don't hate you. You just really piss me off, sometimes."

"I know. You're not easy yourself."

"Not being easy is my best quality."

They loaded her into the ambulance. Claire waved. "I'll drive right behind them. I'll be with you no matter what."

Words that should have made Nicole want to run to the hills, but oddly, they didn't. They actually made her feel kind of warm and fuzzy inside. Which made her wonder what those medics had put in her IV.

Wyatt put his arm around Claire. "Nicole is going to be fine."

"You keep saying that," Claire said with a sniff. "No offense, but I want to hear that from a paid professional. Then I'll believe it."

"She was awake and talking." He was worried about Nicole, as well, but Claire seemed on the verge of losing it.

"What if she's bleeding internally?"

"What if she's not?"

Claire leaned against him. "Sure, use logic when I'm in a weakened condition. That's hardly fair."

He wrapped his other arm around her and pulled her close. "I do what I can."

She felt good in his arms. Under other circumstances, he would have been thinking about that and maybe getting her back into bed. But these weren't other circumstances and they had to talk about what happened.

"I can't believe they're going to have to operate on her knee and that she's going to have another recovery," Claire said into his shirt. "It's so unfair. It should have been me."

"You both fell. She got her knee busted up. It was an accident."

"I know. I just wish —" she sighed "— that we weren't fighting."

He really wanted to be supportive. That's what a decent guy would do. Support during this crisis. He wouldn't be thinking about his own stuff and wanting to discuss it.

Even so, he found himself saying, "We have to talk about what happened."

She looked up at him, her blue eyes filled with concern. "What are you talking about?"

"Us. Being together."

"Oh. I'm fine with that."

She was so damn calm. "I'm not. You should have told me you were a virgin."

She smiled. "Oh, Wyatt, don't worry. It was great. I was too embarrassed to tell you. I probably should have mentioned it, but I didn't and everything worked out. You were very gentle." She drew her eyebrows together. "Is that what you're getting at or do you mean something else? Are you saying you wouldn't have made love with me if you'd known?"

They were alone in the waiting room, but privacy didn't make the conversation easier. "I don't know."

She leaned back. "Then I made the right decision."

"By taking away my choice?"

"I don't know if I should laugh or hit you with a chair," she told him. "You're saying I violated your rights or something?"

This is why men and women should never have emotional conversations, he thought grimly. "There are consequences that should have been anticipated."

Her eyes flashed with annoyance. "I have no idea what you're talking about."

"Which is my point. You're not experienced."

"You weren't complaining before."

Now he was getting pissed. "I'm not making a statement about your performance," he growled. "I'm talking about birth control. You aren't on any, are you?"

He waited for her expression to change to shocked regret. Instead her eyes widened and then she smiled as if he'd just handed her the cure for global warming.

"I could be pregnant?" she breathed. "We could have a baby? I never thought about that. Is it possible? I don't think my luck is that good."

He couldn't believe it. She was *happy* at the prospect?

She flung herself at him and laughed. "Oh, Wyatt, wouldn't that be amazing? A baby. I've always wanted children. Could it really happen my first time? I guess it could. Wow."

He grabbed her and shoved her away. "What's wrong with you?" he demanded. "This isn't good news."

Her smile faded. "Why not?"

How the hell was he supposed to answer that?

"It's a baby," she said. "That would be a miracle. Of course there are logistics, but we'll deal. This is amazing."

He was beyond pissed. Shouldn't she be upset and frantic? "You're not getting it. This isn't good news."

"It is to me. I guess the odds of me being pregnant depend on where I am in my cycle." She clapped her hands together. "But still, a baby. That would be totally cool. What a wonderful consequence."

"Not for me," he snapped. "I'm not interested in more children. I don't do relationships, remember? If you think you're going to trap me the way Shanna did, you're in for a big disappointment."

The happiness fled from her face. "Is that what you think of me?" she asked. "I'm not like that."

"I don't know you well enough to make that judgment."

"I'm not interested in trapping you, or any man. I'm very comfortable being a single mother."

"What do you know about raising a kid?"

"As much as you did when Amy was born. I'll learn."

She was so defiant, he thought, fighting

frustration. Didn't she understand what this could mean?

"With your travel schedule?"

"I'll hire a nanny."

Typical, he thought in disgust. "I'm not paying for that."

"No one's asking you to." She glared at him. "I'm sorry you're upset about this, Wyatt, but I refuse to be. I've always wanted children. Maybe this isn't the way I would have chosen, but it's still a miracle to me. I promise whatever happens, you won't be inconvenienced, which is really what this is about. If I need help, I'll hire it. Without asking for any money from you. I'm more than capable of paying for whatever I want."

"If only," he muttered.

She tilted her head. "You really don't get it. I'm just some woman who plays the piano, right? This may surprise you, but I'm actually very good at what I do. Between concert dates and CD sales, last year I earned about two million dollars. It was a good year, but not my best. Money isn't an issue for me. I'm sorry you're upset about the chance that I might be pregnant, but I refuse to be."

With that, she turned and walked away.

Wyatt stood alone in the waiting room, wondering if he could have screwed things up worse than he had. If there was a wrong way and a disastrous way, he'd obviously gone down the latter.

He shouldn't have attacked her like that. What were the odds she was pregnant? He'd been a first-class jerk and he knew it. He'd reacted because of what had happened with Shanna. But Claire wasn't anything like his ex-wife.

She was also rich, he thought, not happy about the news. He considered himself a confident guy, who didn't worry about impressing the women in his life. Yes, he had a successful business and money wasn't an issue for him, but damn, had she really made two million last year?

"How do you feel?" Claire asked.

Nicole managed a smile. "I've been better. I'm glad I'm going to have an orthopedic surgeon, instead of the one I had last time. Otherwise he would think I was doing this because I had a crush on him."

Claire shifted to the front of the chair she'd pulled up beside her sister's hospital bed. "Would that be such a bad thing? A doctor. Our parents would be so proud."

Nicole started to laugh, then pressed a hand to her midsection. "No. Don't be funny. It hurts."

Claire didn't want to hear that. "Are you sure you're okay? Nothing was ripped open when you fell?"

Nicole smiled. "There's a visual designed to make me happy. Nothing ripped open. I'm sore because I pulled on the healing skin. There was a little oozing but nothing serious."

"I wish it had been me."

Nicole's smile broadened. "Me, too."

They looked at each other. "I'm sorry," Claire said.

"Don't apologize. We both fought. We were both reacting. I shouldn't have yelled at you about Jesse. You were right. She's your sister, too. I should have at least mentioned putting her in jail before I did it. Even though I'm so mad at her."

"I know you are and you should be. You were right about consequences. I didn't think that through. When Jesse called, I just reacted."

"I'm not sure I would have done any different," Nicole said.

Claire hoped that was true. She didn't want her sister going back into surgery with the two of them still fighting.

"It's probably good that you're around with all that's happening with Jesse," Nicole admitted. "Someone needs to be the voice of reason."

"I'm far from that," Claire said, "but I want to help." She clutched her sister's hand more tightly. "I'm sorry I said you were a victim. You're not. You've done so much on your own, with no one to support you. I totally respect that."

Nicole blinked several times. "I don't mean to play the victim. It's just lately it seems like there's always a surprise waiting around the corner and it's rarely good."

That made Claire think of other surprises.

"What?" Nicole asked. "You're thinking about something. I can tell."

Claire didn't know if this was the time. "It's nothing."

"I'm trying to keep my mind off my impending surgery. Please, tell me."

"Okay." Claire sighed. "I had a big fight with Wyatt. When I was gone the other night, I was with him."

"I sort of figured that."

"He's not happy about the virgin thing."

"Did you tell him before or after?"

"After."

Nicole winced. "Did he freak?"

"Pretty much. I don't know what the big deal is, but he was all having a hissy fit."

Nicole laughed. "I've never seen him have a hissy fit. That would have been fun."

"I guess. He seemed okay with it at the time. But since then he's had more than second thoughts." She paused, remembering what he'd said, what she'd never considered. That there was a chance she was pregnant.

"We didn't use any birth control. Now he's worried there might be a baby."

Nicole's mouth dropped open. "Oh, wow. He didn't use a condom? Are you serious? Am I going to have a talk with him when I get out of here. It's bad enough he slept with my sister, but to not use protection? That is totally unacceptable."

Nicole was being protective. Who would have thought? Claire smiled. "For me, a baby would be a good thing."

"Are you sure?"

"Yes, but Wyatt isn't. He's pretty angry. He started talking about how he wasn't going to take responsibility and that I couldn't trap him into marriage." She still hurt when she thought about it. As if she would ever do that.

"Guys get weird about that stuff. Especially one who has been burned before."

"Maybe. I don't know. The thing is, I'm really excited about the thought of being pregnant. I've always wanted children. We argued about how that would happen. It was a mess."

"I'm sorry he was a butthead."

"Me, too."

Nicole squeezed her hand. "Do you really want to be pregnant?"

Claire grinned. "It would be a miracle and yes."

"Then I hope it happens for you. Hey, I'll be an aunt."

Another connection, Claire thought. Another tie. She wanted her life to be interwoven with those she loved.

"If I am pregnant, I'm going to have to work on my emotional health. I want to be a good mother."

"There's nothing wrong with your emotional health."

"You said I was useless," Claire reminded her. "I'm not holding that against you. I didn't know how to exist in the real world."

"Right. You didn't. But you came here anyway. You drove on the freeway to get to me. You learned how to cook and run a washing machine. You're great at the bakery, you're babysitting. You've done all this without any help in a matter of weeks. Claire, I think you're the most emotionally strong person I know."

Claire didn't know what to say. Her chest tightened, but this feeling had nothing to do with panic and everything to do with the affection filling her.

Nicole continued with, "Even now, you're taking care of me. No one takes care of me."

"I'm so amazing you should worship me," Claire said with a laugh that was a little too close to a sob. "I want to take care of you."

"I know. You're a good person. A great sister and . . ." Nicole shrugged. "Okay. Here it is. Brace yourself. I love you."

"I love you, too," Claire told her, leaning close so they could hug. "I can't believe you finally said it."

"Me, either."

CHAPTER SIXTEEN

"I prefer this tile pattern," Alice Grinwell said firmly. "With the slate."

Wyatt counted to ten. Mrs. Grinwell was building her third house with him in ten years. She'd also referred more than a dozen wealthy clients to him. Unfortunately she was one of those people who had more money than sense. In her mind, her life's work was building and decorating beautiful houses. Her husband supported her activities.

Complicating what should have been a dream job was the fact that she changed her mind constantly. Every house took twice as long as it should have and cost three times as much. Not that Mrs. Grinwell cared.

"I want it to look like this," she said pointing at the picture in the magazine showing the fireplace of a custom home up in Bellingham.

He had to admit the work was beautiful,

315

but his tile guys had thrown up their hands, not sure how they would get the same look. Which meant he was going to have to hire the person who did it in the first place and pay for her to come down and work at Mrs. Grinwell's place.

It wasn't the cost — his client would cover that. It was the time and effort and the fact that he was still pissed at himself for how he'd handled things with Claire and angry with her for not recognizing the disaster that would follow her being pregnant.

"I'll make it happen," he said firmly. "I don't know how long this will delay things, but I'll get back to you as soon as I get the details worked out."

Mrs. Grinwell smiled. "You're always a pleasure to work with, Mr. Knight. I appreciate that."

"Thank you."

They talked about a few other details, then his client left. As she walked to her Mercedes, he stared after her, wondering what she would think if he asked her what it was like to be rich.

She probably wouldn't know how to answer the question and in reality, he wasn't sure he cared. He had his own business, he was comfortable. He supported himself, his daughter, provided employment for a couple dozen guys. He contributed.

Unlike Claire, he hadn't personally made over two million last year.

He told himself that her money was the least of his problems. But it still fried him and he couldn't figure out why. He'd always thought of himself as a man who was comfortable in his own skin. He respected women. Other people's success didn't change how he felt about himself. So what was the deal?

Was it because they'd gone out? Did he expect to make more than any woman he dated? Was he that backward emotionally? Or was it something more subtle? If it was, he was in trouble. Getting in touch with his inner anything wasn't his strongest skill set.

"Screw it," he muttered and turned back to the blueprints of the house and the magazine pictures that had created the current hell of his day. He would figure it out later, or not at all. Claire wasn't likely to be pregnant. Once they knew for sure, he could let it go. Move on. Find someone easier to deal with. Or maybe swear off women for a while.

Claire held open the back door while Nicole carefully maneuvered on crutches.

"I can't believe I'm going to have to

recover from another surgery," her sister grumbled as she made her way to the sofa and collapsed. "I was doing so well getting over the first one. Now look at me."

Claire did her best not to wince. They'd both been fighting, they'd both fallen. It was just bad luck that Nicole was the one who'd been injured. Still, she felt horrible to know her sister had more pain to go through.

Nicole looked up and wrinkled her nose. "Don't you dare apologize again."

"I won't."

"If you try, I'll scream. It's a scary, shrill sound and you won't like it."

That made Claire smile. "I won't apologize for anything ever again."

"Let's not get too wild." Nicole sighed. "What a mess. Could my life get worse?"

"That's the wrong question," Claire told her. "Don't tempt fate. Although I wouldn't play the lotto if I were you. It doesn't seem to be the right time."

"I know." Nicole slowly, carefully lifted her bandaged leg up onto the coffee table. "Another scar."

"But this one will look like a sports injury or something. That will be cool. Men love women with scars."

Nicole shook her head. "No more men for

me. I'm done with those games."

Claire hoped her sister was caught up in dealing with Drew and didn't actually mean that. Nicole deserved to be worshipped by some great guy. Actually, they all deserved it.

"Do you want help upstairs?" Claire asked.

"I want to recover right here. The view will be different. Besides, I don't think I could make it up the stairs."

"I could help," Claire told her, trying not to sound doubtful. She had a sudden image of the two of them tumbling to the ground.

"Let's not." She looked at Claire. "I'm sorry you're stuck here."

Claire sat in the chair across from the sofa. "I'm not stuck and I'm happy to help. This is why I came here in the first place."

"At some point you have to return to your regularly scheduled life."

"Maybe." Probably. "But not this week. *You're* stuck with *me*."

"I'd be lost without you," Nicole said, then sniffed. "Damn. I am so not going to cry. We had our emotionally touching moment in the hospital."

Claire smiled. "We can have more than one."

"No, because I don't want to cry again."

"I can handle it. Are you saying you can't?" Claire remembered Nicole being unable to resist a challenge. She doubted that had changed.

"You're baiting me."

"Uh-huh."

Nicole clenched her teeth. "I can handle it better than you. Bring it on. I'm really glad you're here. No one ever takes care of me."

"I'll always be here when you need me."

Nicole's eyes filled with tears. She brushed them away. "Dammit, Claire."

Claire smiled, feeling a little smug. "It's okay. I can deal with your emotional outburst."

Nicole glared at her. "I should throw something at you."

"But you won't. What can I get you?"

Nicole sniffed, wiped her eyes, then cleared her throat. "Pizza and painkillers. In that order."

"Shall we argue about mushrooms on the pizza now or later?"

Nicole laughed. "Let's argue now."

Wyatt flipped over the waffle maker and set the automatic timer. While Amy poured her own juice, he set out syrup, then turned over the vegetarian breakfast sausages she

320

liked so much.

He'd tried to explain that most humans enjoyed the real thing, not some tofu-spiced scary vegetarian fake sausage, but his daughter could be stubborn. He knew she got that from him so it was hard to mind too much.

"I'm excited about my spelling test," Amy signed when he glanced at her. "I know all the words."

"You practiced a lot. And last night you got all of them."

She nodded several times, her ponytail bouncing with the movement. That morning she'd picked out a blue sweater to wear with black jeans and boots. She was growing up so fast. It was just a matter of time until she was rolling her eyes at him and sighing heavily all the time. But for now, she was still his little girl.

The waffle maker dinged. He opened the top and used a fork to lift up the perfectly cooked waffle. After setting it on the plate, next to the veggi-sausage, he passed it across the counter to the breakfast bar where she'd already settled.

"Thanks, Dad," she signed.

"You're welcome," he signed back.

She took a bite and chewed. When she'd swallowed, she said. "I want a cochlear implant."

He stared at her. "What?" He shook his head. "I understood the words." A cochlear implant?

He knew what most parents of deaf kids knew about the surgery. That it wasn't a substitute for hearing, that it was very successful for what it was, that technology was always changing and that once done, it couldn't be undone.

He and Amy had only talked about it a few times, mostly when one of her friends had it done. He'd explained why he thought it was a better idea to wait until she was older. Maybe there would be another leap in technology.

"Why now?" he asked.

"I want to hear Claire's pretty music," she said, then switched to signing, which was faster for her. "I didn't mind not hearing before because there wasn't anything I wanted to hear that much. But I want to hear her play."

Claire had done this? He'd talked to her about the surgery and had explained why it wasn't a good idea and she'd talked to Amy anyway?

"Daddy, are you mad?" Amy asked.

He was beyond mad, but not at his daughter. "I'm surprised," he signed. "We talked about waiting. I think we should wait."

"It's my hearing," she signed back. "It should be my decision."

Which didn't sound like Amy, so she'd either gotten the comeback from one of her friends or from Claire.

"You're eight. You don't get to decide about surgery."

"You don't understand, Daddy. You can't."

Ouch. Now she was shutting him out?

He wanted to tell her that he was the adult and he could make any decision he wanted. But to what end? If Amy was serious about the implant, for whatever reason, they would have to deal with it. But fighting wasn't going to help.

He gave himself the standard "I am the parent," lecture, the one that reminded him to stay in control of his emotions, then said, "Amy, you have to eat your breakfast and go to school. I need to think about this. Let's talk later."

She scowled, then nodded slowly.

Not much of a victory, but then he felt like putting his fist through a wall. Not actually a mature decision.

He dropped off his daughter, then called his office to say he would be late. It took him less than twenty minutes to get to Nicole's house, during which he allowed his temper to grow until it was nearly spilling out of the car.

He walked up to the front door and rang the bell. Claire answered.

"We need to talk," he said, pushing past her into the house. "Now."

"Yes, of course it's not too early," she told him. "Thanks for asking. And how are you?"

He recognized that he'd barged in, but he didn't care. "Sleeping with me doesn't give you the right to mess with my daughter's head. It doesn't give you access to either of our lives. Is that clear?"

"Perfectly, but I have no idea what you're talking about. And while we're on the subject, you *asked* me to look after your daughter, which I was doing as a favor. I believe that means you handed me access to her life, if not yours. Now what is your problem?"

She sounded so innocent, he thought, hating how he was aware of the fact that she was in pajamas and not wearing a bra. It seemed that certain parts of his psyche didn't care about anything but getting naked.

"Amy wants a cochlear implant because she wants to hear your music. She never wanted one before. It's pretty sick to use a kid to make yourself feel better."

Claire felt the earth shift beneath her feet

and wondered if it was an earthquake.

Apparently not, she thought, because Wyatt didn't seem fazed. Although he was very comfortable thinking the worst of her.

"I doubt you'll believe me," she said, determined not to get angry, "but I never discussed cochlear implants with Amy at all. She never mentioned getting one, and I certainly didn't. I didn't know much about them until you and I discussed them on our date. What you decide should and shouldn't be done medically to your daughter is your business. Having her hear my music in the traditional sense isn't important to me."

She planted her hands on her hips and raised her chin. "What I really don't get is why I have to be the bad guy in this. I'm not Shanna nor am I any twisted view of a woman, as you see the gender. I am someone who has only cared about you and your daughter. I have taken care of her and genuinely like her. I will not have you make that into something ugly, because it isn't. Amy's a great kid."

He started to speak, but she held up her hand. "I'm so not finished with you. I'm willing to admit that I didn't tell you I was a virgin. Assuming that it's still my body, I'm not even sure I owed you that information. But for the sake of your current rant, let's assume I did. I have already apologized for that. And for the record, you were the one who started the whole 'I want to have sex with you,' thing. I simply took you up on your offer. So you should stop being pissed off at me because the real person you're mad at is yourself. Amy is growing up and you're starting to realize you won't be able to control everything about her life. Big whoop. That's part of being a parent. But you don't want to accept that. You want someone to blame. Like me. Just like you blame me for not bothering to take one hundred percent of the responsibility about using birth control when we did it."

She leaned in and pointed her finger at his chest. "Stop putting the blame on me. Accept your share of the responsibility and stop thinking the worst about me. I'm a good person, dammit, and you know that. I've been nothing but sweet to your daughter and you know that, too. Now get out of here."

For a second she thought he wasn't going to move. She waited for the verbal explosion to follow, but Wyatt simply muttered something under his breath and walked out of the house.

Claire stared after him until the door slammed, then she sank onto the small chair in the foyer. She felt as if she'd had a run-in with the energy vampire and he'd just about sucked the life out of her.

Her heart pounded in a way that should have made her worry about panicking, but she didn't. She'd handled Wyatt, she could handle a stupid panic attack, too. She was done being afraid or judged based on half-truths and stories. She was going to stand up and be counted on her own merit. Just as soon as she had the strength.

Nicole clumped in from the kitchen. "Impressive," she said. "You really took him on."

"He annoyed me."

"I got that. So did he. Men can be such idiots. I hate to put Wyatt in that category, but I sort of have to. Are you okay?"

Claire drew in a breath, then stood. "I'm fine. He's not going to get me down. I'm stronger than he knows."

"Apparently. You're practically self-actualized. Soon you'll be living on a higher plane."

Claire grimaced. "I can't wait."

Rather than go into work and snap at people who hadn't done anything wrong, Wyatt went home to cool down.

He stood in his study and wondered what

was wrong with him. He was the guy who thought first and then reacted. He made it a rule never to say anything stupid enough to require an apology. He kept his life simple, his relationships straightforward. When it came to women, no one got close, no one got involved with his daughter and no one got to him.

Except Claire.

She pushed buttons he didn't know he had. She made him crazy without even trying, which meant he didn't want to be around when she decided to deliberately push him over the edge.

He crossed to the cabinet against the far wall, opened it, stared at the liquor there, then reminded himself it was barely after nine in the morning. A little early to start, even on a bad day.

He slammed the door shut and walked to his desk. Instead of sitting in the chair, he stared down at the surface, as if the answers were there. The hell of it was, he didn't even know the question.

Did he really think Claire had been the one to bring up the cochlear implant with Amy? She was right — what did she care how Amy heard her music. The child already loved her playing. Claire had faults, but being a raging egomaniac wasn't one of them.

He'd trusted her with Amy but he wasn't willing to trust her to be a decent person?

He'd been mad at her since they'd had sex, he reminded himself. Since finding out she was a virgin. So what about that got to him?

He ran through a dozen or so reasons. That not telling the truth was like lying, that he didn't want the responsibility, that it was all too strange. But he knew he was bullshitting himself. The real reason was that Claire was unpredictable. She had been from the first second he'd seen her and nothing about that changed.

He didn't like unpredictability, especially in women. If he didn't know what was going to happen, then he couldn't stay in control.

Was that what this was all about? Being in control?

Asking the question made him uncomfortable, which meant he was probably close to the truth.

His past had a lot to do with his need to be in control. He couldn't risk caring and making another Shanna-like mistake. No male in his family had ever had a successful relationship. Why should he be any different?

None of which was Claire's fault. He

seemed to be on a roll, screwing up at every turn. He was going to have to do something to make that better.

CHAPTER SEVENTEEN

When Amy flew into the house that afternoon, Claire knew there was a good chance that Wyatt wasn't far behind. While she was annoyed with him, there was a still a part of her that wanted to see him. Which was just plain stupid. True, but stupid.

Amy hugged her and signed, "How was your day?"

"Good. How was school?"

"I got an A on my spelling test."

"Yay, you!"

Amy went tearing into the living room to greet Nicole. Wyatt walked into the kitchen.

He was big and tall and handsome enough to make her breath catch. All part of his appeal, she reminded herself. She knew nothing about having a type, but she would guess he was hers.

She leaned against the counter, determined to make him speak first.

"Got a minute?" he asked.

Did she want to have another conversation with him? The last couple had been awful. And yet she found herself nodding.

They went downstairs, into the studio. Claire settled on the bench in front of the piano while Wyatt pulled up one of the stools in the corner.

She waited.

"It's possible I've been an ass," he began.

Despite her lingering hurt and annoyance, and maybe because of her powerful attraction to him, she smiled. "When are you going to decide?"

"Really soon."

"Let me know when you do."

He looked at her. "You're not like anyone I've ever known. I like my women easy. You're not easy."

She wasn't even sure she knew what easy meant in that context, but knowing she wasn't made her happy.

"You push all my buttons," he continued. "The hell of it is, I don't know how to fix that. I like things predictable and you're not that, either."

Safe, she thought. He wanted relationships safe and meaningless. Did that mean he cared about her? He sure put a lot of energy into being mad at her.

"I would never get between you and

Amy," she told him.

"I know. I'm sorry. It's what you said before. I don't want to lose control. I don't want her to grow up and away and that's what's going to happen."

She didn't totally understand his pain — after all she didn't have a child of her own. But she could imagine it would be uncomfortable.

"Amy loves you," she said, rising to her feet and crossing to him. "You're everything to her."

"For now. In a few years, some kid is going to show up and try to steal her heart."

"That won't change how much she loves you."

"Maybe not." He looked her in the eye. "I don't want you getting close. It's one of the rules. I tried to be clear about that, but after we were together, I figured out you didn't play by any rules."

Meaning she was too innocent to have rules or she just didn't bother? She wasn't sure and . . . She frowned. "Wait a minute. It's not up to me if I get close to you or not. You control that."

"I know."

There was something in the way he said those two little words. Something dark and sexy that made her toes tingle and her blood heat.

"I'm getting to you." She wasn't asking a question. For the first time in her life, she felt sexually powerful.

"More than you know."

Electricity snapped between them.

She didn't know what to do. Rush toward him and risk it all? Run in the opposite direction?

One corner of his mouth turned up. "Don't sweat it, Claire. It doesn't have to mean anything."

But it meant something to her. Then the floor overhead creaked and she remembered they weren't alone and could be interrupted at any moment.

"A safer topic might be better," she told him.

"How about that piano you're sitting next to? Did you practice on it when you were little?"

"Until I went away." She opened the cover and pressed her fingers lightly against the keys. "It's been unused for so long, it's hard to keep tuned. The strings keep wanting to go back into their old position. But we'll get it right."

"Hard to make magic with an instrument that isn't in tune."

She stiffened in surprise. "I don't make magic."

"What would you call it?"

"I don't know. Everything used to be so clear to me. My life was mapped out for me, one concert season at a time. I was always busy. Practicing, traveling, recording. Now I'm not doing anything."

"Which is better?"

"Neither," she said without thinking, then realized it wasn't true. "I miss playing."

He seemed to squirm in his chair.

"What?" she asked.

"Knee-jerk guy reaction. See problem, fix problem. I want to say, 'so play,' but I know it's not that easy for you."

"The panic attacks," she murmured. "I haven't had one since that first morning I worked at the bakery. I came close when I played at Amy's school. I know I'm better, at least in my regular life, but could I perform again? I don't know."

"You need to, Claire. It's what you were born to do. It's your passion."

Maybe, but she wouldn't mind something else being her passion, too. A man, children, a family.

"I miss playing, but I want more in my life this time."

"So make that happen. Aren't you in

charge?"

"Not according to my manager."

"Get a new one."

As easy as that, she thought, knowing if it were him, he probably would. "I've been with Lisa since I was twelve years old. That's more than half my life."

"It's business," he told her. "You had to sneak away to get time off to help out Nicole. You've given away all your power. Do you want to keep doing that?"

The easy response would be to get mad at him, but he was only telling the truth. She let Lisa run her life because it was easier than doing it herself.

"I've never stood up for what I wanted," she said slowly. "I can't tell you why. Maybe fear or inertia." She gave a harsh laugh. "I've always prided myself on not being a diva. I never made demands. I didn't need certain foods or special flowers in my dressing room. But I let Lisa handle the most important decisions — the ones about my time and my talent. I'm twenty-eight years old. Shouldn't I be more grown-up than that?" She sighed. "Be careful how you answer. I'm feeling vulnerable."

"You are grown-up. You've been lazy until now. That's all. Decide to do things differently."

If only, she thought. "You make it sound easy."

"Why does it have to be hard? Decide and then follow through. Or go back to things the way they were."

"No. I won't do that."

"Then you're halfway there."

She smiled. "You're coming across as very sensitive and understanding. You probably don't want that being spread around."

"No way."

"So I can hold something over you."

"You like having power, don't you?" His voice was teasing as he spoke.

"Who doesn't? Power is good."

"In the right hands," he told her.

She had the feeling they switched topics, but she wasn't totally sure. She did know that the electricity was back and it was taking every ounce of her self-control not to stand up and walk into his arms.

She wanted to feel him holding her, have his mouth on hers. She wanted him to kiss her as if he couldn't help himself.

Before she could stand and make her fantasy reality, she heard footsteps on the stairs. Amy clattered into the studio and crossed to the piano.

"Please play for me," she said.

Claire laughed and pulled her up onto the

bench. "How could I refuse? You're my favorite audience."

Wyatt watched his daughter snuggle close to Claire, then close her eyes as she rested one hand on top of the piano.

Did she hear anything at all or did she just feel the music?

The beautiful sound filled the studio, vibrating through him. How was it possible for Claire to create that with only her fingers and her memory? Why had she been singled out for her gift? What combination of genes or DNA or God had picked her?

Did it matter? She simply was. Talented, feisty, irresistible. Dangerous. He knew better than to get involved, yet he felt himself being drawn in closer and closer. Did he want to get out while the getting was still relatively easy?

Instead of answering that, he turned his attention to Amy. His beautiful daughter. While he ached at the thought of any part of her being destroyed, he knew he couldn't deny her what she asked for. The compromise lay in doing only one ear, leaving the other available for future technology. Now she wanted to hear Claire play the piano. In time she would want to hear more of the world. A friend's laughter. A man's voice. A baby's cry.

It wasn't when or what he would have chosen, but he couldn't say she was wrong to want that. Like Claire's music, his daughter was a miracle.

"You're restless," Nicole said after dinner. "Do I want to know what's wrong?"

"I need to play," Claire told her. She'd been feeling the urge since her conversation with Wyatt.

No, that wasn't true. She'd been feeling it for a while now. She'd finally admitted it to herself after her talk with Wyatt.

Nicole looked confused. "I thought you were playing before. You had the studio door propped open. I heard you."

"I mean in public. I have to play for other people." She held up her hand. "This isn't about my ego. I don't need an audience to feel special about myself."

"I wasn't going to say anything."

"You were scrunchy. You had scrunchy face."

"I don't even want to know what that is," Nicole grumbled. "And hey, I'm sensitive, too. I get it. You need to play in public to figure out if you've conquered the panic thing. If you haven't, you're totally screwed." She paused. "I don't mean that in a bad way."

"Of course not." Claire sighed. "You're right, though. I have to fix this stupid panic thing. So I need to play in front of strangers. A lot of strangers."

"What's the plan? You could set up shop on a street corner. You might even earn some extra cash in tips."

Claire ignored that. "I was thinking of a ·bar. It's contained, anonymous. Do you know any around here that have pianos or like a talent show or something?"

Nicole picked up one of her crutches and pointed it at Claire. "You are so not going to play in a bar."

"Why not?"

"You're not the bar type."

"I'm not looking for a second career. I just want to practice being in public. So are you going to help me find a good place or do I have to do it by myself."

Nicole set down the crutch. "Fine," she grumbled. "I'll give you a couple of names. Are you going by yourself?"

"I'll be okay. I'm going to order a glass of white wine, ease over to the piano and start playing. What's the worst that will happen?"

"I don't want to imagine it. When are you going?"

"Tonight. Right now."

Nicole waited until she heard Claire's car backing out of the driveway, then picked up the phone.

"There is a serious problem," she said when Wyatt answered. "You won't believe what Claire's going to do tonight."

She told him, then interrupted his string of swearing by saying, "I know exactly what you mean. Bring Amy over. She can spend the night here. Then you can go and check on Claire. Don't be obvious about it. Just hang out in the back and make sure she's all right. I'm sure she'll be fine —"

"Did she ever tell you about Spike?" he asked, interrupting her.

"Spike who?"

"Some guy at my construction site. Convicted felon, still on parole, tattoos, married. He asked her out and she nearly said yes."

Nicole's vague unease shifted to elephant-size worry. "Hurry."

"I'll be right there."

The Greenway Tavern was better lit than she'd expected, relatively clean and kind of crowded. Claire made her way to the bar, settled on an empty stool and waited for the bartender to make his way to her.

She had no idea if the place was typical or not. There were a couple of pool tables, several televisions showing a baseball game with the sound down, and music playing through speakers in the ceiling. A lone piano stood covered in the far corner of the room. The crowd seemed evenly divided between couples and groups of guys. There weren't a lot of women on their own. In fact, she couldn't see any except for a table of them by one of the posts.

"What can I get you?" the bartender asked.

"Glass of . . ." She hesitated. She had a feeling this wasn't much of a white wine kind of place. "Um, a beer. Whatever you have on tap is fine."

The guy nodded and walked away. Claire had no idea where she'd ever heard about draft beer, but as it had been the right thing to say, she was only grateful.

A couple of guys smiled at her while she waited for her beer. She gave them a slight nod, not wanting to get into conversation. She was here for the pain and nothing else.

When the bartender returned with her beer, he said, "Three bucks."

She passed him a five. "Would you mind

if I played the piano?"

The guy hesitated. "You any good?"

That made her smile. "I've taken a few lessons."

"Sure. But if people complain, you're going to have to stop."

Claire was less concerned about anyone's opinion than having a panic attack of some kind. She'd felt strong for a few weeks now, but she also hadn't tested herself since the school. While she'd gotten through that performance, it had been by sheer force of will.

She waved for the bartender to keep the change, then picked up her mug and walked toward the piano. As she passed a table, a guy grabbed her hand.

"Want to join me, honey?"

"No, thanks," she said without looking at him.

She tugged off the cover, then stared at the black upright. There was a coaster on one end and a tip jar on the other.

She sat on the bench and felt her chest tighten. This time there was no Amy to distract or save her. She was going to have to save herself.

Her breathing became more shallow. She deliberately slowed and deepened it, but she still felt as if air wasn't filling her lungs. She couldn't breathe, she couldn't . . .

"Stop," she said aloud, not caring if anyone else heard her. "Just stop it."

She was fine. She could breathe and she wasn't going to die, no matter how it felt otherwise. The only way to get over this was to play until playing was easy again.

Ignoring the tight chest and the sense of panic, she put her hands on the keys and lost herself in the sound.

Rachmaninoff, she thought with a sigh of relief. One of her favorites. It always calmed her. The way the music —

"Hey, lady. Shut the hell up. No one wants to hear that."

Claire opened her eyes and glanced around to find several people glaring at her. Oops. This wasn't a Rachmaninoff kind of crowd.

"Sorry," she said with a smile. "How about this?"

She transitioned into "Uptown Girl" by Billy Joel and when that was done, played "Accidentally In Love," a song she'd adored from the moment she'd heard it in the second *Shrek* movie.

She played Norah Jones, several popular show tunes and then started taking requests.

She wasn't sure how much time passed. When she felt her body begin to tremble with exhaustion, she knew it was time to stop. But before she could finish her current song, some guy walked up and put a buck into the empty jar.

"You've got yourself some talent there," he said.

She started to laugh. "Thank you."

After she finished the last song, she collected her now-warm beer and her dollar, and stood. Several people clapped, a few yelled for her to keep playing. She shook her head. She was tired, but in the best way possible. Weary from her work.

It would take time to heal completely, she thought. Maybe going back into therapy for a few weeks would be a good idea. But she sensed she'd turned a corner. The healing had begun. She might still be afraid, but she wasn't going to be immobilized anymore.

She walked toward the bar to set down her drink. A guy grabbed her by the wrist. "Want to join me?"

She was about to refuse when every cell in her body went on alert. She glanced down and saw Wyatt.

"What are you doing here?"

"Listening to the show."

Somehow she doubted that. "And before the show?"

"Seeing if you were going to need any moral support."

A kind way of saying he'd thought she might need rescuing.

She smiled. "It could have gotten ugly. Thanks for coming by."

He stood, still holding on to her wrist. "You had them from the second you sat down."

She looked around at the crowded bar. "Almost."

"How did it feel to have them all in your power?"

She remembered the flow of the music moving through her, the rightness of creating every note. "Good," she admitted.

He stared into her eyes. "Amy's spending the night with Nicole. Want to come over for a drink?"

He was inviting her for a whole lot more than liquor. Her insides tensed slightly at the thought of him touching her again. Kissing her, holding her. She wanted to feel those amazing sensations again. She wanted him inside of her, connecting them.

"I'd like that," she said.

He took the mug from her hand and set it on the table. "Then let's go."

As they walked into the house, Claire tried

to figure out how to tell Wyatt she wasn't interested in a drink or polite conversation. What she really wanted was to have him rip her clothes off and have his way with her. She wanted to be taken in the best way possible.

As that conversation hadn't been covered in any how-to book she'd read, she braced herself for a long, frustrating evening until they got to the good part.

But instead of heading to the kitchen or even the family room, Wyatt took her hand and started upstairs. Once in his bedroom, he turned to her, pulled her close and began to kiss her.

She'd thought about teasing that she was actually thirsty, but what was the point? There wasn't anywhere she wanted to be except in his arms. Preferably naked.

He stroked his tongue against her lower lip and she parted for him. As he deepened the kiss, he tugged at her shirt, pulling it out of her jeans and going to work on the buttons. At the same time, she reached for him, which meant they bumped more than unbuttoned. When she clipped him with her elbow, she pulled back.

"This is dangerous," she said.

He grinned. "You're lethal. Tell you what. I'll race you."

"What?"

Instead of answering, he undid his shirt, then shrugged it off. "You're losing," he said.

She shrieked. "I have more clothes on than you."

"Always an excuse."

She jerked the blouse over her head as she kicked off her sandals. She undid her bra and pushed off her jeans and panties in one, quick shove. Then she straightened only to find him still dressed.

"Hey!"

His smile faded as hunger replaced amusement. "Damn, you're beautiful."

He grabbed her and pulled her against him. She went willingly, wanting to feel his hands on her. She wanted it all — the touching, the stroking, the intensity as he took her to paradise and back.

They tumbled onto the bed. Wyatt rolled her onto her back and leaned over her, then bent down and kissed her. Even as their tongues touched and played, he ran his fingers down her belly. She happily parted her thighs.

He slipped between her legs and immediately found that one special spot. He rubbed it lightly, making her squirm to get more. Harder, she thought. Faster.

She soon discovered he had his own agenda. Instead of listening to her psychic commands, he continued to kiss her. Then he moved lower and took her nipples in his mouth, which turned out to be very nice. She had to admit the combination of him sucking on her breasts while touching between her thighs worked in a big way.

Jolts of sensation shot through her. She got hot all over and her breathing quickened. She recognized the rising tension, the pulsing of her muscles and sank into the bed to enjoy the ride.

Then Wyatt stopped.

She opened her eyes and looked at him.

He touched her nose. "I want to try something."

"Another woman? I don't think I'm up for a threesome."

He grinned. "No way I'm sharing you. I want to see if you can come with me inside of you."

As she had experienced exactly one serious sexual encounter in her life, she was more than willing to play. "Tell me what to do."

"Relax and let me take care of things."

An excellent quality in a man, she thought as Wyatt got up and stripped off the rest of his clothes. But before moving back on the bed, he reached into the nightstand drawer and pulled out a condom.

Claire's stomach clenched. Protection. It's what any sensible person would use, under the circumstances. But it reminded her of the last time, when he hadn't and the fact that there was a teeny, tiny chance she was pregnant.

She pushed the thought from her mind. Now was not the time to deal with that, she told herself as he knelt between her legs. He braced himself with his arms and slowly slipped inside of her.

It was more comfortable this time, she thought as she parted more for him. He filled her all the way, which was incredibly intimate.

But instead of pulling out and pushing in again, he straightened and, while still inside of her, reached between their bodies and began to touch her.

His fingers found her center and rubbed it. He circled and pressed in a steady rhythm that quickly had her breathing hard again. She tightened her muscles, which made him groan.

"You can feel that?" she asked.

"Oh, yeah."

Cool. She liked that she could make him experience what she was feeling, then the tension increased and it was more difficult to think about anything beyond how good she felt.

He touched her with a sureness that allowed her to relax. She closed her eyes and gave herself over to the moment. It was different, him touching her while being inside of her. She felt more full, more sensitive. She pressed down on him slightly and moved her hips, drawing him in. He groaned again, but she ignored the sound.

Over and over, he touched her. Circling, brushing, making her strain and shudder. Her muscles tightened again and again. She got closer, then had the urge to move against him.

She pulsed her hips. He answered by withdrawing slightly, then pushing back in. Closer, she thought frantically. She was getting closer and closer. She strained to part her legs more, to have him touch all of her. She rocked her head from side to side, then sucked in a breath as everything inside her went still again.

There was a single heartbeat, then she shattered into her climax. He continued to touch her, while moving in and out, carrying her forward on a tide she couldn't control. She groaned her release, breathing his name, her muscles contracting over and over again.

Then he wasn't touching her with his fingers. He'd knelt over and began to fully move in and out. She hadn't known what to expect . . . but what stunned her most was how each stroke pushed her orgasm on a little more. She came again and again, trembling in rhythm with his thrusts, sure this was going to kill her, but what a way to go.

She was still climaxing when he shuddered and was still. He collapsed on his side, pulling her with him. They lay there, a tangle of arms and legs, breathing hard, holding on to each other as if they were never going to let go.

The sunrise started shortly before six. Claire knew because she and Wyatt were already in the kitchen, making coffee. She wore one of his soft, warm plaid shirts and nothing else. She felt sexy and wicked and more satisfied than she'd ever felt in her life.

She leaned against the counter while he turned on the machine, then put his hands on her waist and drew her close.

"You're always beautiful," he murmured as he kissed her. "Even first thing in the morning."

"Thank you," she said, knowing she

wasn't. Not really. But if he thought she was, she wouldn't do any complaining.

He slipped his hands under the shirt and touched her bare waist. She began to tingle in anticipation. But instead of exploring further, he released her and tucked her hair behind her ears.

"You're going to have to be careful when you go back to New York," he said.

"Go back?"

"Won't you? Eventually?"

She'd never thought about it specifically. "I guess. My apartment is there. My career." Her life had been, until recently. Now she was less sure.

"You'll need to learn how to protect yourself. You're going to be dating and when the men you go out with find out about your financial success, you run the risk of them wanting to take advantage of you. You'll need to be careful."

Claire didn't know what to say. There were so many assumptions in his little speech, where was she supposed to start?

"I don't know that I'll be dating," she said, finding that the easiest one to address.

"What man could resist you?" he asked.

Good answer, but still. "Why would I pick someone like that?"

"Some men are good at hiding that they're

bastards."

"You'd never want my money."

"Agreed. But I'm not talking about me, I'm talking about the next guy."

Next guy? Because they weren't going to be going out anymore?

One corner of his mouth turned up. "I'm the guy you met on vacation. I live in Seattle. I have a kid. You live in New York and travel the world."

Meaning, what? They had nothing in common? It would never work? She felt a sharp pain in her chest and it had nothing to do with being scared or worrying about a panic attack.

"I want the best for you," he told her. "I don't want you to get hurt or have regrets."

Too late for that, she thought, as the truth crashed into her. She was already in a world of pain. Wyatt had been straightforward with her from the very start, and now he was trying to do the right thing and take care of her. It didn't occur to him that she wanted more. Someone who would care about her enough to insist she stay, no matter how difficult it might be to work out the logistics. Someone who would love her . . . the way she loved him.

Chapter Eighteen

Nicole did her best not to spend the morning sulking, but it was hard. She was tired of being stuck in the house, tired of being the one left behind. Last night Claire had gone off to conquer her fears so she could return to her exciting life in New York. She'd also had fabulously hot sex with Wyatt. It wasn't that Nicole cared about Claire sleeping with Wyatt specifically, it's just that she was soon-to-be divorced, unlikely to trust a man with her heart anytime soon and therefore not going to ever have sex again. She wasn't the type to simply take a man to bed, not that they were lining up, asking. All she had to show for the last three months of her life was a cheating ex-husband, a stealing, backstabbing baby sister and two ugly scars.

She slumped down on the sofa and tried to tell herself the news wasn't all bad. She and Claire had reconciled.

"Now that I like her, I know she's going back to New York," Nicole muttered, feeling crabbier by the second. "Then I'll be all alone again."

She hated feeling like this and was willing to risk watching daytime television to change her mood. But before she could reach for the clicker, she heard a knock at the door.

Nicole pushed herself up onto her crutches and walked to the door. She opened it, expecting to see the mail carrier, or a package delivery. Instead Jesse stood on the front porch.

Nicole's first emotion was relief, followed by a rush of love. She hadn't seen Jesse in weeks and despite everything that had happened between them, she'd been worried. Which just went to show Claire wasn't the only one flirting with crazy.

Nicole was careful not to show any emotion as she said, "What are you doing here?"

"I heard about your surgery." Her baby sister shifted on the porch. "I wanted to see how you're doing."

The initial rush of affection quickly faded. All of Jesse's betrayals lined up in her head, making her want to lash out. She didn't care that her sister looked tired and contrite and even a little sad. She wanted revenge.

She also wanted to talk to Jesse. Damn.

"I'm fine," Nicole said at last. "Healing."

"Can I come in?

Instead of answering verbally, Nicole stepped back. She led the way into the house, two parts hoping things could go back to how they'd been before and two parts knowing some wounds took more than a few weeks to heal.

Nicole sank onto the sofa. Jesse stayed standing. She looked around. "The place looks the same."

Nicole shrugged. She didn't want to talk about decorating.

"I thought maybe we could talk," Jesse mumbled.

"About?"

Jesse sucked in a breath. She raised her head. "I'm sorry," she snapped. "I'm really sorry and you're not making this easy."

Nicole pushed down the hope that sparked inside of her. "Making it easy isn't my job."

Jesse rolled her eyes. "When are you going to stop taking every opportunity to teach me some stupid moral lesson?"

"When you stop needing them. Come on, Jess, convince me." It wouldn't take much, but Nicole wasn't about to admit that.

"I'm sorry I hurt you. I'm sorry you got upset."

The hope died and anger grew out of death. "How about 'I'm sorry I stole from you?' or is that too much like accepting responsibility?"

"It's a family recipe. No matter how much you might not like it, I'm still a part of this family. The bakery is half mine. I had the right to take it."

Nicole wasn't going to admit that. "The recipe belongs to the business. Instead of talking to me or trying to make some equitable arrangement or even ask, you just took what you wanted, then set up a Web site almost exactly like the bakery's."

"When was I supposed to talk to you? You threw me out of the house."

If Nicole had been even a week further along in her healing, she would have stood up to face her sister without crutches, but there was no way her knee would support her.

"You're right. I wasn't talking to you. Why is that? Oh, yes, I remember. You slept with my husband. In my own house. Oh, wait. Was he like the recipe? Were we sharing him, too?"

Jesse blushed, then ducked her head. "That's not what happened."

"Sure it is. Worse, I lied for you. When Matt called I didn't tell him why you'd moved out. But know this. If he calls again, all bets are off."

Jesse started crying. "I deserved it. I know that now."

What? Punishment? Drew? Nicole felt the anger fading as exhaustion claimed her.

Without meaning to, she remembered something she hadn't allowed herself to do. She remembered walking up the stairs late in the evening. She hadn't even noticed Jesse's door was partially closed until she'd heard a weird noise. Then she'd crossed the landing and pushed it open.

They'd been in Jesse's full-size bed. They'd both stared at her, wide-eyed. Everything about that moment was burned into her brain. The way Drew had been on top of Jesse, his hand on her bare breast. How sharp and intense the sense of pain and betrayal had felt. They were supposed to be the two people in the world who loved her more than anyone. She'd been wrong to trust either of them.

"I never wanted to hurt you," Jesse said, brushing the tears from her face.

"Really? Well, then, that makes everything all right."

"I hate it when you get like this," Jesse said. "You're so cold."

"You're still sorry you got caught but not

359

sorry you did it. That's what gets me, Jess. Not Drew, but you. I raised you. I've been there for you every day of your life. I sacrificed for you and you were never grateful. You only wanted to know what else I could do for you. You never cared about any of it."

"I cared," Jesse yelled. "I cared a lot and I would have been grateful, but for what? My mother leaving because it was more fun to be with Claire? Should I be grateful that my father didn't care about me? Or how about for all you did? I can give you the list. You know why? Because every damn day you talked about all you were giving up for me. All you had to do or take care of. Your life was one big pain in the ass because of me. I get it!" she screamed. "I ruined your life, okay!"

Nicole didn't know what to say. Jesse had to be kidding. "You twist everything around to suit yourself."

"Who do you think I learned that from?" Jesse yelled. "You know what? I'm glad I slept with Drew. Glad. If he wasn't such a loser jerk asshole, I'd do it again. But he's not worth the trouble. I should have figured that out. He married you. And now you don't even have him." Jesse's eyes filled with tears. "I'll hate you forever."

Nicole's anger returned, burning bright and hot like the sun. "Back at you," she snapped. "Get the hell out of my house."

"Gladly."

Jesse stalked away. The front door slammed and then there was silence.

Claire arrived home to find Nicole fuming.

"Jesse was here," she announced. "Our conversation didn't go well."

"What happened?"

Nicole filled her in on the details, then said, "Don't you dare take her side."

"I won't. I know this has been hard for you." For both of them, but Claire knew better than to say that. It was easy for her to be rational and see both points of view, but much harder for Nicole. And while she cared about Jesse, she had to agree that her baby sister had messed up big-time more than once in the past few weeks.

"It sucks that it's too early to get drunk."

"You're on pain medication," Claire said.

"I'd pass on it for a vodka tonic. At least I would if it was four, or even three. What time is it?"

"About nine-thirty in the morning."

Nicole groaned. "I have hours to wait." She hobbled over to the sofa and collapsed. "I'm glad you're here."

Claire settled across from her. "Me, too. Whatever happens, I want us to stay close. We should have before."

Nicole's face scrunched up.

Claire smiled. "What are you holding back?"

"I want to jump into my 'you left me' routine, but I won't. You were six. No one gave you a choice. I missed you more than I could say."

"I missed you, too. We'd never been apart. I felt like someone cut off my arm. I was so lonely. That never went away."

"Me, too, though I was busy. Jesse was born a few months after they took you away. She changed everything."

For Nicole, Claire thought. Not for her. She learned about her new sister from her grandmother and saw a few pictures.

"I wanted to call more," Claire admitted. "But we didn't have the money back then. I'm sure it was expensive, plus with the time difference." Later, when she'd been able to make her own decisions about calling, Nicole hadn't wanted to talk to her.

Her sister sighed. "Okay, I was very annoyed with you and unforgiving."

Wow — an apology from Nicole? "I believe the word you're looking for is bitch."

"Maybe."

362

"There's no maybe, honey. You were the queen bitch."

"I'll accept being in the royal court, but I won't accept being the actual queen."

"Works for me."

They smiled at each other. Claire risked the moment by asking, "What are you going to do about Jesse?"

"I haven't got a clue. I want her to be different and that isn't going to happen. I want her to accept responsibility. Another chance for me to be disappointed. I wish she'd grow up, which makes me zero for three." She pulled a throw pillow to her stomach and wrapped her arms around it.

"I don't know what to do about the charges. One side of me says to drop them. She's family, blah, blah, blah. Another part of me wants her to understand that there have to be consequences for what she's done. Your thoughts?"

"I don't know," Claire admitted. "I agree with you. She is family and she has totally messed up. I'm the wrong person to ask."

"You're as right as I am. Which is part of the problem. I'm in such a weird position," Nicole admitted. "I'm as much her mother as her sister. I never know what role to play or what I should be doing. I can't help thinking I really messed up somewhere for her to have done what she did."

"No," Claire told her. "You're not at fault. Nicole, you're only six years older than her. You are her sister and not her mother. You did the best you could."

"I don't think it was good enough. That's my guilty secret. Want to share yours?"

Claire hesitated. Nicole's eyes widened. "You have one?"

"Maybe. I'm in love with Wyatt."

Nicole looked stunned. "The sex was that good?"

That made Claire laugh. "It's not about sex."

"It's always about sex. Especially for you. Wyatt is your first. It makes sense you'd feel something for him. Are you sure it's love?"

"I'm not sure of anything anymore. I know I've never had these feelings before. I know I want to spend every minute with him and not just while he's in a good mood. I want to learn about him, plan a future. I want to get so tangled up with him that neither of us knows where we start individually or where we end as a couple." She paused. "Does that make me a stalker?"

"Not unless you start spray-painting that on his garage wall. Wow. You really have fallen for him. Does he know?"

"No. I realized this morning when he was

talking to me about the other men in my life."

"What other men?"

"The ones that are supposed to follow him. He says he's just my vacation fling or something. That we have nothing in common."

"Wyatt does always resist getting involved."

Not words Claire wanted to hear, but ones she needed to accept. "You told me and he told me. No relationships. He's convinced he's bad at them. What does he say? That he comes from a long line of men who pick the wrong woman?"

"Something like that," Nicole admitted. "But it's just what he says. It doesn't have to be what he believes."

"You're his friend," Claire said. "What do you think?"

Nicole hesitated for a second. "That he's so used to hiding that he has no idea what he wants."

"The politically correct answer. You're sweet to try to make me feel better."

"Wyatt could change. People change."

They could, but they didn't all that often. "Do you really believe, in your gut, that Wyatt could fall in love with me?"

"Yes," Nicole said firmly.

Claire didn't believe her for a second, but the fact that her sister would be so supportive was enough. At least for right now.

"Mrs. Olive says the counselor will talk to Daddy and me," Amy said, so excited that she was difficult to understand. "I'm going to need . . ." She paused to finger spell at the speed of light.

"Slower, please," Claire signed. "You're going to need what?"

"T-h-e-r-a-p-y."

"Oh, like what Nicole is getting for her leg but for you it will be your ear and your brain."

"Uh-huh." Amy grinned. "Daddy says we'll do my bad ear. It's a comp . . . Compy something."

"Compromise."

She nodded again. "After the counselor, we'll meet with the doctor."

Amy climbed out of the car and ran up to the front door of Nicole's house, where she would wait until Wyatt came by to pick her up.

Amy hurried over to the sofa to greet Nicole, then signed about her impending surgery.

"Are you happy with just one ear?" Nicole asked. "One and not two?"

"Uh-huh. I need to wait until there's better ways for me to hear with the other ear. I'll still be able to hear good with the one implant."

She spoke with a combination of signing and speaking.

"You're very mature," Claire told her.

Amy dimpled.

"Go in the kitchen," Nicole told her. "There's a surprise."

Amy raced in that direction. When she'd left, Nicole said, "I agree. She's very together. I wouldn't have been at her age."

"Me, either."

Nicole rolled her eyes. "Oh, please. Of the two of us, you have the best shot at the title of mature child. You were practically living on your own as you studied and toured the world."

"I couldn't have handled what she's doing. Amy has backbone. I would have listened to the adults around me and done what they told me to."

"If only that were still true," Nicole said with a sniff.

Claire laughed.

Amy burst back into the room. "You made cookies! Can I have one?"

"Of course," Claire said. "My first attempt at baking. Be kind."

"They'll be fine," Nicole told her. "Baking is in your blood."

"I hope so."

"As long as you didn't use too much salt." Claire remembered the unfortunate incident the first day she'd gone to the bakery. "We're not going to mention that."

"Aren't we?"

"No."

Claire led Amy back into the kitchen and served her a couple of cookies, along with a glass of milk. She sat across from her at the table and listened to the details of her day.

As the girl spoke and signed and laughed, Claire realized something. She didn't just love Wyatt. She loved his daughter, too. Leaving them both behind, not to mention Nicole and even Jesse, was going do more than hurt. It was going to break her heart.

Claire hovered impatiently, dancing from foot to foot, counting to herself. She'd used three different tests at the same time and then lined them up on the bathroom counter on a paper towel. Now came the hard part — waiting.

The sticks offered her nothing at first, then one by one they changed and gave her the same message. She shrieked and ran into Nicole's bedroom.

Her sister was still in bed. It was barely after six, so Nicole being asleep wasn't a huge surprise. But Claire didn't care. It was only in deference to her sister's still-healing knee that she didn't jump on the mattress. But she did yell.

"Get up! Get up. You have to be awake so I can tell you myself."

She pulled back the drapes and opened the blinds. Sunlight spilled into the room.

Nicole sat up and blinked at her. "What's your problem? It's early." She glanced at the clock. "Dear God, I'm going to have to kill you."

Claire didn't care. She spun in a circle, her happiness giving her speed and momentum. She couldn't possibly be expected to contain all the happiness bubbling up inside of her.

"I'm pregnant," she announced. "I peed on three different sticks in three different tests and I'm pregnant. I'm having a baby. Isn't that the best?"

Nicole's mouth dropped open. "Since when?"

"This morning. Oh. I guess technically since that first night Wyatt and I, you know. I'm so happy. I've always wanted children. I never thought I could get pregnant so easily. I thought I'd have to work for it more.

This is going to change everything. I get to be a mom and start a family." She stopped spinning and planted her feet until the room stopped moving, too.

Nicole laughed. "Too bad no one can harness that energy."

"I know. You'll be an aunt. I hope I have a girl. Is it okay to hope that? Except a boy would be great. I definitely want a boy."

"I know you haven't been drinking, but you are totally out of it."

"I'm happy! I've always wanted kids but that seemed impossible, like I would never be that normal." Claire laughed. "I should have gotten pregnant years ago."

"Apparently."

Claire settled on the edge of the bed and grinned. "You're worried. I can see it in your eyes."

"Just about Wyatt."

The man who was probably not going to be so happy about this, Claire thought, bubbling too much to have anything break her mood.

"He'll come around or he won't. Either way, I'll deal."

"Good for you," Nicole told her. "He may surprise us both. And if he doesn't, I'll break his kneecaps. I happen to know that can be really painful."

Claire leaned forward and hugged her. "I love you."

"I love you, too. Even if I am a little bitter."

Claire pulled back. "Why?"

"Because I always wanted a family, too. Don't get me wrong. I'm grateful Drew and I never got around to the kid thing. But a baby would be nice."

She sounded wistful as she spoke.

"So go get pregnant," Claire told her. "It's easy."

Nicole laughed. "So I've heard. I appreciate the advice, but I think I'll wait a bit. Things are a little complicated right now. But I'm happy for you."

"Me, too!" Claire sighed. "I'm also terrified, but in a good way. I'm filled with possibilities and anticipation."

"What are you going to do about your career?"

"I don't know." While thoughts of Wyatt being unhappy didn't affect her mood, a sharp longing to play again seemed to shave off a couple of layers of happiness.

"I miss it," Claire admitted. "More and more. Can I do both?"

"Why not? Aren't you rich? Can't you hire help if you need it."

"Sure."

"Honey, then I say go for it."

Claire laughed again. "I will."

CHAPTER NINETEEN

Claire called ahead to make sure Wyatt was at his office, then drove over before he could head out to a job site. She spent the thirty-minute trip alternating between total happiness and a gnawing worry about what he was going to say.

In a perfect world he would be as excited about the baby as she was. She wasn't going to hold her breath for that, though. She figured the best she could hope for was neutrality.

She walked into the building and was directed back to his private office. Wyatt hung up the phone as she entered, smiled and moved toward her.

"An unexpected pleasure," he told her, pulling her close and kissing her. "The best kind."

His mouth was warm on hers, making her tummy clench in anticipation. Blood moved faster and the instant desire made her want to throw herself at him.

She pulled back, laughing. "How do you do that? Turn me on with just a kiss?"

"I'm gifted."

He was more than that. He was everything she'd ever wanted. Strong, yet gentle. Caring, determined, even stubborn. She loved so much about him, including how much *he* loved his daughter. Would he be willing to give their child the same amount of caring?

He put his hand on her waist and kissed her again. "If you're here for something quick on my desk, I can tell you that I'm open to the possibility. In the name of making all your fantasies come true."

She touched his face. "You're so generous."

"I know."

"While I appreciate the offer, I stopped by to tell you some happy news."

Wyatt stiffened. "Okay."

"What?"

"Your happy may not be my happy. Are you leaving?"

She hadn't expected him to say that. "Leaving for New York?"

"You will eventually. Your work is there. You can't give up the piano forever."

A fierce longing gripped her. She was less

surprised by it this time — it seemed to happen more and more lately. The need to create, to be one with the music. To let it fill her up and spill out of her.

"I'm not leaving," she told him. Not yet, a voice whispered. She ignored it and looked at Wyatt. "I'm pregnant."

Everything about him seemed to freeze in place. Then he was moving, putting space between them.

"You're sure?"

His words sounded so cold and distant. She held in a shiver.

"Yes. Very sure."

He nodded once, then swore. The bubble of hope she'd barely allowed herself to admit was there burst.

"Wyatt," she began, "this doesn't have to be a bad thing."

His expression turned angry. She could see him visibly trying to get control. "It is for me. I never wanted any part of this. Not a baby. I can't believe it's happening again."

She knew the "it" was his sense of being trapped. Of being forced into a relationship, a marriage, a responsibility he didn't want.

He glared at her. "I know you didn't do this on purpose, but it sure as hell feels that way to me."

"That's not fair and you know it."

"You're right. Just like I know you're going to expect me to marry you, then you'll go back to your fancy life, leaving me with another kid to raise."

Even though they weren't a shock, his words still hurt her.

"I'm not trapping you," she said, wishing he could have been at least a tiny bit happy, if not for himself, then for her.

"So you say."

He didn't believe her? "You don't know me at all, if that's what you think."

"I know enough. I know you're used to getting what you want."

What? "Since when?"

"When have you not?"

It wasn't a fair question. She thought of all the things in her life she hadn't wanted. But he wasn't in the mood to listen. "I thought . . ."

"That I would be happy?" he asked, interrupting. "Why? I should have used protection. I shouldn't have assumed. Not that I was thinking that day. Look, it's fine. We'll deal. Somehow."

He sounded resigned, as well as angry. He was being magnanimous enough not to blame her totally, but he still expected to get screwed.

It hurt, she thought sadly. It hurt to have

him so disconnected from the joy. They'd made a baby. Didn't that matter to him at all? They'd created life. They should be celebrating. But he didn't see it that way and she wouldn't see it any other.

"You don't have to be any part of this," she said, trying to keep her voice from shaking. "I thought you might want to be a father to our child, but if you don't, that's perfectly fine. I can be a single mother."

He didn't look convinced. "You mean you'll hire staff. Isn't that what you said you'd do? Hire a nanny?"

She'd known there was a chance he wouldn't be excited. More than a chance. But she'd never thought he would be deliberately mean. She squared her shoulders and raised her chin.

"I can see this is a bad time for us to discuss anything," she said, determined to keep her voice calm. She didn't want him to know how deeply he'd cut her. "We'll talk later. For the record, I don't want anything from you. I also don't expect you to believe that. I'm sorry you're not happy but I can't ever be sorry there's a baby."

She turned then, and left without saying anything else. She had to hurry to get to her car before she started to cry.

Claire bit down on the Kidd Valley onion ring and waited for the yummy flavor to brighten her mood.

"You want to talk about what's wrong or do you just want to eat and sulk?" Jesse asked from across the table.

Claire smiled. "I'm not sulking. Not seriously, anyway. I'm just . . ." She sighed. "I'm pregnant."

Jesse dropped her hamburger back on the paper. "You're what? Are you sure?"

"I'm triple sure."

"Who's the guy? Some musician back in New York? A married conductor?"

"You're the one who seems to favor married men," Claire said.

Jesse took a bite of her hamburger. "Sure," she mumbled. "That's what you all think."

Claire waited until her sister had swallowed, then said, "Wyatt."

Jesse's eyes widened. "Are you serious? You slept with Wyatt? Does Nicole know?"

"Yes to both. She knows about him and she knows about the baby. She's not the problem. He is."

Claire gave a brief rundown of her last conversation with him. "He's so distant and

378

cold. I would almost wish he was angry because then I would know he was feeling something. He thinks I'm trapping him, which I'm not. I'm so happy about the baby, but he doesn't see it that way."

Jesse put down her burger and wiped her hands. "Nicole isn't mad? She doesn't care that you slept with Wyatt? I can't believe it."

Claire couldn't, either. "That's all you got from what I said?"

"What? No. I mean, yeah, it's too bad about Wyatt."

"Talk about too little too late," Claire grumbled, feeling a little of Nicole's annoyance with their baby sister.

"Hey, I've got my own troubles."

"Maybe you have them because you only think of yourself."

Jesse pulled back. "I don't need this from you."

"An opinion on your behavior? I can see why you wouldn't want one."

"Look, don't get all pissy with me because your life is messed up."

"Is that what you think this is? I couldn't possibly have a valid insight? You're wrong about that. I know exactly what's going on with you. You take the easy way out. I wonder if you always have. Jesse, you're getting too old for this game. It's time to take responsibility. Do the right thing."

Claire thought Jesse might get angry and stalk off, but instead she stayed in her seat.

"I've tried," Jesse grumbled. "I apologized to Nicole but she's still mad at me. She won't listen. What if I didn't do it? What if nothing happened?"

Claire held in a sigh. "Were you in bed with Drew?"

"Yes."

"Naked?"

"I had my panties on."

For how long? So what if there hadn't been actual intercourse? They'd been on the verge. That was enough. "He was touching your breast."

Jesse tossed her burger on the tray. "Okay, I get it. I'm the big bad?"

Even now, Jesse wasn't taking it seriously, Claire thought in annoyance. "Guess what?" Claire snapped. "You're the one who screwed up. She gets to be mad as long as she wants. Just because you're sorry doesn't mean the pain goes away. You need to keep showing up until she knows that you're serious. Right now she thinks you're just saying what she wants to hear and I kind of agree with her."

"Figures you'd take her side. You're just like her, you know. Stupid twins."

Claire knew Jesse hadn't meant the comment as a compliment, but that's how she took it. "I want to be like Nicole."

"You're more than halfway there."

"She's smart, capable, loving and successful."

"Bossy, annoying and a real pain in the ass."

"You miss her."

Jesse nodded slowly. "I know what you're saying, Claire, but it's not like that with Nicole. Once she gets mad, she doesn't get over it."

"You're wrong. She got over it with me."

"I'm not you."

"You're not trying. There's a difference."

Jesse slid out of the booth and grabbed her purse. "I don't need this crap. Not from her and not from you. You're mad at me for something that didn't happen. Go to hell."

With that she was gone.

It was, Claire thought sadly, the Keyes sisters' day for running away.

Wyatt knocked once, then let himself into Nicole's house. "It's me," he called, then found her sitting on the sofa, her foot propped up on the coffee table.

"How are you feeling?" he asked Nicole.

"Ready to take you on."

Her eyes were bright with annoyance and something else he couldn't identify. He didn't need to ask if she knew about the pregnancy. That was obvious. She probably knew how he'd reacted. Even if Claire hadn't told her, Nicole knew him well enough to guess his reaction.

"What did you expect me to say?" he asked, feeling anger rise up in him. He'd been numb earlier, but now he was feeling it all. "This shouldn't have happened."

"You're right. It shouldn't have. But it did. And whose fault is that? What the hell were you thinking, Wyatt? You slept with my sister and didn't use a condom? Who does that?"

He didn't have an answer for that. It had been the night, or morning, and the moment. He'd been carried away by a wave of passion he'd never experienced before. But there was no way he was going to say that to Nicole.

"I thought she was covered."

"She was a virgin and the person supposed to be doing the covering is you. What right do you have to take those kind of chances?"

"I don't usually do that."

"So Claire just got lucky? This is all your fault and now you're whining about taking responsibility."

"I'm not whining."

"Sure sounds like it to me. Worse, you're punishing her. You were there, big guy. You wanted to play escaped convict and the warden's wife. Now you take responsibility for your actions."

Wait a minute. Nicole was supposed to be his friend. "You're taking her side?"

"Absolutely. You couldn't be more wrong. Dammit, Wyatt, I expected a whole lot better of you. Now get out."

He stared at her. "You can't mean that."

"More than you know."

He left the house, then stood by his car. What was going on? The whole world was screwed up.

He glared at the house. If Nicole wanted him gone, he was gone. He didn't need her or Claire or any of them.

Claire arrived at the house to find Nicole waiting with an assortment of pints of Ben & Jerry's ice cream.

"Normally we'd both get drunk on margaritas," Nicole told her. "But in your present condition, that's probably not a good idea. We're going to have to settle for ice cream."

The sympathy in her sister's voice told

her she'd heard about her conversation with Wyatt.

"How'd you find out?" Claire asked.

"The bastard came here looking for a shoulder to cry on. I told him that was reserved for you, then kicked him out." Nicole held open her arms.

Claire crossed to her and allowed herself to be hugged. Nicole held on tight, as if she would never let go.

"I'll find someone to beat the crap out of him," her sister told her.

Claire fought tears. "I love him too much to want him hurt. How sick is that?"

"Pretty sick. So I won't tell you when it happens. But I'm still having it done."

Claire straightened. "Thanks."

Nicole shrugged. "What else can I do? For what it's worth, I'm sorry he's taking this badly."

"But not surprised?"

"No. I'll admit his family isn't exactly functional, but Wyatt's usually the good guy. Still, he believes he can't do relationships and Shanna's pregnancy and subsequent disappearing act hardly made him feel better about the process. Then you came along."

"The virgin piano player?"

Nicole smiled. "Something like that. He

didn't know how to handle you. He still doesn't. It's easier for him to get angry."

Claire tried to understand, but she couldn't. "He doesn't care about the baby."

"You've spent a lot of your life looking for family. This baby gives you that and more. He's been a single dad for eight years. His dreams are different. He'll come around."

"To what? Reluctantly accepting responsibility. I don't want that."

"What do you want?"

To be swept away, she thought sadly. She wanted Wyatt to realize he was madly in love with her, couldn't live without her and desperately wanted their child. She wanted everything he'd accused her of . . . love and marriage. But the difference between her and Shanna was that she didn't want to win him by default and should she be lucky enough to have him want her back, she would never leave.

"I want a happy ending."

"Sometimes we have to make our own," Nicole told her. "Starting with ice cream. What flavor do you want?"

The doorbell rang. Claire's whole body clenched as she hoped it was Wyatt. Maybe a beam had fallen on him at one of his jobs and the head injury had made him come to his senses. If only.

"I'll get it," she said as she left the kitchen and walked into the great room.

She didn't find Wyatt on the doorstep. Instead Lisa, her manager, stood there.

While Lisa was as well-groomed as ever, she looked tired. And old.

"Claire," she said with a tentative smile. "I was hoping to find you at home. Can we talk?"

A couple of weeks ago, Claire would have told her no. They had nothing to say to each other. Now, she wasn't so sure. The sense of longing swept over her again, the need to play, to perform. Along with that yearning was a determination to make things different, to not be the frightened, obedient client she'd been before. She wasn't who she had been when she'd arrived in Seattle. But who was she now?

"Sure, we can talk."

Lisa followed her into the house, then closed the door. "You're looking well."

"I feel good."

"Are you —" Lisa pressed her lips together. "Never mind."

"Am I practicing?" Claire asked, then laughed. "Yes. I've played a little, but I'm not on a schedule. I'm not taking classes, either."

She missed all that, too, she realized. The

regular sessions with her music, when it was just her and her coach and the perfection she could create.

"You probably want to yell at me now," she said, prepared to hear it all and deal with it like an equal, not a subordinate.

Lisa only nodded slowly. "I didn't think you were playing much. You're on vacation." She swallowed. "Is it just a vacation? Are you coming back? Before you answer, I need to say something."

Claire waited, trying not to feel nervous. She was an adult, she reminded herself. She needed to act like one.

"I was wrong," Lisa told her, clutching her handbag in front of her. "You were so young when we started working together. I treated you like a child, because you were. But you grew up and I didn't notice because it was easier for me if I made all the decisions. You kept trying to tell me you weren't happy and I didn't listen. I never wanted you to be unhappy. I never wanted you to feel trapped. I'm sorry."

Claire considered her words. "You were doing whatever you thought was right to get a performance out of me. That mattered more than anything."

"Only because you're so gifted. Claire, no one can do what you do. I worried you couldn't see that. I was afraid you didn't respect your gift."

"It's my gift to respect or not."

"I know. I see that now. I just hate to think of you wasting away, not playing."

"Not earning the money."

"That, too. You are my only client, Claire. If you're not working anymore, I have a right to know. This is my livelihood, as well."

Something Claire had never considered.

She led the way to the sofa. Nicole was nowhere to be seen, and probably hiding out in the kitchen with a pint of ice cream. This live performance had to be more interesting than anything she'd seen lately on television, Claire thought, trying to find the humor in the situation. Getting upset wouldn't help anyone. Better to stay calm and rational.

"I have responsibility for what went wrong, as well," she said, looking at Lisa. "I should have been more clear about how unhappy I was. Instead I used the panic attacks to get what I wanted. Eventually they began to control me. I wanted to be treated like an adult, but I didn't act like one. I was a kid faking a stomachache to avoid a test at school. That was wrong of me."

Wow — admitting fault was not her favorite thing, but it had to be done. "I shouldn't have just disappeared and left you hanging," she continued. "That wasn't fair to either of us. I'm sorry."

"I'm sorry, too," Lisa told her. "For everything."

They stared at each other for a couple of seconds, then looked away. They'd never had the sort of relationship that made hugging comfortable and Claire didn't know how to move on.

"Do you know what you're going to do?" Lisa asked.

She realized then she'd been avoiding the truth for a long time. "I'm going to come back to New York and return to my music."

Lisa leaned back against the sofa. "Thank God."

Claire smiled. "Don't get too excited. There are going to be a lot of changes."

"Whatever you say. Seriously, you're in charge."

"Unlikely," Claire told her, knowing Lisa was good at her job, but also stubborn. "We'll have to find a way to compromise. I don't want to be running all over the world for weeks at a time." She was also going to have to eventually avoid air travel. The pregnancy wouldn't allow it. Although she didn't know when that restriction would start.

"You can write your own schedule. There's also studio work."

Claire nodded. "I'll want to spend a lot of time in Seattle. I might buy a place here."

"You can play here or in San Francisco and Los Angeles. Even Phoenix. Also Japan, but only when you want to go overseas." Lisa leaned toward her. "We can make this work, Claire. I want us to be partners."

They would never be close friends, but she would like them to be partners, too. "I have the greatest respect for you," Claire told her. "The change is going to be hard on both of us. We have years of patterns we have to break."

"I can change."

Claire knew she could, as well. She already had.

CHAPTER TWENTY

After Lisa left, Nicole came out of the kitchen. "You're leaving." It wasn't a question.

Claire didn't know what to say. "I'm sorry," she began.

Nicole shook her head, then handed over a pint of ice cream. "Don't apologize. You have to go. It's where you belong."

"I don't agree with that, but it's where I have to face my demons."

"You have mutant hands," Nicole teased. "You'll beat those demons for sure. But just because you're leaving doesn't mean you have to stay gone."

"I know." Claire fought tears. "I meant what I said. I want to get a place here. You'll get sick of me."

"Maybe, but I can handle it." Nicole handed her a spoon. "How does it feel to be in charge of Lisa?"

"I don't know. Scary, but in a good way. It

only took me twenty-eight years to figure out how to be a grown-up."

They moved to the sofa and dug into their ice cream. Claire wondered how it was possible to be both excited and sad about her future. She felt the need to start practicing right away, to know what music she would be playing. She was also thrilled about the baby. But there was also the pain of leaving Seattle and her sisters, not to mention Wyatt and Amy. Speaking of her sisters . . .

She licked her spoon. "You have to forgive Jesse. Not right away, but eventually. She's family."

Nicole took another bite of her Cherry Garcia. "Did I ever mention that she and Wyatt had a brief but highly passionate weekend together? Amy was off at camp. They headed to a B and B on the San Juan Islands. I heard they nearly set the place on fire."

The ice cream formed a hard knot in Claire's stomach, which felt worse than wanting to throw up. Her skin got really hot, while a sense of anger and betrayal crawled through her body. She wanted to scream. She wanted to rip Jesse's hair out.

"When?" she asked, her throat thick with pain.

Nicole took another bite. "Gotcha."

Claire blinked. "What?"

Nicole looked at her. "It didn't happen. I wanted you to experience about a tenth of what it felt like to find Jesse, the person I loved and trusted most in the world, in bed with my husband and then ask you if you still thought I had to forgive her."

Relief rushed through Claire. She thought about being angry with Nicole, but she totally got her point. "I'm sorry," she said. "I won't mention forgiving Jesse again. You have to deal with that in your own way."

"Thank you." Nicole sighed. "You're right, though. I can't stay angry forever. It's going to end up hurting me more than her. But I'm comfortable being really pissed for the next few weeks."

"The hits keep on coming," Claire said, knowing Drew hadn't been the only hurt. Jesse's stealing the family recipe had made things worse.

"I'm swearing off men," Nicole told her. "Pretty much forever. I don't care who the guy is or how he tempts me, I'm not giving in."

"Never say never."

"Watch me."

Claire smiled. "I will, because it will be great fun to say 'I told you so' to you."

They ate more ice cream, then Nicole

said, "I'm sorry about Wyatt. That he's being such a jerk."

"I appreciate that." Claire wasn't sure what to think about all that had happened. "I wish things had gone differently. I wish he could love me back." She managed to get the words out without her voice cracking. Improvement, she thought. But she still had a long way to go.

"Love sucks," Nicole said.

"No. But it's not always easy. I can't regret loving Wyatt and Amy. I tell myself the big hole inside of me will eventually heal. I'm better for having known and loved him."

"You're being really mature. It's kind of annoying."

Claire smiled. "Thanks. I've grown a lot in the past couple of months."

"You've done good. You're not a useless ice princess anymore."

"I was never that."

Nicole grinned. "See. You're standing up for yourself and everything. You're a regular person, with gifts and flaws."

"And a baby," Claire said, knowing that was the greatest gift of all.

Claire waited until she was sure Amy would be in bed before going over to Wyatt's. She parked in the driveway, then walked up to the wide, double door and knocked. She had her car keys in her pocket and a legal-size envelope in her hands. Unfinished business, she thought sadly. Too bad there weren't documents that could fix her broken heart.

He opened the door. "Claire."

She stared at him, trying to memorize everything about his face. The deep color of his eyes, the shape of his mouth. Would their baby have his features or hers? Would people look at the child and know Wyatt was the father by the way he or she smiled?

"This won't take long," she said. "I didn't call first. I was afraid you wouldn't see me."

"I'm not hiding from you." He stepped back to let her in.

"You're not exactly trying to find me, either."

He led the way into the family room. Neither of them sat.

"You here to finish what Nicole started?" he asked, sounding more curious than worried.

Claire welcomed the memory of her sister standing up for her. "No. I'm here to give you this." She handed him the envelope. "I had my lawyer prepare the documents. They're straightforward enough, but I suggest you get your own legal counsel to look them over. The basic idea is once you sign, you will have no legal or financial responsibility for the baby. I'll never ask for anything. Not that I would, but this should give you peace of mind. It will be like it never happened."

Wyatt dropped the envelope onto the coffee table. Is that what he wanted? This to have never happened?

"Look," he began, not sure what he wanted to say. "I know you're not Shanna, but this is a lot to deal with."

"You don't have to deal at all. That's the point."

"Is that what you want?"

She folded her arms across her chest. "Why does that matter?"

"Because we're both involved. Because I want to know where you see this going."

What did she expect from him. Marriage? In his head, he balked at the idea. He should be running in the opposite direction. But maybe it wouldn't be so horrible. Claire wasn't the woman he'd thought. She cared about people. Amy was crazy about her.

"I want it all," Claire told him. "I want the happily ever after fantasy. I want you to love me with every cell in your body. I want us to be a family. You, me, Amy, the baby, more kids. I want forever."

He swallowed and tried not to feel the walls closing in.

"I love you," she said, staring him in the eye. "All of you. Even when you're a total jerk. But you don't love me back. You've made that clear, and I won't settle for less. So I'm leaving. It's time for me to go back to New York, anyway."

His mind was completely blank. He didn't have a single thought. Then they crashed in on him, making it impossible to focus on anything.

She loved him? Seriously? She said it just like that? And she was leaving? "You can't," he told her, not sure if he was telling her she couldn't go or she couldn't love him.

"I'm going to keep in touch with Amy," she said as if he hadn't spoken. "I hope you won't have a problem with that. She's wonderful and there's no reason why she and I can't have a relationship." She paused and swallowed. "I hope you find whatever you're looking for. I hope . . ."

She bit her lower lip, squared her shoulders and raised her chin. "Goodbye, Wyatt."

Then she was gone. She told him she loved him and she'd left anyway. They all left, so he was used to it. But this was the first time he would be sorry.

"You have to promise," Amy signed.

"I promise," Claire told her, then hugged her. "I'll be back for your surgery."

"I want to hear your music."

"You will." Claire straightened and hugged Nicole. "Are you sure you're going to be all right by yourself? I worry about you."

"I'm fine," her sister told her. "I'm practically breaking land-speed records on my crutches. I'm going back to work where I can terrorize my staff. It will be fun. I'll barely notice you're gone."

But there were tears in Nicole's eyes as she spoke. Probably like the tears Claire could feel burning in her own.

"I hate this," she muttered.

"It's the right thing to do. Just don't stay gone long."

"I won't. I love you."

"I love you more."

"Unlikely."

"Don't argue," Nicole sniffed. "I'm two minutes older."

Claire nodded, then hugged Amy again. "I love you."

Amy started to cry, then signed that she loved Claire.

"This is crazy," Claire muttered as she straightened. "We're all going to be puffy. We have to stop."

"You have to go. Call me when you land."

"It'll be four in the morning."

"I don't care. Call me."

"I will."

Claire got into her rental car and started the engine. Still fighting tears, she headed for the freeway, then the airport. She was catching a late-evening flight to New York. Back home, she thought. Except she was leaving her heart in Seattle, so how could anywhere else ever be home?

Wyatt put down his empty beer bottle. "I don't know what to do."

"Don't ask me," Drew told him from across the table in the bar. "I know shit about women. I lost Nicole."

"That was your own damn fault."

"And this isn't yours?"

Wyatt didn't like that his stepbrother was actually making sense. It was his fault that Claire had asked him to sign away his parental rights. Why would she think he would care about their baby? He'd done nothing but accuse her of trying to trap him and complain about what a disaster the pregnancy was.

"I needed more time," he muttered.

"To do what?" Drew asked. "Nothing's going to change."

He might. A baby. He'd never thought of having another child. He had Amy and she was everything to him. What child could be more?

That was his head talking, he reminded himself. In his heart, he knew he could love another kid. Maybe more. But he'd never let himself go there because he hadn't believed it could ever work out. His relationships with women were always disasters. It was his genetics at play.

He looked at Drew. "How'd you get someone like Nicole to fall for you?"

"I don't have a clue."

"Why'd you cheat on her?"

Drew shrugged. "Jesse was always there, prancing around in her little clothes."

"I don't believe it."

Drew took another long drink of his beer. "I couldn't be what Nic wanted me to be. I kept seeing disappointment in her eyes. She never said anything, but it was there. I couldn't stand it."

"So you decided to disappoint her more?"

"I don't know. I'm just telling you what I was thinking when I tried to screw Jesse."

Wyatt wanted to dismiss Drew's words,

but he knew what his brother was talking about. He'd seen the same disappointment in Claire's eyes when he hadn't been happy about the baby.

"She told me it can be like it never happened," Wyatt said.

"The baby? So that's good."

"I can't walk away from my kid."

"Then you have a problem."

Worse, he wasn't sure he could walk away from Claire.

"I could almost see myself with her," he mumbled.

Drew signaled for another beer. "That proposal will make her heart beat faster."

"You know what I mean. I've never been able to see myself with anyone." He finished his beer. "Who am I kidding? It'll never happen."

"That's bullshit and you know it," Drew told him. "It's an excuse not to try. No one else in this family has ever been able to hold a job for more than a year. You've got a business. You're raising a great kid. Do you really believe you can't have a decent marriage?"

Wyatt nearly fell off his chair. "Are you being insightful again?"

"Yeah, don't tell anyone. It doesn't happen all that often. Look, Wyatt, you've stood by me when no one else would. You've given me a job and you didn't kill me when I cheated on Nicole. I don't have what you have. I lost her. I know that. But you still have a chance. Don't be an idiot."

"Words to live by," Wyatt muttered, then stood. "I gotta make a call."

He walked out into the cool night and pulled out his cell phone.

"It's me," he said when Nicole answered. "I need to talk to Claire and don't tell me I can't. This isn't your business."

"I agree, but you still can't talk to her. She's not here. She left a couple of hours ago."

He went very still. "For where."

"New York."

He couldn't believe it. "She left without saying goodbye?"

"You made it clear you didn't want to have anything to do with her. She believed you. The fact that she left shouldn't be a surprise at all, Wyatt. It's what you wanted."

CHAPTER
TWENTY-ONE

Claire left the practice studio shortly after one. It was a perfect early-summer day — sunny, but not too warm. She considered getting a cab, but decided the walk would be good for both her and the baby.

She'd been in New York about two weeks and was surprised at how easily she'd slipped back into her old routine. Practice every morning, lessons a couple of times a week, then meetings with Lisa. They were still putting together the fall tour and deciding which CDs she wanted to be on. The two for charity, of course, but there were other artists who had interesting ideas Claire wanted to explore.

She'd had her first doctor's appointment the previous week and had been pronounced perfectly healthy. She was eating well, sleeping great. Life was good . . . or it should have been. Despite the fact that she hadn't had a single panic attack or even a hint of one, despite Lisa acting like they were partners and actually listening, despite having everything she'd always said she wanted, she felt . . . wrong.

It was as if nothing would come completely into focus. No matter how she turned her head or squinted, she was missing something just out of view.

The music was great. She loved the music. She'd asked Lisa to find her somewhere to play over the summer so she could make sure she'd really chased away her demons. There was a charity concert in a little more than a week, which was exciting. But still not enough.

She paused by the newsstand. "Hi, Billy."

The old man looked up. "It didn't come today, Claire. I called around and found it for you, though." He gave her an address. "Ike there is holding you a copy."

"You're the best."

"I know." He grinned. "That's why you women can't get enough of me."

She hurried down three blocks and over one to the newsstand he'd suggested. After introducing herself to Ike, she took the copy of the *Seattle Times* he held out and gave him five dollars.

"Keep the change."

"Oh, sure, now I know why Billy likes you

so much."

Claire laughed. "You mean it's not my dazzling smile?"

"I'm sure that helps. Have a good day."

"You, too."

Claire found a Starbucks, ordered a decaf latte, then settled in the corner with the paper.

It was silly, she knew. Yet she felt compelled to find out what was happening in Seattle. As always, she read a few articles, then turned to the real estate section and looked at houses for sale.

"I'm just daydreaming," she reminded herself. But if she *were* buying a house, it would be relatively close to Nicole's without getting in the way. She'd want a big deck and maybe a view. Lots of trees and a basement. A yard for kids.

She sighed when she realized she was describing Wyatt's house. The house she couldn't forget, owned by the man she still loved.

Had he already moved on? Did he think of her at all? Did she haunt him the way he haunted her? Did Amy still think about her? She missed the little girl nearly as much as she missed Wyatt.

Everything was different now, she reminded herself. A few short months ago she'd been practically agoraphobic, hiding out in her apartment, terrified of everything. She'd been alone. Today she had her life back and so many people she loved. She also had a baby. She'd been lucky and blessed . . . so why wasn't it enough? Why did she want the one man she couldn't have and how was she supposed to fall out of love with him?

"Am I interrupting?"

Claire looked up and saw Lisa standing by her table. "Not at all. What are you doing here?"

"This is my neighborhood. I live over there."

She pointed to a tall building. Claire knew her manager had moved a couple of years before, but as they didn't socialize, she'd never been to her place. Lisa always came to her.

"You seem to be settling in," the other woman said before sipping on her coffee.

"I'm happy to be back." Sort of. "I've missed playing."

"How was practice?"

"Good. I'm working on the pieces I'll play for the charity concert. Nothing is new, so it's more about refreshing my memory than anything else."

Claire wondered if her manager felt the

faint sense of awkwardness between them. Despite having known each other for years, everything was different now. They were going to have to create a new relationship as they went.

Lisa glanced at the paper. "Still missing Seattle?"

"More than I thought I would." She touched the real estate section. "I meant what I said before. I want to buy a house there."

"What I saw of the city was very nice. And it has to be cheaper than here. Would you keep your apartment for yourself or sublet it? I suppose you could sell it, but you'll still be coming back to New York."

Claire didn't realize how she'd braced herself until she began to relax. Despite their conversations and Lisa's promise to treat her like a partner, she'd expected her manager to protest. "I don't want to sell it," she said. "Or sublet it."

"You can afford to keep it for when you're in town." Lisa set down her coffee. "This may shock you, but I'm glad you're making changes. I had a lot of time to think after my first visit to Seattle. I didn't know if you were coming back or not. What with you being my only client, I panicked. What was I going to do with myself? How would I survive?"

Claire swallowed guilt. She'd never meant to leave Lisa hanging.

"I took a long look at my life." Lisa smiled. "I'm fifty-six. I've never been married. I don't even have houseplants. My life has been my clients. You for the last sixteen years, but others before. I've worked hard, seen the world. Many would envy my life. It does make for excellent cocktail conversation, but I'm ready for a change."

"You're quitting?" Claire asked, not sure how she felt about that.

"You won't get rid of me so easily. But I am going to be taking time off. A vacation or two. Or five. According to my accountant, I don't have to worry too much about money, even the way I shop. I'm nowhere near ready to retire, but cutting back sounds very good." She touched Claire's hand. "You went looking to find yourself and you did. Now it's my turn."

Claire liked the sound of that. She'd always been half-afraid of Lisa and for the first time, she finally saw her as a real person.

"Would you like to get dinner tonight?"

Her manager smiled. "I would. We can celebrate the changes we're looking forward to."

■ ■ ■ ■

Wyatt opened his front door to see Nicole standing on his porch, leaning on her crutches.

He hadn't seen his friend in over a week and he'd missed her. "Tell me you didn't drive."

"Don't ask, don't tell. It works for the military."

"Nicole. You're still recovering from surgery."

"Did you notice it was my left knee? I drive with my right leg." She sighed. "I don't do it often, okay? I just wanted to see you."

"I thought you hated me." She'd been pretty clear on what she thought about him the last time they'd talked. And the time before.

"I thought you were a jerk. There's a difference. That doesn't mean we can't be friends."

He stepped back to let her in. As she walked past him he said, "I've missed you."

She paused next to him, then turned toward him. He wrapped his arms around her and pulled her close.

Hugging her felt good. Familiar. But it

didn't do a damn thing for him. Too bad. Nicole would have been a whole lot easier to handle than Claire.

"I've missed you, too," she grumbled. "Everyone's leaving me. Have you noticed that pattern? First Drew —"

"You threw him out."

"Then Jesse."

"You threw her out, too. You're right. There is a pattern."

"Shut up. I didn't throw out Claire or you."

"If you could have tossed me across the room, you would have."

"Maybe," she admitted, then made her way to the sofa and collapsed. "I'm back to work and maybe not taking it as easy as I should. I hurt."

"Can I get you something?"

She looked at him. "How about Claire?"

"She'll come back if you ask her," he said.

"That's not what I meant and you know it."

He did. "She served me with papers saying I don't have to have anything to do with the baby if that's what I want. Just sign my name and it's like it never happened."

Nicole raised her leg until she could rest her heel on the coffee table. "She told me. I let her think that would solve the problem."

"It won't?"

She rolled her eyes. "You're about the most responsible person I know. You're not letting your own kid disappear from your life. You couldn't stand it."

He'd been avoiding that reality, but Nicole was right. Even if he wasn't crazy about Claire, he wouldn't walk away from his child. He wasn't going to sue for custody, but he would insist they work something out.

"I don't know what to do," he admitted. "I never meant for this to happen."

"I assume you're talking about more than getting her pregnant."

"Isn't that enough?"

"If we were only talking about the logistics of sharing child rearing, you would have already worked out a schedule."

First Drew, now Nicole. Did everyone know him better than he knew himself?

"I miss her," he admitted. "I miss seeing her and talking to her. I bought a couple of her CDs, so I can hear her music, but that's not enough."

He leaned forward, resting his forearms on his thighs, and stared at the carpet. "She haunts me. I don't have to close my eyes to see her. I hear her voice in every moment of silence. Sometimes I think I should go after

411

her, just get on a plane and fly to New York and drag her back here."

"It would get the message across. What's stopping you?"

"A lot of things. My history with women." He remembered what Drew had told him — that he'd broken the family bad luck streak in every other area of his life, why not this one. "Can I make it different with her?"

"You know you can," Nicole told him. "Besides, it's not like Claire has a lot of experience. She won't be as picky as some women would be."

Despite the aching hole in his heart, he smiled. "Gee, thanks."

"I live to be helpful. What else?"

The next one was hard to admit. He sucked in a breath. "Do you know who she is? She's famous and rich. I'm a contractor. I do well. I have a successful business, but what do I have to offer her that she can't buy herself?"

Nicole slugged him in the arm. She didn't come close to hurting him, but she'd never hit him before.

"What?" he asked.

"It's not about stuff, you idiot. It's never about stuff. Why can't guys get that? Stuff is usually a substitute we accept when we can't get what we really want."

"What do you really want?"

He noticed she didn't have to think about the answer. Were women born knowing this kind of thing, or did they come up with it as they got older?

"We want to matter," she said. "We want to be the most important part of your world. We want to know you'd be lost without us, that you ache when we're gone and count the hours until we're back. We'll give you forever, if you just make us believe that."

That was a lot, Wyatt thought. More than a simple "I love you." It was about giving of himself, opening up to the possibility of handing her everything and still having her walk away. It scared the crap out of him.

"Is it too late?" he asked, not wanting to hear the answer, but knowing he had to.

Nicole sighed. "I should tell you it is, because you handled most of this pretty badly. But Claire loves you and I love her, so I'll tell you the truth. No, it's not. You can still win her. But don't expect me to tell you how. I've already given too much away."

Amy ran into the room. She saw Nicole and squealed with delight. "You're here!" They embraced, then his daughter slid onto his lap and hugged him. "Hi, Daddy," she signed.

There was so much affection and trust in her eyes. He could still pick her up and toss her in the air and she only laughed. It never occurred to her he could drop her or hurt her in any way. Because he never had and he never would. He would give his life for hers a thousand times over. She was his world.

Which is exactly what Claire wanted. To be his world. His everything. The woman of his dreams.

She was that and more. The problem was going to be convincing her.

Claire adjusted the headphones she wore before every performance. She did her best to get lost in the music, lost in the sounds and nuances of the piece. All around her, stagehands spoke into walkie-talkies, making sure the lighting was perfect, the stage cleared of everything but her piano, the curtains ready to open. Someone yelled that it was three minutes. She heard that much, then tuned out the rest of it.

She felt the presence of others. Lisa hovered in the background, ready to take the headphones from her, trying not to look nervous. While the performance was for charity, it was a big deal for both of them. It would be the first time Claire had played in public since she'd totally lost it in the early spring and had to be helped off the stage.

Clair opened her eyes. She could see the piano from where she stood. She imagined herself there, the crowd beyond.

Some had come to support the cause. Others were there because they'd heard what had happened before and wanted to know if she had lost it. But most wanted to hear her play. They wanted the gift that flowed from her freak hands.

She looked at her fingers and smiled, knowing she wouldn't change anything about herself, even if she could. She was exactly what she needed to be.

"Are you all right?" Lisa asked. "Should I not say anything?"

Claire took off the headphones and handed them to her. "I'm fine. Nervous, but in a good way. It's anticipation, not fear."

Which was almost the truth. Fear was there, nibbling on the edges of her consciousness, but she ignored it. She knew the music. That was easy. She'd survived the morning rush at the Keyes Bakery. Now *that* had been hard.

She heard the announcer begin to speak

415

and touched Lisa's arm. "Thanks for not giving up on me."

"How could I?"

Life was nothing if not ironic. She and her manager had finally become friends, just when they were going to be working less together.

Claire waited until the curtain began to lift, then she walked to the edge of the stage and out to the center. She paused in front of the piano and faced the large crowd.

There were more people than she'd expected . . . a sea of expectant faces. The applause washed over her.

She drew in a deep breath, then another. She was nervous, but in a way that would give her an edge to help her do her best. There was no terror, no chest-crushing fear. A sense of contentment, of pride, filled her.

She was about to turn to sit when she saw someone wave at her. She stared into the crowd and recognized Amy. To the girl's left stood Wyatt. Their eyes met and he smiled at her.

She felt her heart stumble a beat. Her breath got stuck and her whole body trembled. Wyatt? Here?

He was tall and handsome in a black tux, looking as polished as the rest of the crowd. As if he belonged in the city instead of back home in Seattle.

What was he doing here? Had he come to hear her play? Why hadn't he called?

She wanted to rush into the audience and have him hold her. She wanted him to sweep her away and never let her go. She wanted to know why he'd come to her performance.

Then she remembered the other four hundred plus people who had paid to hear her play. She bowed once and walked to the piano, then sat down.

The concert hall went still. She could feel the expectation filling the space. She put her hands on the keys and began to play.

The music was familiar — an old friend who greeted her with a perfect combination of notes. The ebb and flow of the piece filled her body, then spilled out, transporting her to another plane where there was only amazing beauty in the form of sound.

She forgot about the crowd, she forgot to be nervous. She had found herself again, in this place. It was as it had always been.

No, it was different, she thought in a small corner of her mind. Better. More connected. It was as if by loving, by opening herself to the possibilities, the pain and the hope, she'd become one with the universe.

She was aware of Wyatt, of his watchful

attention. She felt only support, though, and it gave her energy and focus. She moved her body as she played, allowing herself to give everything, and when she touched that very last key, she was drained as she had never been before.

There was silence at the end, as there had been at the beginning, but this was different. She looked up and saw amazement in their faces. It was as if she'd managed to stun even the most seasoned patron. As one, the audience rose to their feet and applauded. They screamed her name. A few wiped away tears.

She stood, her exhausted legs trembling to keep her upright. Satisfaction and pride filled her. She smiled and bowed.

As she rose, she met Wyatt's gaze and saw something there. Need. Maybe even hope and she allowed herself to believe anything was possible.

"Oh, my God!" Lisa cried as the curtains closed for the fourth and final time. "That was amazing. I've never heard you play like that. People are going to be talking about this performance for weeks. Whatever you did out there in Seattle worked."

Claire smiled. "Apparently I really needed a vacation."

"It's more than that. You've changed as an artist. You're more . . ." Her manager frowned. "I want to say mature, but that's not the right word. You've found something inside of yourself that was never there before. You're one with the music."

"Thank you."

Lisa sighed. "Ah, they come. Your adoring public. I'll do my best to keep away the crazies."

Claire turned to greet those who had the inside track to getting backstage. She remembered enough names to make a good impression and appreciated all the kind words, but her attention was elsewhere, wondering when she would see Wyatt and Amy.

"Riveting. I've never heard that piece played so well."

"The best I've ever heard."

"Dazzling."

"Extraordinary."

Claire thanked them, knowing she couldn't take full credit for what had happened. There was a part of her that had finally been set free, but it wasn't a conscious act on her part. She suspected it had a lot to do with facing down her fear and growing up, but she wasn't about to explain that to anyone. Except maybe her family.

At one point, she saw Lisa talking to Wyatt and pointing to the rear of the stage. As that was the way to Claire's dressing room, she relaxed, knowing they would be there when she was finally able to get away.

Thirty minutes later, she escaped and made her way to her dressing room. She opened the door, her heart thundering, her stomach swirling with anticipation.

Amy launched herself. "I miss you," she signed as she flew across the room.

Claire caught her and hugged her. "I missed you, too," she signed, but she only had eyes for Wyatt.

He stood by her dressing table, looking gorgeous and hunky in his tux. She'd missed him so much, she ached, and seeing him now only brought all that pain to the surface. She wanted to go to him, but she knew she had to wait until she found out why he was here. He might simply be delivering the papers she'd left with him.

There was a knock at her door. Lisa stuck in her head.

"I promised Amy a tour of the orchestra pit," her manager said and held out her hand. "We'll be about twenty minutes."

"Thanks," Wyatt said.

Amy grinned at Claire then skipped out the door.

When the door closed behind them, Claire said, "Lisa's not really a kid person, but she should be able to manage a tour."

"Amy's talked about learning to play drums after she gets her implant," Wyatt said.

"Technically, in an orchestra, they're percussionists."

"Amy's thinking more about a rock band."

"Then she'll be a drummer."

Wyatt shoved his hands into his slacks' front pockets. "You were incredible."

"Thank you."

"I've heard you play before. In the studio at Nicole's house and at Amy's school. This was different."

"I had accompaniment."

"Not only because of that. It was something different."

Her heart pounded so hard her chest hurt. She wanted to believe that things were going to work out, but suddenly she wasn't sure. He wouldn't look at her. That couldn't be good.

"This is who you are," he said. "I knew in my head that you were some famous pianist, but I didn't know what that meant."

She wanted to collapse on the floor. Whatever Wyatt *had* been going to say, he'd changed his mind. Something about the night had scared him away.

She wanted to scream out her protest. They could still make it work. Only that wasn't her decision alone. It had to be his, too, and if he couldn't handle who and what she was, better to know now.

Which was a great intellectual argument, but it made her heart scream in protest.

"I was going to ask you to come back to Seattle," he said, finally looking at her. "To relocate there. I was going to try to convince you that you belonged there. With your sisters and with me and Amy."

Was? Was? And now what?

"I was going to tell you that I've been a total ass about the baby, about us. My only excuse is that you scare the hell out of me, Claire. You make me feel things. I can't play by my rules when it comes to you because I can't not care. You're exactly who I've been waiting for all my life."

He pulled his hands out of his pockets and moved toward her. "I was going to tell you that I love you. I've never said that before, not romantically. I didn't love Shanna. Maybe that's really why she left. I figured I'd never fall in love. Then you showed up. You were so beautiful, but you were also so giving. You're smart and funny and you love my daughter. You said you even love me."

She felt tears burning in her eyes. It was everything she wanted to hear and she knew it still wasn't going to be okay.

"I can't ask you to give this up," he continued. "That's what I didn't get before. I can't ask you to move your life to Seattle."

She wanted to tell him that of course she could. There were flights to New York all the time. She could live anywhere. But maybe he was looking for an excuse. As much as it hurt, she had to let him back out if that's what he'd decided.

"You're having a baby," he said. "We're having a baby. I'm not walking away from our child, or from you. So we'll figure it out. I can't leave my business right now, but I'll finish up the projects I have and Amy and I will join you here. I can get a job, or start a new company. Or open a branch office. Whatever. My point is, Claire, I'm not going to ask you to give up anything for me. I love you. I want to be with you. I want you to be happy, and if you need to be in New York, then Amy and I will move."

He paused, and took another step closer. "If you still want us. Me, I mean. I know you love her."

Tears spilled from her eyes. She was too happy to speak or breathe or do anything but stare at him.

He shrugged. "I know what you're thinking. I should have to work harder to prove myself. I will. I'm sorry about what I said about the baby. I know you weren't trying to trap me. I didn't expect to fall for you and when I did, I . . ." He looked away, then back at her. "I got scared, okay. I'll admit it. I'd never let anyone else matter as much as you did. I was looking for reasons to push you away. I want our baby. I want you. I want us to be a family. I love you, Claire. If you can forgive me for what I put you through, I'm hoping you'll marry me. If you want to get married. If you don't, we can just live together. Whatever you want."

She brushed away her tears, then surprised them both by starting to laugh. She rushed toward him.

Wyatt held open his arms and she flung herself into them. They held on to each other.

He was strong and warm and oh, so familiar. Everything about this felt right.

She raised her head and smiled at him. "I love you."

"I love you more."

She laughed again. "Let's argue about that forever, but first, I don't want to live in New York. Wyatt, I can work just as well in Seattle. I want to move back. I want to be near Nicole and Jesse and the bakery and your family. Even Drew, who I'm not sure I like right now. I really appreciate the offer, but I love Seattle."

"Are you sure?"

"As sure as I am about loving you."

He touched her face, then kissed her. "I was a total jerk."

"I forgive you."

"You don't have to. You can make me squirm for a while. I deserve that."

"Do you love me?" she asked.

"More than anything. You're everything I've ever wanted. I don't know how I got so lucky to find you."

"Good answer," she whispered. "Consider your squirming days at an end."

"Does this mean you'll marry me?"

She nodded.

"Do you believe me when I tell you I'm happy about the baby?"

He sounded so worried and anxious. She could see the concern is his eyes. Concern and love and hope.

"Yes," she told him.

"I'm kind of hoping for a boy," he admitted.

"Of course you are."

She smiled and he pulled her close.

"I love you," he said. "Let's go find Amy

and tell her the happy news. She's always wanted a stepmother and a brother or sister. You're going to score big points with her."

"I'm glad. Then we'll book a flight back to Seattle," Claire said as they walked out of her dressing room. "I'm ready to go home."

CLAIRE'S COCONUT KISSES

1 cup brown sugar
2 stiffly beaten egg whites
2 cups corn flakes
1 cup moist shredded coconut
1/2 cup chopped walnuts
1/2 tsp vanilla

Beat sugar into egg whites. Fold in corn flakes, coconut and nuts. Add vanilla. Drop by teaspoons onto well-greased cookie sheet. Bake in moderate 350°F oven for 15 to 20 minutes.

Place pans on damp towel and remove cookies immediately with spatula. If cookies stick to pan, return to oven to soften. Makes 1-1/2 dozen kisses.

We hope you have enjoyed this Large Print book. Other Thorndike, Wheeler, and Chivers Press Large Print books are available at your library or directly from the publishers.

For information about current and upcoming titles, please call or write, without obligation, to:

Publisher
Thorndike Press
295 Kennedy Memorial Drive
Waterville, ME 04901
Tel. (800) 223-1244

or visit our Web site at:

http://gale.cengage.com/thorndike

OR

Chivers Large Print
published by BBC Audiobooks Ltd
St James House, The Square
Lower Bristol Road
Bath BA2 3SB
England
Tel. +44(0) 800 136919
email: bbcaudiobooks@bbc.co.uk
www.bbcaudiobooks.co.uk

All our Large Print titles are designed for easy reading, and all our books are made to last.